Wicked
Women

Wicked Women

Edited by
Jan Edwards and Jenny Barber

F✦X SPIRIT

www.foxspirit.co.uk

Cover Art by Sarah Anne Langton
http://www.secretarcticbase.com/
conversion by handebooks.co.uk

ISBN: 978-1-909348-69-1

A Fox Spirit Original
Fox Spirit Books
www.foxspirit.co.uk
adele@foxspirit.co.uk

Contents

WIN SOME, LOSE SOME

Juliet E. McKenna

The Martagon is one of those taverns which, while not a brothel, always has enough lasses idling about in low cut bodices to catch a man's eye through its hospitably open door. And there are always plenty of men passing the door, given it's in the middle of a street of rooming houses that cater to country folk on some long anticipated visit to this splendid city of Selerima. Such folk always include plough boys desperate to quench their youthful ardour without the risks of sowing their seed in some local furrow. And then there are the older men whose marriage bed has long since staled. They can often be tempted into a slice from a fresh cut loaf.

'Livak, there's a man asking for you.' One of the lasses sauntered over, hips swinging, hem of her pink gown hiked up to show the golden lace on her petticoats and fine white stockings above her soft yellow slippers.

I swept up the rune bones I'd been casually rolling on the table in front of me. 'Send him for a walk down the Andelane. He'll find what he's looking for there.'

Even dressed in a man's breeches and boots with shirt and jerkin loose enough to disguise my curves, getting the occasional offer is one of the prices of setting up in an inn like the Martagon. Some mistake me for a lad in the candlelight, half blinded by guilt or anticipation or both. Others just see my red hair and green eyes and remember all the whispered stable yard tales about the insatiable appetites of Forest women. Such whispers had mortified my respectable housekeeper mother once I'd reached girlhood, just when she'd thought the gossip about her ill-starred dalliance with the Forest minstrel who was my father had finally faded.

'Tell him she's with me.' Halice was sitting behind me, apparently asleep in a round backed beech wood chair, long, solidly muscled legs stretched out in front of her. She was booted and breeched like me but where I wore a cheerful blue jerkin and breeches she was wearing muted brown and grey, the better to go unnoticed in the shadows. 'If that doesn't put him off, give me a nod. I'll come and get some more ale and set him straight.'

There are precious few men who'll cross Halice. For a start, she'll look all but the very tallest straight in the eye and can stare down most of those. For any who won't back down, she carries a sword in those places that permit it and carefully hidden knives for towns and cities where the Watch say otherwise. Add to that a face as plain as an overcast sky and it's hardly surprising she doesn't get many importunate offers.

'He's not looking to ease his urges.' Tirian shook her head, golden ringlets dancing around her white neck. 'He says he knows a friend of yours.'

'Does he?' Halice's chair scraped on the floor behind me as she sat up straight. 'Who might that be?'

Tirian's brow wrinkled prettily. 'Lady Alaric? Does that sound right?'

'Who is he? Point him out,' Halice demanded.

Tirian obliged and I saw a middle aged man of middling build dressed better than most in this particular taproom. He wore a fine linen shirt with lace at its collar underneath a full-skirted, long-sleeved coat of soft black leather. His breeches were black too; fine broadcloth with silver buckles at the knee, sturdy black cotton stockings below to mask the filth of the streets that nevertheless spattered his square-toed black shoes.

'Merchant's clerk?' Halice hazarded.

'No ink stains on his cuffs or wear on his elbows.' I tossed the yellowed rune bones with their three deeply carved faces from hand to hand. 'Upper servant, I'd say, in a house where he gets silver and gold slipped in his hand by grateful guests, not just copper.' I glanced back over my shoulder to Halice. 'Well?'

'Tell him he can come and drink his ale with us, Tirian' said Halice cautiously. 'Bring us another flagon while you're at it, please?'

Tirian shrugged and for a moment I thought her dainty

pink dress was going to slip right off her shoulders. 'I've nothing else to do, I suppose.'

Halice took the hint and had a silver mark ready when Tirian returned with the flagon and this mysterious stranger in tow. We could afford to be generous to the lass. We were having a most profitable stay in Selerima.

'May I?' The stranger gestured towards one of the empty stools around my table.

I nodded, scanning the tap room as I did so. It was still early enough in the evening for Tirian to have no more than her thumbs to twiddle, so it would be a while before anyone could be tempted into a friendly game of chance with me. A game where they'd put their ill-luck down to distractions like Tirian catching their eye. Most evenings that was even true.

'You reckon we've got acquaintance in common?' I shifted my stool aside a little so Halice could swing her chair around to face this unknown newcomer.

'Indeed. The incomparable Lady Alaric.' He sat on a stool, knees together, both hands cupping his goblet of wine. Me and Halice might merit a second glance in a place like the Martagon but this chap stuck out like a cut finger needing a bandage.

'You've served her on some visit hereabouts?' I queried. This man was plainly an upper house-servant. I'd seen the type often enough, growing up as bastard daughter to a prosperous merchant's housekeeper.

'Let me introduce myself.' The man smiled. He had a thin mouth and circumspect brown eyes beneath black hair showing just a hint of grey and close cropped to disguise its thinning. 'Arle Cordainer.' He held out an uncalloused hand bare of rings. I shook it without comment.

'A name that means nothing to me.' Halice folded her arms, which showed up the muscles of her forearms at the same time as emphasising the width of her shoulders. I'd seen wrestlers envy those shoulders.

'I assure you it's good enough for Lady Alaric.' Cordainer paused then leaning closer, lowered his voice. 'And for Mistress Heraciol.'

'And what would those good ladies have to tell us about you?' Halice's expression didn't alter and neither did mine.

When you keep yourself fed and shod through gambling, you keep a straight face or go hungry and barefoot. All the same, we were playing a different game if he knew two of our mutual friend's many faces.

Cordainer took a moment to sip his wine. 'Lady Alaric would remember me as house steward to Lord Elwyl, when she found herself benighted on the road between Peorle and Duryea. I was able to be of service when she asked me for a direct route to Trebin that would nevertheless keep off the highroads.' He took another drink of wine. 'And to be discreet about her plans.'

I exchanged a glance with Halice. So our distant friend had spotted this man wasn't above taking a little gold to help her out, with a little more besides to keep his mouth shut once she'd made her escape with whatever she'd blackmailed or bamboozled out of his employer.

'As for Mistress Heraciol, we've been correspondents for a year or so now,' Cordainer continued blithely.

Perhaps his finery had been bought with the gold marks she doubtless sent hidden in the seals of her letters, thanking him for snippets of information about the great and the good and the gullible of Selerima, titbits garnered as he waited on table or fetched and carried linen from closet to guest chamber. Who bothers to guard their tongue when a servant is no more to be remarked on than the furnishings? Less so in fact, if some rich merchant or minor noble has some new expensive tapestry brought all the way from Toremal or glittering crystal goblets from the fabled Aldabreshin Archipelago. Mistress Heraciol habitually drank from just such costly glassware in her expensive house in Relshaz, thanks to her talent for turning insubstantial gossip into solid coin.

'So what has she seen fit to tell you about us?' I wondered aloud.

'And why,' added Halice, her voice hard.

Cordainer smiled again and sipped at his goblet. 'When I wrote to wish her a fortunate Winter Solstice, I asked if she knew anyone who might be travelling this way in the first half of summer. Someone who had certain particular talents and none too many scruples about using them. She mentioned your names.' He looked Halice straight in the eye.

'In my youth, I spent some time in the Duke of Marlier's household. I can quite believe any daughter of Lady Lifinal more than merited your chastisement. I only wish I'd had the spirit to give her ladyship a slap in the face myself.'

'Heraciol told you about that?' Halice sounded amused but her eyes stayed wary. 'Well, I'd had about enough of playing watchdog for the duchess anyway. Being turned out to take to the road again was no great hardship.'

'But you didn't go back to the mercenary life,' Cordainer remarked with a glance at Halice's dun coloured hair which she still kept cropped as short as the soldier she had been. 'You've been travelling with your charming companion here.' He made me a half bow remarkably elegantly for a man sitting on a stool. 'And I gather you also know all the trials and tribulations of the servant's life.'

'Enough to know it was never going to be the life for me,' I answered with a sunny smile. Not that I'd had a notion in my foolish head as to what I might do instead, when I'd fled my mother's fate. Setting my face against Tirian's trade, I'd been barely scraping a living playing games of chance in grubby inns when I first encountered Halice working her way from town to town teaching swordplay or challenging the locals to wager their purses on their boasts that they could beat her. Both our fortunes had improved since then, now we had a practised routine for shading the odds in our favour over the course of a game of runes.

I gestured around the Martagon's taproom before throwing a spread of bones on the table. 'This is where we do our business and while it's pleasant to reminisce about old friends, you're keeping us from getting a game in play, so unless you've something more to say?' I raised my brows at Cordainer as I leant forward to gather up the runes.

He sipped at his goblet and set it down, losing his amiable smile as he leant closer once more and lowered his voice to a murmur. 'I've been house steward to Master Barazon since the turn of the year. He's head of the Tailor's Guild and the richest liveryman in this city. He has a beautiful young wife whose fondness for him is equalled only by her fondness for jewels – and I've noticed if he wants her to open her bed curtains to him, she expects to close her fingers around something more lasting than his manhood.'

'Which may interest Mistress Heraciol,' said Halice with distaste wrinkling her nose. 'What's it to do with us?'

'Master Barazon has decided it's time he got himself an heir,' Cordainer replied crisply. 'And he has some concerns about standing at stud, given he's wed two wives already and neither had so much as quickened before they quit his house, never mind borne a child. He intends to cover his new filly as often as he can and that has meant dazzling her with something truly spectacular.' He paused and looked from Halice to me and back again. 'Something that would fund a nice retirement for me and set you ladies up with fine houses and servants of your own.' He looked back at me, dark eyes penetrating. 'I gather your fingers are as nimble with locks as they are with rune bones and with upper story window catches besides.'

'Is that so?' I said, non committal. 'But you'll have keys and permission to be in the house besides. Why should you share the spoils with anyone else?'

'Because I would be the first person Barazon would set the Watch hunting, if I disappeared in the same night as his wife's newest treasures. I need to be there lamenting with the rest of the household.' Cordainer spread his hands. 'And while I know how to turn chance heard words into coin thanks to our friend Mistress Heraciol, I've no notion where to sell gems without awkward questions. That's one of the talents I believe you ladies have?'

'It depends if the gems are worth the trouble,' said Halice baldly.

'Diamonds.' Cordainer looked for a response. He just about hid his disappointment at not getting one. 'Of the first water and set in white gold. A necklace in the eastern Archipelagan style, hanging earrings to match and a crescent of diamonds fit for an empress's hair. I've seen them and believe me, Madam Barazon would lay down, hoist her skirts and let her husband take his pleasure on the steps of the Conclave Tower at noon for their sake.'

'Getting hold of them isn't half the task,' Halice pointed out. 'They'd have to be got well away from here.'

'And still most likely broken up for sale,' I agreed, with a rueful shake of my head.

'And how do you know we won't just disappear with

them, leaving you looking foolish?' asked Halice with cold malice.

'And have me write as much to Mistress Heraciol?' Cordainer leaned back from the table, picking up his goblet for a final swallow. 'I think we can trust each other to keep honest, given how widely she could spread the word we weren't to be trusted. Well, I imagined you'd want time to consider such a proposal. Perhaps we can share a drink and discuss it further later this evening?'

'Perhaps.' Halice inclined her head as Cordainer stood up.

We watched him walk over to the counter, confident without being confrontational as he asked a trio of men in country jerkins to let him by. He set down his goblet and turned to smile at one of Tirian's fellow flowers in a flame coloured gown. Discreet silver changed hands and he left with the lass on his arm. As soon as his back was turned, Tirian swept up the goblet and drained it.

'Giving Mynna a quick joggle gives him a reason to be here,' I remarked to Halice. 'Just in case anyone's got their eye on him.'

'If we get a hint that anyone has, we don't touch this,' she warned.

'You think we should touch this in any case?' I looked at her, my surprise coloured with exasperation. 'Care to explain why?'

'He's obviously a friend of Charoleia's.' Halice studied one broad blunt fingered hand.

'Who doesn't know her by that name,' I pointed out with some asperity. 'I wouldn't call him much more than an acquaintance, if the only two faces he knows are Lady Alaric and Mistress Heraciol.'

'He's done her enough good turns for her to pass on our names when he went asking for help with this,' Halice countered. 'And if we do him a good turn, you know that'll be credit in our ledger with Charoleia.'

Which was always worth having. Among other things, Charoleia, who had more guises than a troupe of travelling players, generally knew which noble and wealthy sons had an exaggerated and consequently expensive belief in their own abilities at the gambling tables. It was remarkable how often they would fall into a friendly game of runes with a harmless red-headed lass who just happened to be stopping at the same respectable inn on some byway. And if they took exception to their losses or felt inclined to try snatching their coin back, that's when they would discover I was travelling with that uncommonly tall, plain-faced and far from harmless woman who'd taken a seat at the gaming table once the runes were well in play.

I shrugged and snapped my fingers to attract Tirian's attention. She came over, eyebrows raised. 'I'm not your personal pot girl.'

'The old crow who just left with Mynna,' I jerked my head toward the door and then gestured towards the counter. 'How much wine was left in his goblet to quench your thirst?'

'More than half.' Tirian was puzzled. 'I don't know why he should be so fussy. That's a good vintage. Menk knows better than to serve bitter lees to someone dressed like that.'

'His loss, your gain,' I shrugged.

'I'll take all the luck I can this evening,' Tirian perched her rump on the edge of our table. 'It's cursed quiet, isn't it?'

'It is that,' I agreed.

'Not for long.' Halice nodded towards the taproom's outer door.

Two men entered, evidently brothers from their colouring and features but distinct in dress and manner. The first was stocky rather than tall and with flaxen hair that would be the envy of every girl lounging around the room. He was dressed with a style to catch the eye, boots well polished, breeches of dark green broadcloth, silver studs on the belt that circled his waist and his shirt of crisp new linen clasped at the throat with an emerald brooch. He scanned the room with sapphire eyes, well aware of the effect of his appearance.

'Doesn't he ever feel the cold?' I asked Halice. According to whichever Almanac you used, the season had turned from Aft-Spring to For-Summer three or four days ago but I still didn't find it warm enough to go around in shirtsleeves once the sun had set.

Halice shrugged. 'No, neither of them do.'

The second man was slighter in build than his brother

and nowhere near as dapper in his dress. His boots were scuffed, his old leather belt was stretched, the brass tag from the end long since lost and his shirt was open at the neck. All the same, he was attracting just as much attention from the lasses around the room with his air of raffish charm, eyes as blue as his brother's and twinkling with impudence.

They came over and sat at our table. Tirian swiftly appeared with a fresh flagon of ale, two earthenware cups and a coquettish smile even shared between the two of them. 'Master Sorgrad,' she dimpled, setting a drink down before the taller of the pair. 'Sorgren.'

The rumpled brother slid a wiry arm around her waist and pulled her onto his knee. 'Good day to you, sweetness.' He used his free hand to brush the ringlets back over her shoulder and kissed her just below her ear. She blushed vividly.

'Give us a moment please, Tirian,' Halice asked. 'We've some business to discuss.'

'Gren caught up her hand and kissed it before releasing her. 'Later, sweetness?'

'I'll be waiting.' Tirian smiled at him with happy anticipation before returning to her position at the counter, more than one envious female gaze following her.

Sorgrad held out his hand and I dropped the rune bones into it. 'So, are we playing decoy pigeon for you?' It's a fact that men who'll baulk at proposing a hand of runes with a woman can be tempted when a table's already in play.

Halice shook her head. 'The evening breeze brought us the whisper of a richer game.'

'Runes? White Raven?' Sorgrad hazarded.

Halice lifted her drink to mask her mouth from curious eyes. 'Gems.'

Sorgren's eyes brightened. 'This sounds like fun already.' He leaned forward, elbows on the table, lacing his fingers together.

'This isn't a good city to fall foul of the Watch in.' Sorgrad sounded wary, unobtrusively checking to be certain no one was close enough to eavesdrop on this conversation.

'We've got a man on the inside,' Halice offered. 'Charoleia put him on to us.'

'Did she?' mused Sorgrad.

I hadn't known these brothers for long but I already knew he could count the people he trusted absolutely on the fingers of both hands with a couple to spare. Charoleia merited the first forefinger when he made that count.

'What kind of gems?' asked 'Gren, persistent as always.

'Diamonds,' Halice answered simply. 'Aldabreshin. Of the first water and set in white gold.'

Sorgrad raised his golden brows. 'That's from your man on the inside?'

Halice nodded. 'House steward to the head of the Tailor's Guild.'

'Who sits and pretends to drink but leaves more than half his wine untested,' I chipped in.

'You don't trust him?' Sorgrad looked at me, azure eyes piercing.

'I don't know,' I shrugged. 'And I don't know him.'

And I was still getting the measure of these two. While I will have various thefts to answer for when I finally face Saedrin at the door of judgement, at least I'll be able to plead I'd only even stolen when the alternative was starvation. Well, mostly. But Sorgrad, Sorgren and Halice had quite a different attitude, having served together in various mercenary bands in the interminable Lescari civil wars. They wouldn't plunder peasants, not least because 'Gren said they never had anything worth taking, but if they came across someone rich enough to stand a loss without harm, they were never averse to weighting their purses at his expense.

Halice was telling the two of them about Cordainer. 'So he's trusting us to shift the gems for him,' she concluded. 'That should keep him honest.'

Sorgrad nodded slowly. 'Col, that would be the best place to take them. Each piece to a different merchant.'

I noted Sorgren frowning. 'You don't like the idea?'

'What?' He looked at me, brow clearing. 'No, it sounds like a fun game. I've been trying to think where I heard this man's name before.'

'Cordainer?' I queried.

'No, Barazon.' He looked at me exasperated before scowling again, eyes distant. 'He's more than head of the tailors' guild. He runs more sheep on the uplands than any other man in the city.'

'Does he now?' Sorgrad's otherwise handsome face turned ugly for a moment. 'Then he's got plenty to pay for.'

I thought about asking if they would be handing over their share of the loot to those uplanders dispossessed by the wealthy of Selerima eager to profit from the burgeoning wool trade. I decided against it. Their appearance marked them out as Mountain Men clearly enough but I'd never heard anything to suggest they ever looked back at whatever home they'd fled any more than I did.

'So we're agreed?' Halice looked round the table. 'We'll talk to this Cordainer when he's done with Mynna?'

Sorgrad and Sorgren nodded and I held my tongue. There was no point in finding myself outvoted three to one.

Guild Master Barazon lived in a part of the city where even the back alleys were paved and clean. Fortunately they were also deserted. Halice and I kept to the shadows as we approached the back wall of his sizeable dwelling, belligerently spiked against unwelcome intruders. There was the big main gate, wide enough to accommodate the biggest wagons laden with barrels and sacks of provender to keep his household fed and his guests impressed. Set into it was the narrow wicket door grudgingly opened to let the servants out to whatever hard-won leisure they spent their drudgery dreaming of. A slight shadow detached itself from a recess opposite.

'Are they all gone out?' Halice asked softly.

'Gren nodded, a hood hiding his fair head from the inquisitive moonlight. 'Every last one of them. Cordainer locked up himself.'

Halice nodded at me. 'Let's see what kind of lock Barazon spends his coin on.'

'Aren't we waiting for 'Grad?' I rubbed my hands down the sides of my dark grey jerkin to rid them of sweat.

'Here he comes.' Sorgren turned to watch his brother lope down the alley.

'All gone off in their carriages to enjoy,' he confirmed under his breath.

'Let's be about it then,' Halice said tersely.

I slipped across the alley to press myself in the scant

shadow afforded by the arch of the gate. My hands shook slightly as I sorted the lock picks Sorgrad had given me for a Winter Solstice gift. I took a deep breath and my hands stilled, my fingers deft as I felt my way through the unseen workings of the lock. It was a good one. Barazon might scorn the Mountain Men as he sent his shepherds and their bully boys to drive them from their pastures but he was still prepared to pay for their unequalled metalwork. Fortunately, Sorgrad had been picking Mountain made locks since his curiosity first outstripped what few scruples Maewelin has blessed his birth with. Better yet, he was an excellent teacher and I was an apt pupil.

With a last snick of well greased brass, I had the lock open. Even before I'd turned to wave the others across from their hiding place, 'Gren was at my side.

'Have you got it?' I demanded under my breath.

'Just watch this.' Moonlight caught his mischievous grin.

I stepped back to let him slip through the gate, Sorgrad hard on his heels with a naked dagger in his hand. Halice stood at my back, glancing up and down the alleyway, hands seemingly casual in her pockets.

'Cordainer will get a flogging for this,' I said, not for the first time. 'For letting the porter go to the shrine dedication along with all the other servants. I don't suppose Barazon will think much of such piety when he sees he's been robbed.'

'There are the dogs. Who'd have imagined thieves would feed them meat doused in some apothecary's draught?' Halice shrugged, unconcerned. 'And if he does get flogged, his cut of the proceeds should pay for plenty of salve.'

Sorgrad reached through the wicket gate to tug at my sleeve. 'Come on.'

I slipped through and Halice ducked after me. 'Lock it,' she ordered before following 'Gren across the clean swept cobbles of the yard.

I glanced at the motionless heaps that were the hapless watchdogs, dark against the moonlit ground. At least Sorgrad's blade had still been clean. 'Gren's friend the apothecary had unwittingly supplied something potent enough to save the poor hounds from a throat slitting to silence them.

The yard was ringed by single storied workshops and

storehouses. By the time I had the wicket gate locked, Sorgrad and 'Gren were up on the stone slates of the roof closest to the windows of the main house. 'Gren was keeping an eye outwards while Sorgrad worked to foil the shutters' catches from the outside.

'Up you go.' Halice gave me a boost and I crept carefully across the treacherous slates towards the concealing shadow cast by the house. With surprising stealth for a woman of her size Halice swung herself up to join us.

Sorgrad eased the shutter open and now concentrated on the window within. I looked out across the yard, the roofs and out to the back alley beyond. There were more back yards, some butted up close to their neighbour, some separated by a narrow run giving access to the high road flanked by these expensive houses. A few windows in the garrets opposite were golden with candle light but they were too far away for anyone to pick us out of the shadows. Besides, the maids behind those meagre muslin curtains would hardly be staring idly out over the city. All they'd be thinking of was getting as much sleep as possible before the relentless sun called them to another day of tedious labours.

'In we go,' ordered Sorgrad, shoving the shutter back. 'Gren was in first, me next and then Halice. Sorgrad jumped lithely down from the sill and immediately turned to pull up the shutter.

Halice lit a small shuttered lantern to show we were in a neat sitting room furnished with a well polished table that didn't match its chairs and an upholstered daybed whose silk was faded and worn at the foot. 'Housekeeper's domain,' she confirmed with a grin.

Sorgrad was lighting his own lantern. 'Let's find the stairs.'

The housekeeper kept her preserve guarded with a locked door but it was the work of a moment to undo that. Beyond was a corridor carpeted with a strip of drugget to muffle servants' hurrying feet. I pictured the map Cordainer had drawn for us in my mind's eye. The house steward's room was off to that side, where our friend held court among similar cast-off furniture. That door on our other hand would lead to the servant's dining hall.

'Gren wrinkled his nose.

'What?' I demanded.

He looked down at his hands. 'I must have got some blood on my cuffs from that offal I fed the dogs.'

'Never mind that.' Sorgrad was already half way up the first flight of the back stairs ahead of us. A short corridor with an expensive Dalasorian carpet led towards the front of the house and the expansive salons where Barazon would entertain his fellow guild masters and Selerima's richest merchants. We carried on up the back stairs, soft soled boots silent on the coarse carpet.

Sorgrad halted at the next floor. 'We'll take his study. You take her parlour. Then we'll hit the bedchambers.'

Halice and I turned to the double doors of Barazon's wife's personal sanctum. She was either too idle to lock them, or too confident in her servants' loyalty or in their fear of her wrath.

'Nothing too identifiable,' Halice reminded me as she set her muted lantern on a round table inlaid with florid marquetry. 'Silver for preference.' She was already breaking the beeswax fingers out of a delicate candle branch.

I tugged a soft cloth bag out of one pocket and began emptying the herbs from an array of silver canisters before dropping them inside it. Mistress Barazon would find her tisanes already blended for her when the maid brought hot water for her morning drink tomorrow. The herb canisters were fine work, modern but Tormalin made all the same. It was a shame to think of them getting scratched and dented as they jostled in the bag. Still, they were going to be melted down anyway. We weren't going to waste time trying to get a fair price for them, not when their theft was merely a feint to cover the fact we'd been after the diamonds all along.

'That'll do.' Halice caught up the lantern and headed for the door.

I followed, stifling a sneeze from the heady dust of the herbs.

Outside, 'Gren slipped like a shadow out of Barazon's study. 'I'll see you upstairs.' In sharp contradiction to his words, he ran lightly down to the floor below.

Sorgrad appeared at the study door, his own cloth bag bulky with their spoils. 'Let's get these gems.'

'Where's 'Gren going?' Halice demanded curtly.

'Thought he heard something,' Sorgrad shrugged. 'Let's get this done and get clear of here.'

I followed him and Halice up the stairs. My heart was pounding like a festival drum and my breath came fast and shallow. I rubbed one hand on my thigh to rid it of sweat and swapped the bag of tisane canisters over, so I could do the same to the other.

'I'll take the boudoir.' Sorgrad turned to me when we reached the floor where the master bedrooms were. 'I imagine the lady will have the best lock she can on her treasures. You go and see what the guild master might have to lose.'

'I'll wait for 'Gren.' Halice waited at the top of the stairs, frowning as she looked back down.

I took her lantern and hurried into Barazon's bedroom. His bed stood four square against the far wall, dark brocade curtains caught back with silken cords, linen pale where the sheet had been turned back for him by some dutiful chambermaid. The air was still and heavy with the scent of a sickly pomade just undercut by a sharp suggestion of the artemisia and the orris root that hid powdered in linen sachets to protect his clothes from vermin. There was a table by the window littered with oddments of parchment, a book with gold on the binding catching the moonlight cutting through a crack in the heavy drapes hiding the window. Somewhat unexpectedly, a glass fronted case of books stood against one wall.

There would be precious little in here worth taking. I cut across the caressing thickness of the carpet to the door of the dressing room. Ignoring the tall clothes presses set into the wall, and the marble topped washstand with its ewer and basin, I headed straight for the heavy painted coffer under the window. That would be where he kept his jewels; chains to add lustre to a chest already puffed with importance, brooches to adorn his hat and cloak, buckles for his shoes and breeches.

Unsurprisingly, the coffer was locked. I fished out my lock picks and bending over it, I set to work. There had to be a few things in here a man this wealthy could stand to lose without too much pain.

'Livak!' Halice startled me. I jerked upright and caught

her reflection in the tall looking glass where Barazon admired himself. 'Come on?'

I abandoned the chest and ran. Halice was already out of the bedchamber and on the stairs. 'Did 'Gren hear something?' I asked, abruptly breathless.

'He found something,' Halice replied grimly.

I followed her down the stairs, Sorgrad appearing at my elbow.

'Did you find the diamonds?' I demanded.

'I found the coffer,' he answered, voice tight with fury. 'Just where Cordainer said we would. Double locked, just like he said. I got it open and the cursed thing was empty.'

I was too astounded by that piece of news to say anything as we hurried down the stairs.

'Gren was waiting for us. 'In here,' he said tersely.

In there was the house steward's sitting room. In there was an acrid smell of blood compounded with voided bowels and the scorched polished wood of a side table where a candlestick had toppled over. The main table was thrown on its side, a chair splintered beside it. A body lay sprawled across a daybed the twin of the one in the house keeper's room. There'd be no saving the upholstery on this one and the whole room would have to be repainted besides. The walls were spattered with blood.

'So who do you suppose that is?' rasped 'Gren. 'Because it's not Cordainer. Look at those hands.'

One showed the unmistakeable indentation of a scholar's ring and there was the raised ridge of a pen callous on the middle finger of the other. The corpse was wearing the clothes we'd last seen Cordainer in, down to the last detail. That fine linen shirt wasn't crisp and white any more. It was ruddy with clotted gore. Whether or not the dead man was Cordainer was anybody's guess. His face was a nauseating pulp of torn flesh and smashed bone puddled with blood still wet enough to shine in the dim light of Halice's lanterns. Another glint showed up the poker used to do the murder tossed back into the hearth.

'Cordainer must be long gone, with the gems in his pocket,' Sorgrad breathed with ominous calm. 'We've been set up to swing for this.'

'Not if we get clear,' said 'Gren fervently.

'Drop the loot,' Halice's bag dropped to the floor with a clatter.

We were back in the housekeeper's room when we heard the main door to the street below crash open, hobnailed boots screeching on the flagstones of the entrance hall on the floor below. Sorgrad smashed the window to get to the shutters and flung them open, heedless of a cut on his hand. We were out onto the low roof beyond as whoever was in pursuit came thundering up the stairs, their yells and threats indistinct. The voices in the alley beyond the back yard were all too clear.

'Stop where you are!' 'There's no use in running!' 'Hold for the Watch!'

Sorgrad looked one way, down into the yard next door. 'Gren considered the herb garden on the other side. It was no use. Candle lanterns swinging crazily on watchmen's poles threw light into every corner as they poured through the houses on either side. Barazon's neighbours' voices followed them with querulous questions and complaints.

The Watch had a key to Barazon's back gate. It swung open on dutifully greased hinges and a whole detachment of bully boys in their heavy coats and broad brimmed hats came flooding through. There was no escape. Sorgrad sat down on the roof and unobtrusively slid his scabbarded dagger inside his breeches while ostensibly ripping a length from his shirt tail to swaddle his cut hand. Halice pushed me down beside him, her hand on my shoulder inexorable. Then she spread her hands wide in the moonlight, in apparent surrender. 'Gren stood on the ridge of the roof, hands on his hips, defiance in every bone of him.

'You come on down and let's be having no nonsense.' A watchman with a white cockade in his hat peered up at us, quarter staff gripped purposefully in hands that could cover a dinner plate.

'Cry,' Sorgrad murmured beside me.

'What?'

'Weep, snivel, tell them how you never meant-'

'Shut your mouth!' shouted the man with the white cockade, his tone hardening.

He might have said more but uproar in the house interrupted him. The rest of his little army had found the body in Cordainer's room.

'All right, captain, we'll come quietly.' Sorgrad got to his feet and as he did so, quite deliberately trod on my hand. That was enough to startle tears to my eyes and by the time my turn came to clamber down to the waiting watchman and their manacles, I was grizzling quite convincingly. Not that it saved me from the same chains as Halice. I traded a swift glance with her. Her stolid face was unreadable but I could see apprehension in her eyes as well as her warning. Then she was shoved on towards the gate by guards who held their quarter staffs ready, just in case this woman who topped most of them by a head should try something unexpected.

'Gren was the last one down from the roof, jumping lithe as a cat to land beside his brother.

'Give us your hands,' barked the watch captain.

'Make me,' 'Gren challenged.

Sorgrad said something in what must have been the Mountain tongue and looking mutinous, 'Gren held out his wrist for the irons.

'Where are you taking us?' I wailed as we were ushered towards the gate, a solid wall of brown coated watchmen surrounding us.

'Lock-up, copper top,' said one behind me, with an unpleasant relish in his voice.

It wasn't the first lock-up I'd been in. There had been selfish market towns here and there on the road where being caught without the price of a bed for the night made you a vagrant.Such refuse wasn't allowed to clutter up their doorsteps or ginnels. Some would simply send you on your way whatever the chime of day or night, with a kicked arse if necessary. Others would throw you in a cell till morning, one deliberately filthy and cramped enough to be no kind of welcome lodging.

The Selerima lock-up was comparatively clean by contrast; a large cellar in the watch house divided up with walls of lath and plaster, each pen with a door of iron bars. A watchman dozed on a stool by the door we'd been dragged through earlier, oblivious to the drunken maunderings of some other inmate.

I ignored him as well, all my attention on the stairs beyond the outer door. 'Where do you suppose they've taken him?' At least the rambling drunk's lament covered my words.

'Somewhere where they can wash the blood away easier.' Halice was lying on one of the two palliasses we'd had tossed in to us. The sackcloth was grubby and stained and the straw within was crushed and rank. 'Can you see 'Gren?'

'He's still just lying there.' I couldn't keep the anxiety out of my voice.

'He's tough as old boots,' Halice assured me.

'He's covered in blood,' I retorted, uncomforted.

Unsurprisingly Sorgren's uncrushed cockiness made him the watch captain's first choice for questioning. He'd swaggered out as if the men flanking him were some escort rather than guards. They'd carried him back in between them a while later, his fair hair plastered to his forehead with blood, his lip split and bruised, one eye swollen shut. His jerkin was gone and there were boot marks plain as day on his soiled shirt.

Then they'd taken Halice, who'd come back unbloodied but walking stiffly and dropping down to lie on her palliasse without speaking, not even turning her head as they dragged the limply unresisting Sorgrad away.

At least they'd taken the punishingly heavy manacles off us in here, along with every blade we'd carried between us, including the one tucked down Sorgrad's breeches. I rubbed at my sore wrists and wondered what chime of the night it might be. We'd let the five bells of midnight come and go before we'd set out for Barazon's house. It had to be getting on for dawn. How long had they been trying to beat some answers out of Sorgrad? When was it going to be my turn?

With what felt like sickening promptness the lock to the cellar turned with a deliberate clunk. The dozing guard sprang from his stool as the door opened to reveal a pair of broad shoulders in a watchman's leather coat. There were two of them, carrying Sorgrad between them. He looked as badly beaten as 'Gren. The drunk fell silent for a moment then resumed his meaningless litany in a low mumble.

'Open up.' The one carrying Sorgrad's feet nodded at the cell where 'Gren still lay motionless.

The guard from the stool fished at his belt for a ring of keys and unlocked the metal door. They threw Sorgrad inside and he landed on the stained palliasse with the dull thump of a sack of turnips hitting a barn floor.

'And her.' The guard jerked his head at me.

I stepped back as the watchman with the keys unlocked the door. Waiting on the threshold, he reached inside but I was too far away.

He looked at me patiently. 'Come on love, don't make it worse than it already is.'

I took a hesitant pace forward and he gripped me around the upper arm, not cruelly but firmly all the same. The two men waiting to escort me to whatever fate awaited me watched. One was impassive, the other openly anticipatory, greedy eyes on my breeched legs, lingering on my chest before he turned to lead the way up the stairs.

'Up you go,' ordered the impassive one.

I obeyed. There was nothing else I could do. Weary to my bones after a day and a night without sleep, it took remarkably little effort to summon the tears that Sorgrad and Halice had both advised in the brief deliberation we'd managed under cover of the drunk's riotous singing. That was without acknowledging the gnawing fear that we weren't going to find a way out this.

The watch house was dull white plaster walls in sore need of a new coat of lime wash. Candles in sconces caked in wax were adding to the soot stains already reaching up the wall to join the scorch marks on the ceiling. The wainscoting was the same brown oak as the stairs which were wide and dusty and hadn't seen a coat of polish since I'd discarded my housemaid's apron. They took me to a room on the second floor and took up station either side of the door once they'd closed it behind us all.

The man inside wore a coat of brown velvet and sat behind a broad table stacked high with parchments and ledgers. He nodded to a single stool set in the empty expanse of a threadbare carpet in the middle of the room. 'Sit down.'

I did as I was told, an abject picture of misery.

He got up from his round backed chair and came to offer me a handkerchief. 'Dry your eyes.'

His tone made that paradoxically harder to achieve; stern but not cruel, regretful rather than wrathful. I mopped and wiped and drew a shuddering breath.

'I'm willing to believe you had little enough to do with this,' the man in velvet said calmly as he returned to his chair. 'Mountain Men like those two always have glib tongues to go with their light fingers. Forest maiden are you? Not really used to all the deceits and counterfeits of the city? I'm willing to believe you were talked into what you thought was just to be simple housebreaking. I don't imagine you ever thought it would end in murder. That should be enough to save you from the gallows if we can recover Master Barazon's diamonds for him.'

'I don't know where they are,' I stammered.

The man in velvet shook his head and continued as if I hadn't spoken. 'We've searched the house and the yard. You didn't get far, any of you, so where could you have hidden them? Or was there another one of you, someone who got away before we arrived? Was it him who killed Master Cordainer? Tell us where he is and where he's got the diamonds and it'll be him on the gallows tree instead of you.'

'There wasn't any one else,' I said slowly. 'Apart from Cordainer. It was him found us and told us about the diamonds. Find him and you'll find them.'

'We found him, didn't we? With his face smashed in and your yellow haired friend with blood on his cuffs,' said the watch commander with faint impatience.

I shook my head stubbornly. 'That can't be him.'

The watch commander rested his forearms on his table and steepled his fingers together. 'I could just about believe Cordainer got greedy for those diamonds himself, if they're as fine as everyone says. Did they look like a lord's ransom to you?'

'They weren't there.' I realised I was explaining this badly. 'When we got to the coffer, they were already gone.'

'You saw the empty box?' asked the commander.

'That's what Sorgrad told me.' I heard the hard note of defiance in my words and wondered if I should start crying again.

'Who could have had the gems in his pocket all along and been lying to your face,' commented the commander. 'While that brother of his found Cordainer had repented of some folly or loose words to a tavern whore. He told the other servants he was leaving the shrine dedication early just to make sure the house was secure.'

'Who roused the Watch?' I asked, trying for a sob in my voice.

'Cordainer told one of the footmen to come looking for him at the end of the prayers and to go and find a watchman if the house was still dark,' the commander explained obligingly.

I slumped on the stool and studied the toes of my boots as I thought about that. The footman can't have been too pleased. When the prayers were done was when the ale donated by local brewsters would be sold to fill the new shrine's poor chest for the first time. We'd been counting on that keeping the servants carousing long enough to let us get clean away. We'd discussed the timing with Cordainer in detail.

'I've been fair with you,' the commander said, stern now. 'Told you exactly where you stand. We'll be searching that house, the yard and the ones on each side again at first light. Tell me where your thieving friend threw those diamonds and I'll make sure it's to your credit. You need to understand, my lass, that keeping faith with those Mountain Men will just see you hanged alongside them.'

I nodded dumbly, still studying my boots. The watch commander waited for me to say something more. I swear I could hear the chains and gears grating inside the time piece on the wall, as its finger measured out my silence down the long length of its graduated scale.

'Take her back down,' he finally ordered with disgust.

I followed the guards meek and mute down to the depths below. The lecherous one unlocked the cellar door and the stolid one followed me inside. There was neither sound nor movement from Sorgrad or 'Gren. The drunk had finally fallen silent and the one noise was the slow rhythm of Halice's snores.

'You'd better go and get some sleep in a real bed,' he

told the guard now dozing again on the stool with some exasperation.

As the yawning watchman departed, handing over his keys so the stolid one could return me to my cell, I found I was holding my breath. Was my luck going to take even a faint turn for the better this disastrous night?

As he locked the iron bars behind me, the stolid one turned his head to address the lecher with curt disapproval that I guessed must stem from some earlier incident. 'You can see out the night here. Come and get me when tenth chime sounds.'

The stolid one stumped off up the stairs. I unbuttoned the front of my jerkin and tugged at the laces of my shirt before turning round to press myself against the iron bars. 'Please, you have to believe me, I don't know where those diamonds are,' I hissed at the guard with wide eyed desperation. 'Please, I never meant to be any part of this. You've got to get me out of here. I'll do anything.' The neck of my shirt just revealed the creamy flesh that the sun never saw. 'Please. You've got a kind face.' I managed to summon a few tears to turn my eyes to glistening emeralds.

His greedy eyes fastened on the as yet concealed delights beneath my shirt. 'Now then, lass, you heard what the captain said.'

'But I don't have anything to tell him,' I lowered my voice, glancing back into my cell with apprehension for a moment. Halice snored on. 'I only went along with them because it sounded a better way of filling my purse than lifting my heels. I only want to get back to my people.' I ran a distracted hand through my tousled auburn hair.

'I might be able to put in a word for you.' The lecherous guard licked his lips and rubbed a grimy hand over his stubbly chin. 'If you make it worth my while.'

'Please, I'll do anything,' I repeated, trying to look like the kind of half-wit who'd believe a lowly turnkey could have any influence on her fate.

He rose from his stool, adjusting his breeches as he did so, eyes fixed on my breasts as I pressed against the bars. 'Kneel down then.'

'No, what if she wakes,' I threw a terrified glance in the direction of Halice's palliasse.

Lust had her claws deep in him now and he fumbled for the keys as he hurried over. I took a pace back as he unlocked the door, hands at the neck of my shirt to keep all his attention on me.

As the iron bars swung open, he reached for me and Halice grabbed him by the collar, dragging him into the cell, her other hand clamped mercilessly over his mouth. She smiled, finally abandoning the feigned snoring. 'I thought he was never going to take the bait.'

'I thought I was going to have to strip naked for him,' I agreed.

He struggled in Halice's grip as she twisted his collar tight around his neck. A button pinged away to be lost in the scraps of straw littering the flagstones. His struggles didn't last long, his face suffused with red, outrage vanishing behind screwed tight eyelids, tears mingling with the sweat from his forehead.

Halice held his limp body up against her own, one hand still over his mouth. 'Get his coat off, quick.'

I struggled to pull it free, tugging the heavy leather down over his shoulders and arms. 'He isn't dead, is he?' We were in enough trouble over the body we weren't responsible for. We'd definitely hang if there was another one added to our tally.

'No. Rip his sleeves off.'

As I did so, releasing a rank sourness, Halice seized the grimy linen and gagged the watchman. He was already beginning to stir as we laid him down on the palliasse, using the other sleeve from his shirt to bind his wrists behind his back.

'Come on.' 'Gren rattled the bars of his cell door impatiently.

'Tie his bootlaces together.' Halice shrugged on the watchman's leather coat and the leather protested as it stretched across her shoulders. She pulled the keys free from the lock and went to release Sorgrad and 'Gren as I did so.

As I left the cell, I realised the drunk was awake and watching us, eyes bright in an unkempt tangle of grey beard and hair. He grinned, showing me stained and rotten teeth. 'Didn't see a thing, my girl, nor hear nothing neither.'

'Livak.' Sorgrad was already at the top of the steps.

'They've been locking this from the outside. You'll have to open it.' When I opened my mouth to demur, he held up his hands. The watchmen must have stamped on his fingers to leave them so bruised and swollen.

'They took my picks.' I looked at him aghast.

'Use the loop from the keys,' Sorgrad ordered tersely. 'It's a piss poor lock.'

I untwisted the thick wire that bound the keys together with shaking fingers. With our second turn of good fortune that night, Sorgrad was right. It was a crude and clumsy lock easily tripped.

Halice licked finger and thumb and snuffed the candle in its sconce by the door. 'Ready.'

'What if there's some one out there?' I couldn't help but ask.

'Then we'll be hanging on the nevergreen tree before sunset,' shrugged 'Gren.

It was hard to tell, given the bruises staining his face but I fancied there was a hint of uncertainty in his bloodshot eyes. Perversely that put new heart into me.

'We've just got to chance it, my lass,' Sorgrad said calmly. 'Remember what I told you?'

I nodded briefly. It had sounded like madness then and it felt like madness now.

'Let's get out of here.' We moved to let Halice open the door and did our best to hide behind her, the skirts of the watchman's coat adding to her bulk. The corridor beyond the cellar stairs was empty and Halice hurried to snuff the candle burning out here.

Wordlessly, she halted at the bottom of the stairs, so the rest of us could slip up with her at the rear, hopefully no more than a watchman come in from the streets to any casual glance from below. She took the stairs two at a time, footfalls still soft all the same. Sorgrad and 'Gren were hurrying on ahead, pinching out candles as they went. Every bone, every muscle must have been screaming with pain after the beatings they'd taken. Still, better this agony than the slow choking death of the hangman's noose.

We left the floor with the commander's office behind us without incident but the runes rolled against us on the next floor. A door opened and a watch man dressed only in his shirt appeared, rubbing his eyes and frowning at the unexpected gloom. 'Who put the candles out?'

'Run!' growled Sorgrad.

We did, heedless of the noise. We took the next flight of stairs and the next. The slam of doors and confused exclamations drowned out the sound of our boots on the floorboards. We ran up the final flight of stairs and faced a blank wooden door. Halice kicked it open, barely breaking step. Just as Sorgrad had predicted, there was a garret running the length of the building. The pale light that presaged dawn spilled through cramped dormer windows. Halice stripped off the watchman's coat and draping it over her two fists, punched out the glass in the closest. 'Gren scrambled out with the thick leather protecting him from the bottommost shards.

He leaned back in and held out a hand. 'Let's be away from here,' he grinned, teeth filmed with blood.

I climbed out onto stone slates, treacherous with moss and blinked in the pallid light. The commotion below was rising as watchmen reached for boots and breeches before starting the chase. We'd been counting on them being unwilling to chance a fight with their shirt tails flapping around naked thighs. The watchmen dressed to stop us were wrong footed and all the way down the empty street below, their shouts echoing from building to building. I didn't look down.

Halice followed Sorgrad out of the window, her head bumping his thigh. 'Gren was already on the ridge of the roof, running lightly along to the next building. Sorgrad had been right; these houses were all built hard up against one another. I followed 'Gren, stepping lightly up onto the next roof.

Sorgrad was hard on my heels. 'Quick as you can,' he said coolly. 'Before someone down there thinks to find a cross bow.' With dawn building, he looked even worse than he had in the cellar's candle light.

'They're out,' called Halice and I chanced a glance over my shoulder to see three watchmen cautiously emerging from the window we'd smashed, hands and feet clinging to the slope of the roof.

Turning to look straight ahead, I concentrated on running, on keeping my footing on the rough slates, on not looking down, on not thinking what the fall would do to me. End my troubles, that's what it would do. I wasn't ready to settle for that, not yet.

The shouts in the street rose to a frustrated screech. We were outstripping our hesitant pursuers. A long building boasting angular chimneys stacked in fours and sixes offered some concealment and we took a brief pause.

'Down?' Halice wondered.

Sorgrad scanned the mismatched eaves and gables ahead. 'See there, that house with the wing running down to the back. We can get down onto that outhouse roof and then on that wall.'

Halice nodded. 'Keep down, so they don't see us from the street.'

We slid down the far slope of the roof on hands and knees, pressed close to the slates. I began to breathe easier. There was no sound of any watchmen tackling the tangle of alleys and blind entries running along the back of these merchants' marts and warehouses as yet. Crouching, running bent double, hands steadying ourselves as we went, we made it to the building Sorgrad had spotted without mishap. We dropped down onto the outhouse roof without any cry of surprise from an early rising housemaid to set the Watch's dogs on our trail. It was a nerve-wracking jump to the narrow, sloping coping of the wall. We made it and down to the alley below. The others were panting and trembling just as much as I was.

'Time-' Sorgrad paused to catch his breath. 'To leave town. I know where we can get horses on the Kadras road.'

'We'll have to get down to the river. Swim for it.' Halice turned to face the unseen river. She always had an unerring sense of direction.

'I can't swim!' I protested.

'You'll float,' Sorgrad assured me. 'I'll do the rest.'

'Gren smiled widely at me, setting the split in his lip oozing again. He licked it. 'So, going to say you told us so?'

'No, because I didn't.' Relief and anger were a heady mix, loosening my tongue like fine wine. 'I cursed well should have,' I told him in no uncertain terms as we ran. 'It's a solid gold certainty I will next time, before I let you drag me into something like that.'

'Good girl,' 'Gren approved.

I didn't have the breath to answer him. We ran through the empty streets. Men delivering coal and kindling shouted questions after us. A baker walking slowly home after a night making the city's morning bread stopped to look at us, face appalled at 'Grad and 'Gren's injuries. The Watch would easily be able to map our course later that day if they so chose. That was no matter. We would be long gone. We climbed ivy covered walls and trampled through vegetable plots, cutting across the gardens that backed onto the ancient and lofty wall that held the river back from the city. As soon as we found one with a gate to the bank and no sentry in sight on the wall walk above, Halice and Sorgrad broke it down with swift, measured violence.

Out on the broad grassy swathe, laundresses setting great swags of linen to dry on the elder bushes watched, astonished as we plunged into the wide river with its gravelly shoals and willow crowned islets. Sorgrad was right, I did float, just about, as he dragged me across the stretches too deep for me to wade. I scrambled out half drowned on the far side, coughing and spluttering like an unwanted kitten thrown into a stream.

We found the horses where Sorgrad said. We didn't steal them, leaving Sorgrad's silver and emerald brooch pinned to a halter left hanging from the stable door. We'd made enough enemies in Selerima without adding to them.

'Where do you suppose Cordainer's got to?' I wondered when we felt far enough from the city to slow and let the horses choose their own pace. I was riding pillion behind 'Gren.

He shrugged, adding venomously. 'Wherever it is, it can't be far enough away.'

'We need to get a letter to Charoleia as soon as we can,' commented Sorgrad coldly. 'She'll be out for his blood just as much as us.'

'He'll pay us back, sooner or later,' agreed Halice ominously. 'And we'll repay him with interest.'

'Sooner or later,' I echoed.

THE SHABTI-MAKER

Christine Morgan

'Why is my husband's tomb not yet completed?'

'There was an accident, oh merciful one, oh jewel in the crown of Isis. A terrible accident.'

Ateb, overseer of construction, abased himself before the queen and her company. The other workers did likewise, folding their bodies to the ground, bowing their heads. Sweat gleamed on their bare backs and dripped from their shaven scalps.

She had come among them with little warning. Her arrival caught them in the midst of the day, Ra's great sun-disk burning white-hot in the sky and the date-palms rustling, desultory in an arid eastern breeze.

Kepu and Tamit had run in breathless from the fields, having seen the dust-cloud stirred up from the road by the royal procession. There'd been time, just barely, to gather everyone together, labourers and villagers, elders, children, and slaves. Tools were put hastily aside from work-roughened hands. Bread was pulled from the ovens, stew-pots swung from the coals so that they would not boil over.

Goats and pigs roamed freely, the streets strewn with dark piles of their droppings. Geese honked and waddled atop the mud-brick houses, their own droppings streaked yellow-brown against the faded white-lime plaster on the walls. A dog sat, leg-raised and licking himself, in the shade of a squat stone block carved on all four sides with the likeness of the grinning god Bes. Dung-baskets, heaped high and stinking, half-blocked the gate into the humble market-square.

Into this came their queen, the pharaoh's eldest sister and chief wife, Queen Nefersiu. She rode in comfort upon cushions in a covered litter, carried by Nubians in leopard-skins. Servants, scribes, soldiers, handmaids and priests accompa-

nied her. So did a nurse, in whose charge was young Prince
Utsef, the pharaoh's son and heir.

The Nubians had held the litter low enough for Nefersiu
to step down, which she did once her handmaids spread out
cloth of linen so that the queen's golden sandals should not
be soiled. She stood proud and beautiful before her sub-
jects, and even as they grovelled, few could help sneaking an
admiring glance.

'An accident,' Nefersiu said, in response to Ateb the overseer's words.

'Yes, revered one, carer of Egypt,' said Ateb with a vig-
orous nod. 'We lost two donkeys, thirty-one workers and
almost a dozen slaves.'

'How did this happen?'

Atep nearly fell all over himself in his too-eager rush to
explain. As he did so, the other workers remained bowed
low. Some had brought their families with them, wives and
children – or widows and orphans now – and these clustered
nearby with sorrowful expressions. Several wept silent tears.

The tragedy was but a few days past, the memories fresh
and raw in their minds.

All had been well, the work going as usual. Old Sakhmet,
listening to Atep tell the queen, even remembered which of
her figurines she'd just finished – a fat, funny little monkey
to tumble and caper and do tricks to amuse a child – and
how she'd been trying to decide if she would start the next
right away, or go over to the stall where Ib-Hathor sold
melons first.

Any walk was a long walk for an aged woman on a hot
afternoon, but the prospect of a juicy slice of melon, and
perhaps a juicier slice of the latest gossip, had Sakhmet
reaching for her trusty stick when disaster struck.

So sudden. A warning shout from the direction of
the worksite, a strange groaning noise, a grinding crack,
and then such a tumult it sounded as if a mountain had
shattered.

It was not in fact a mountain, but the shattering effect
had been much the same.

Though she had not arrived soon enough to witness anything but the aftermath, hobbling along on her stick as fast

as her stiff legs and aching hips could carry her, Sakhmet found she could envision it in all too vivid detail.

Great chunks of stone smashing and bouncing, cracking apart on each other when they struck ... the creak of wood as scaffolding gave way, collapsing in a jumble of timbers, planks and poles ... snapped ropes lashing like whips ... a clattering rain of tools and sun-baked bricks ... men falling, screaming ... tremendous earth-shaking deafening crashes...

Then silence. Silence and a billowing gritty sand-storm of a dust cloud, gradually settling, gradually clearing to reveal the destruction. Followed by the feeble struggles and cries for help of those not killed instantly. Dirt sticking to the bloody streaks and smears, making a muddy reddish plaster. Thick puddles soaking into the dry, thirsty sand.

Some of it she had not needed to witness with the senses of her body. Some, she knew even from afar – hearing the high, shrill cries of the ka-spirits flown swift from their mortal abodes. Others, she saw when she came to the site, when she saw what few else in the village could see, only those such as Hamun-Ra, the priest, touched with the gifts of the jackal-god. She saw the ba-spirits, crawling and slithering, flowing low and oily like liquid smoke, over and around the places of death.

All other activity in the village and at the worksite went forgotten until much later, when the demands of the living finally overpowered those of the dying and the dead. There had been scant sleep. Chores were neglected. Meals were indifferently taken when opportunity allowed.

They tended to the injured as best as could be done, but, for some, no amount of tending would do. The piercing shrieks of their departing ka-spirits were followed by the sight – to the eyes of those who had such sight – of the ba-spirits issuing forth. They squirmed from breathless mouths, blind and plaintive. Even those who could not perceive them *knew* of them. Knew they were there and would *be* there, and would remain as long as the dead went unburied. Growing stronger. Growing dangerous.

The survivors gathered, hungry and tired, unwashed... hardly fit to be in the presence of their glorious, gold-adorned queen.

And their little prince, the next pharaoh.

Sakhmet smiled to see the boy. She liked children, though she'd had none of her own. They, in turn, tended to like her, or at least the cunning figures she made. Sometimes, to please them, she set her skilled hands to the task of crafting toys for them to play with, toys of wood or clay, brightly painted.

Looking at Prince Utsef, she supposed that he had thousands of toys, far finer than anything she could ever hope to create. Clever toys with jointed limbs and moving parts; valuable toys set with precious metals and jewels, armies of tiny soldiers; toy chariots with wheels that rolled.

At the moment, however, the young prince seemed bored. He fussed and fidgeted, clearly uninterested in the adult conversation. Now and then he tugged at the wrist of his nurse, but the girl only patted and shushed him before going back to taking coy glances at a handsome guard.

The children Sakhmet knew, the sons and daughters of villagers and workers and slaves, were lean and wiry, already accustomed to toiling in the fields or doing other labour. On all but the coldest of days, they went naked more often than not, and their hair was kept cropped short or shaved except for a side-lock.

Not so Prince Utsef. The more she watched him, the more splendid he appeared. Plump and well-fed, his limbs almost chubby, dimpled at the knees and elbows. His skin smooth, unscarred, soft-looking, sleek as if regularly bathed and rubbed with scented oils. Beaded braids of black hair framed his round-cheeked face, long ringlets tightly curled and waxed hung to his shoulders in the back. His lips tinted ripe-red, his wide eyes outlined by kohl. He wore a pleated kilt of white linen bound with a gold-and-scarlet sash, sandals to match his mother's, and a pectoral necklace set with ebony, turquoise and green copper.

Oh, he had never known a day's want or deprivation. He had never gone to bed with an empty belly. This was a boy-child coddled and indulged. His nurse, when not making eyes at soldiers, must fawn and dote on him, feed him sweets, pet and pamper him. All those around him would treat him as the living royal god-blood incarnate he surely was, their next pharaoh, their next king of the lands of the Nile.

As if he detected her scrutiny, the prince's head turned, searching her out. Their gazes met. His was fearless, inquisitive. Sakhmet smiled more widely, feeling her thin old skin crease along its wrinkles at the corners of her eyes and mouth. To her delight, after a moment's dubious inspection, the boy gave a smile of his own. It beamed like Ra's shining rays, flashing teeth white as chalk.

Perhaps he wouldn't snub a small gift? A trinket that might not be so fine as whatever toy-treasures filled his palace chamber, but might please him nonetheless?

Atep, having described the collapse at the worksite, went on to tell the queen that they had cleared away most of the debris already, as well as retrieving the corpses; though there had not yet been the time to do more than the most basic of burial preparations for the workers.

Nefersiu raised a beringed hand in a regal gesture to silence him. Thin bracelets clinked and jingled on her slender wrist. She was a tall woman with a long, elegant neck and a stately profile. Her dress, of linen so sheer it might have been woven from moonbeams, fell from a pectoral banded with lapis and carnelian. Both her hair and cosmetics were elaborately done and sweet fragrances surrounded her. She might have stepped whole from a wall-mural, or been a statue brought to life.

'And the tomb?' she inquired. 'When will it be done?'

'Soon, oh fairest flower of the earthly gardens,' Atep said. 'Soon.'

'My husband does not have time for further delays.'

An anguished cry took them all by surprise. '*Your* husband?'

'Tsst!' someone hissed in warning, but it was too late.

Shaking off the neighbours that sought to dissuade her, Inubet pushed her way through the crowd. The widow was dishevelled, hair unkempt, her face harrowed and eyes reddened from grieving. Several alert guards stepped forth, but she hardly noticed.

'What is the meaning of this?' Queen Nefersiu's voice was as obsidian – dark, sharp and cool.

'*Your* husband does not have time for further delays? *Your* husband yet lives! He has the best physicians, and every medicine… he may live for *years*! He lives, waiting for his tomb to be fitted out like a palace, while *our* husbands rot in a trench."

'They have not even been wrapped in the winding cloths'. Tchah added, clutching two scrawny children to her sides.

The guards closed ranks between the distraught women and the queen, not brandishing their spears but neither holding them entirely at rest. Sakhmet saw the nurse lift the young prince, hoisting him onto one ample hip.

'How many more?' cried Inubet. 'How many men must die to appease Pharaoh's vanity?'

The queen regarded Inubet, eyes glittering through kohl. 'How many do you have?'

Shocked gasps from several villagers greeted this, and were met by some smirks from the royal company. Atep, the overseer, interposed himself and performed another unctu-ous, abasing bow.

'Pardon them, most gracious daughter of Ra,' he said. 'They forget themselves. They forget their place.'

'Hmf.' Nefersiu sniffed. She flicked her fingers. 'See that they remember.'

At once, the insolent women were seized and dragged before the queen. Tchah shrieked as she was torn from her children. Inubet lashed out, raking a soldier's face with gnawed, dirt-caked nails. No one objected or dared move to intervene, except for Tchah's sister-in-law darting forward to collect her nephew and niece.

Sakhmet grimaced, wishing she did not have to watch, but that was a luxury to be denied the workers and villag-ers. It was not the whip, there was that mercy at least, but ten strokes each from a length of knotted rope. When their backs were striped and bloody, Tchah was permitted to scurry to her family, but Inubet was made to grovel before Nefersiu so that her tears fell like desert rain to sparkle upon the golden sandals.

Then Inubet, in a madness of defiance and rage, spat on the queen's feet.

For a moment, the only sound was that of beetles whir-ring in the dry grass.

'Death,' Nefersiu said.

The guards used the same knotted rope that had striped Inubet's back bloody, looping it around her throat and twisting it tight. It was over fast, but not fast enough, her body thrashing in the dust the way a goose's did when its neck was wrung. Then came the swift-winged keening passage of the ka-spirit, all but unnoticed. Finally came the ba-spirit, worming its way through Inubet's slackened lips to creep and writhe in restless searching.

Sakhmet looked away, glimpsing as she did so the look of astonishment upon the visage of the young prince. Then his nurse swept down, scooped him into her arms, and hastened him from the market-square, crooning to him. 'There, there, Sefi. The bad, ungrateful creature got what she deserved.'

Handmaids hurried to attend the queen, removing her befouled sandals, washing her feet with clear water, rubbing them dry with soft cloths. As they did so, Nefersiu began issuing orders. Everyone sprang to obey without hesitation or dispute.

There were many arrangements to be made for the accommodation, housing, and feeding of their guests. Considerable activity followed.

Ptahotep, uncle of Atep, was the village headman; his house was nothing compared to the pharaoh's grand palaces, but it was the best available and so would have to do: news which sent his wife and household into a flustered panic. Dozens of pails of water and bundles of firewood had to be fetched. Bed-linens, chairs and stools would have to be borrowed from every home. The queen's servants had brought along some stores of provisions, but would need use of the bread-ovens and cook-pits. So much to be done.

Meanwhile, Atep instructed that Inubet's body be taken to the trench and placed with the others. Hamun-Ra and his sons would just have to see to her, as well. She was lifted, carried away. The ba-spirit lingered where the royal guards had throttled the breath from her. Its smoky, oily substance roiled around the legs and sandals of those who walked through it, unknowing.

Another among the dead.

Another body to be prepared for burial; such as it would be. A full burial befitting a Pharaoh, with embalming, mummification, canopic jars and a sarcophagus, a funeral, a tomb, was a lengthy and expensive process. Even the quicker and cheaper alternatives were more than could be managed here and now, with so many dying at once. Hamun-Ra and his sons were already overwhelmed with the sudden work-load they'd been given.

Another soul followed the sun's journey west, to the great Seven Gates, to the underworld, through realms of fire and serpents to reach the court of Osiris. Where, if the soul passed judgment before the gods, and if it was weighed against the Feather of Truth and not found wicked, it would go on to dwell forever in the land of Tuat. To dwell forever, as best a soul could, once reunited with a body that might or might not be in the most well-preserved of conditions.

It was a sad matter to think on, that Inubet and the others must spend the eternity of their afterlives bound to imperfect forms and untreated flesh. But, such was the way of it. Those who could not afford full mummification, or lavish tombs stocked with every luxury, would have to make do with that which Osiris provided. It would still, of course, be a comfortable existence with no fears of illness, injury, famine, flood or attack. That alone set Tuat far above the worldly realm of the living.

In Tuat, the souls of the dead reunited with their family and loved ones. In Tuat, the most worthy of all might be chosen to sail with Ra on the golden sun-boat through the dark caverns of the twelve Hours of the Night. Best of all, in Tuat, a life of endless hard labour and toil could be set aside in favour of rest and leisure, sports and games, and all manner of pleasant activities, pastimes and entertainments.

Sakhmet sighed at the prospect. Not that she minded the work of her craft. She enjoyed shaping each figurine, seeing their postures and features give each its own person-ality; bringing them to their vivid semblance of life with her paint-pots and colourful glazes. That, in her mind, was far different from the daily tedium of hauling wood and water, cooking her meagre meals and cleaning the lonely hovel where she slept. It was far different still from those seasons when every villager able to pick up a dredge, pail, hoe or seed-bag was ordered to the fields from dawn until dusk.

To be free from those duties; to be freed from the bur-dens of age and infirmity; to meet her parents and sisters after so very many years, she doubted she would have to confront her former husband, if ever a man had a sin-heavy heart, that man was Thatek, who surely had been devoured by the Gobbler of Souls. But her friend Ayaba had died only last summer, and it would be good to see her again.

Ah, but her time would come when it did. In the meanwhile, the fruits of her art were needed for the others, to help give them the afterlife of relaxation they had earned. When they were called to work, the shabti would answer for them.

Leaning on her stick, she made her way to her house. It was of a single room, built so as to share walls with the larger homes on two sides, and had a yard with a reed fence shaded by straw mats held aloft on a framework of poles. This yard faced the marketplace, and was where she sat to both make and sell her wares.

Her most prized possession was a long low cedar wood box that had been her father's, and her grandmother's before that. Like Sakhmet herself, it was old, scuffed and scarred, worn at the edges and corners. She lifted the lid. Inside, packed on layers of hide scraps and dry grasses, were the shabti she had made.

She smiled on them much as she had smiled at the young prince. That these were the closest she would ever come to having children was a knowledge that had not escaped her notice. Sometimes she named them, or talked to them, and why not? Was it any stranger than Ayaba and her cats?

'Inubet,' she murmured as she sorted through the contents of the cedar wood box, recalling the young widow, the occasions they'd spoken, and what of her life Sakhmet knew.

The shabti she chose was of a woman drawing water. Because Inubet had been a wife, she included figurines of Taweret the benign hippopotamus and the grinning god Bes, to ensure a happy home in the next world. Lastly, remembering that Inubet had a special fondness for dates, she selected a wooden carving of a date-palm, ripely laden.

There would be little payment, if any, of course. Kha'ut, Inubet's husband, had been a common tomb worker, not a skilled artisan. They'd been as poor as anyone in the village, newly married and still childless.

Perhaps, when they were together again in Tuat, the gods would grant them that blessing.

'Isis and Hathor be praised,' Sakhmet said.

She folded the shabti and figurines into a packet of papyrus-leaves, and placed it with the others in her carrying-basket. Later, when the heat of the day began to wane, she would take them down to the Beautiful House, where Hamun-Ra and his sons did their grim work. Not that it was much of a Beautiful House, just a tent that had been raised beside a sandy trench at the worksite.

The normal sounds of an afternoon had doubled, with the queen's company of soldiers and attendants going back and forth. By the snatches of conversation overheard through her windows, she surmised that Queen Nefersiu had ordered a feast to be held that night, after she and the pharaoh's architect had made their inspection of the tomb. Pigs squealed, being led to the slaughter. Boys ran along the river to check the fish-traps, and girls gathered goose-eggs. Ptahotep's wife and Ib-Hathor fell to shouting over the quality of melons. Urbu the brewer, a notorious miser, walked by complaining bitterly to someone how many jugs of his best barley-beer the guards had already depleted.

Despite these noisy distractions, Sakhmet ate a simple meal of bread and dried figs, then lowered herself onto her sleeping-rug. As she often did, now that age wrapped her bones like winding-cloths, she reclined with the slim handle of a willow-wood ankh curled loosely in her fists and resting upon her scant bosom.

If the cedar wood box had come to her from her father, the ankh had been a gift from her mother, when Sakhmet became a woman. She and each of her sisters had been given one. Though time and touch had long since worn away the paint and smoothed the intricate carvings, it seemed to glow with warmth and life.

She felt the painless rising tug as her ka-spirit took flight, unseen on falcon's wings.

It was not death, not for her, not yet. It was somewhere beyond waking thought and sleeping dream, a travelling, a release. The sudden freedom from walls, from world, from weight of flesh. This, she knew, was why ka-spirits cried out as they did when parted from their earthly bodies. The shock of it never failed to be both terrifying and exhilarating.

Shadows surrounded her. The vast and gloomy caverns of the Hours of the Night stretched along the river that flowed in the depths far beneath Tuat. In the distance, the Seven Gates glimmered, promising oases of light. Closer still burned the eternal flames and molten pools of the lakes of fire.

But here, here where the dead souls waited, cold wet darkness ruled.

Water dripped from fanglike formations. Crevices gaped in the walls, in the floor, promising the threat of hungry mouths and swallowing throats. Scaled backs split the river's surface, serpents in undulating ripples, crocodiles lurking.

Sakhmet, a ghost among ghosts, unnoticed, glided over the gathered souls. Most were incomplete, their ba-spirits still clinging to their places of death, awaiting decent burial. Any who dared try to go onward in such a fragmented state would be at even greater risk of being devoured by the beasts of the river, or at the mercy of clawed demons eager to rend them with searing fire.

Others *were* complete, but hesitated. The wicked, perhaps, who knew that their hearts would sink the scales against the Feather of Truth, and were reluctant.

The confused, who could not realize they were dead; the frightened; the lost and the mad; those with unfinished business, unrequited love, and unavenged wrongs; those who were not ready, or did not wish to go: they were the saddest of all, the most tragic.

She recognized those from her village. Workers and slaves who'd died in the collapse, or shortly after from their wounds. Kha'ut was there, seeming more bewildered than glad to have his wife Inubet beside him.

It would be better soon, Sakhmet wanted to tell them. To reassure them, as they shivered, soul-naked on the river-banks with the black caverns looming around them. Their bodies would be seen to, their funerary rites done with at least the minimum of decent burial. Their ba-spirits would not be doomed to haunt the earth forever.

They would go on from here, pass the Seven Gates, stand in judgment before Osiris and Anubis, and, because they were good people, honest and hard-working, they would be granted places in Tuat. Fine homes where they could rest, and enjoy the eternal rewards of lives well-lived. When they were needed to do work, they could call upon their shabti, and the shabti would answer for them.

Unable to comfort the dead, sensing the stirring of serpents nearby and aware that her own ka-spirit was at risk from malicious demons the longer she lingered, Sakhmet flew silent and unseen back to the upper world.

Just as the departure from the mortal body was always a shock, so too was the return to it. The heavy solidity of even her thin and frail old flesh; the entombment within skin and bone; a heartbeat that had been slow and somnolent jarred to a sudden, frantic pace; breath that had gone shallow becoming harsh gasps...

Her eyelids flicked open. Sunbeams slanted in through her window, dust-motes and chaff wafting lazily in them. All was bright light and sharp edges and stark detail. Each sound rang clear and loud and distinct. The scents of dung and sweat and cooking food struck strong and pungent. Every knot in her sleeping-rug and every bump in the ground beneath it pressed into her like hard stones.

Sakhmet clutched the ankh tight in both hands, feeling the rapid drumming of her heart begin to calm itself again. Her gasps steadied into regular breathing.

A shudder passed through her, a shadow, a chill.

Something...

Something was not right.

Spine creaking, neck crackling, she sat up.

She hadn't slept long. Not more than an hour. She looked around her room. All was where it should be, as she'd left it, undisturbed.

And yet...

Hurry.

Whispers from nowhere, from everywhere. A soft, hissing urgency.

It gripped her, and she did not know why, but was powerless to resist.

Her walking-stick was near at hand. She pushed herself upright, went to her carrying-basket, and slung it over her shoulder. The contents, wrapped though they were in papyrus leaves and carefully packed, shifted. Stirred.

As if they moved?

Moved on their own, rustling like mice in the straw?

Which was impossible, of course. She might name them, talk to them, think of them in a strange way as the closest she would have to children, but she had never imagined them coming to life.

Not in this world.

Hurry. Take us. Give us.

She'd meant to wait until the heat of the day had waned, but those whispers, that urgency, the shadowing and shuddering chill; these would not be denied.

Hurry?

As best she could, at a hobble.

Outside, everything still bustled with activity, preparing for the feast that the queen had ordered. Greasy smoke rose from the butchered carcasses of pigs, sizzling on spits. Women wrapped grain-stuffed fish in grape leaves to bake in the coals. Girls pulled dozens of loaves of bread from the ovens. Vegetables and eggs boiled in leather kettles. Ib-Hathor arranged platters of melon slices, fruit, dates, and figs. Urbu the brewer kept a shrewd watch on slaves bringing out jug after jug of barley-beer. What appeared to be every pot of honey had been fetched from every house.

It was more food for one meal than the entire village might otherwise consume in a month. Even taking into account what provisions the royal company had brought with them, the granaries and storerooms must be sorely depleted. What they were to do after? How they were to feed themselves? Yet as surely as the Nile rose and fell, surely as Ra was reborn each morning, the gods and Pharaoh would look after the people of Egypt.

This, Sakhmet overheard as she made her way through the market-square. And this, she wanted to believe, as she'd believed since she was a child no older than the little prince.

Yet, as she hobbled, the end of her walking-stick and her cloth sandals scuffing in the dirt, she felt those shadowy, shuddering chills again.

Hurry.

'Yes,' she whispered in reply, hardly aware she did so.

None of her neighbours, busy with their tasks, paid her any notice. Some soldiers, leaning idle on their spears, only glanced at her in passing. An old woman, bent and poor and useless, muttering to herself, senile or mad; not worth their interest.

Dust hung in the air and the path to the worksite showed the recent tracks of many feet, signs that a group had come this way just ahead of her. Atep the overseer, taking Queen Nefersiu and her attendant priests and scribes and architect to inspect the tomb?

Sakhmet trudged downhill, following a curving descent into a narrow, winding, sandy-bottomed gorge between reddish rock cliffs. At the far end, the path widened into a road, beaten down by the plodding hooves of donkeys dragging blocks of cut stone from the nearby quarry.

It was here that Pharaoh Tehenut had chosen as the spot for construction of his tomb. Passageways and chambers had been carved into the cliff-face, shaped with careful chisels. Intricate murals, painted and engraved, covered the inner surfaces. There were pillars, slabs, obelisks. There were niches cut to hold sacred jars, and places for the vast wealth that would be buried with the pharaoh. Once Tehenut's sarcophagus had been set within, thick walls and hidden doors would be sealed to deter vile tomb-robbers.

The unfinished grand causeway seethed with dark, writhing shapes. They moved not with the organization of bees at their hive, but with the disorder of ants unable to make sense of a broken hill. The debris had been cleared away, the bodies retrieved, the blood soaked in and vanished into the dry soil. This was where they had died, the workers and slaves, and so this was where their ba-spirits remained, and would remain; growing stronger, growing angry and more dangerous, the longer it took for their fleshly forms to be decently buried.

Atep, out front gesturing and talking in a manner more suited to a merchant desperate to sell dubious goods than an overseer, could not them. Nor could the queen, or most of those who had accompanied her. Two of the priests seemed able to, however, and side-stepped uneasily whenever the crawling course of one of the smoky, oily shadows came near.

Flanking the entrance were statues fifteen cubits high. On one side stood the jackal-headed death-god Anubis, on the other, noble Osiris held the crook and flail in crossed arms. The structure between them, the squared-off arch-ways and columns meant to hold aloft a less-than-modest step-pyramid topped with a sculpted limestone bust of Tehenut himself, was what had collapsed, crushing so many men.

Queen Nefersiu looked impatient with Atep's explana-tions. He, for his part, dripped now more with sweat than he ever did during a regular day's labors. The architect conferred with the scribes. The priests conferred with each other. Again, no one noticed a lone old woman passing by, back bent beneath her burden.

Sakhmet observed that Hamun-Ra and his sons were not present at the gathering in front of the tomb. She found them further on, at the shoddy tent that had been erected to serve as a makeshift Beautiful House. Not that any full embalming or proper mummification would take place here.

At the long table, Hamun-Ra worked on Inubet's body. He was a tall man, and thin, with a jackal-mask covering the upper half of his face. As she approached, he pushed it up on his head so that his tired eyes peered at her from under the scuffed black leather muzzle.

'Ah, Sakhmet,' he said, in a manner both exhausted and relieved. 'I was about to send a boy to ask you to come.'

'What has happened?' She glanced at Inubet, who might have looked peaceful now if not for the bruised welt circling her throat.

'The queen.' Hamun-Ra sighed. His lips drew together in a tight line, as if pulled by one of his own corpse-stitches. 'She commands we bury the dead at once.'

'Today?'

'Before the feast.'

'Are their bodies prepared?'

He sighed again, pained. 'As well as we could, but…' A hopeless wave of his hand said the rest.

She thought of the ba-spirits, how they crawled and squirmed. She thought of the ka-spirits, flown ahead to the next world, and the souls in the dark river-caverns of the Hours of the Night.

'It will have to do, then,' Sakhmet said.

'You brought the shabti?'

'I did.' She touched the strap of the basket. 'Something told me I needed to hurry.'

The priest nodded. 'Good. At least there is that. See to them.'

'These are for Inubet.' She handed him the packet containing the four figurines she'd chosen: the shabti woman drawing water, Taweret and Bes, the date-palm. Then she left Hamun-Ra to his own task and went out from the Beautiful House by way of a tent-flap on the other side.

The stink of spoilage, rank and meaty, wafted up from a long shallow trench that had been dug in the sand. The dead were laid out there in rows, workers shoulder-to-shoulder with slaves. Though an outcrop of the cliffside shaded the trench from much of the sun, the inescapable heat of the day took its toll.

Their bodies had been washed of the worst of the blood-stains and filth. They still wore the simple garments in which they had died. The sudden violence of their endings showed in bones jutting from mangled limbs, misshapen ribcages, caved-in skulls, features battered almost beyond recognition.

Their legs were bound at the ankles and their arms folded over their chests. A gum made from sap sealed their eyelids. A stitch of coarse thread held shut their lips. Around each man's neck, on a loop of cord, hung a wooden, clay, or papyrus cartouche inscribed with that man's name.

Little else had been done. Little else could be, for so many, in so short a time.

Sun-darkened brown skin had gone the greyish hue of old liver. Untreated flesh had begun to swell and bloat with soft putrefaction. Seeping fluids had dried, caked and crusted.

No incisions marked their abdomens. Their intestines had not been removed, or even flushed with water, let alone filled with cedar oil to cleanse out the dissolved viscera. There would be, for these unfortunates, no preserved organs. Their corpses would not spend the requisite seventy days soaked with natron. They would not be wrapped in strips of linen treated with aromatic spices, or have amulets and protective spells and scarabs tucked into the winding-cloths at crucial points.

They would simply have their faces draped, their bodies sprinkled with salts, and then the sand would be shovelled over them, burying them together in this single mass-grave. Thirty-one workers, a dozen slaves, and Inubet.

The two donkeys had been another matter. A pharaoh might be buried with mummified horses, a sacrificial ox, his best hunting-hounds and his favourites of the palace cats. Theirs was a poor village, these had been merely donkeys, and meat and hides were hard enough to come by.

Hamun-Ra's youngest son moved along the rows of the dead, ceaselessly waving at the buzzing flies with a palm-frond. One of his brothers set clay dishes of grain, bread, and beer by the head of each corpse; another placed tools or other items at their feet for use in the next world. A few of the dead had small bundles of personal effects brought by their families.

It was not much. Hardly luxurious. Hardly vessels of wine, barges and chariots, or golden death-masks banded with precious gems.

Sakhmet frowned, troubled by the bitter flavour of her own thoughts. Never before had she pondered the differences so much, never before had she felt such a sense of dissatisfaction. This was the way of the world, of life and death, the will of the gods. It simply *was*, and was to be accepted.

She set down her basket, knelt, opened it, and began sorting through the leaf-wrapped packets of shabti and figurines.

This earthly life was often wretched and short, filled with struggle and suffering and hardship. In the next world, in Tuat, the souls of the dead could rest at their ease –

'What are you doing?'

The youthful voice startled her so that she dropped the shabti she held. It landed unharmed in the loose dirt. A small, soft-fingered hand picked it up.

Prince Utsef examined the shabti as Sakhmet blinked at him in surprise. He stood unconcerned, fearless, his dimpled legs bowed, his plump belly rounding forward. The light sparkled from his golden ornaments and gleamed on the waxed black ringlets of his hair.

'My Prince,' she said, bending her head.

'I asked what you were doing.'

Her glance darted past him and found the nurse some distance off, sharing a goatskin of wine with the handsome guard as they kept watch over the pharaoh's son. Why they were with him *here*, of all places …

'I am Sakhmet, the village shabti-maker,' she said. 'I brought the shabti to be placed with the dead.'

'They smell,' he announced. 'Nurse said they would, but I wanted to see for myself.'

In his other hand, he clutched a cloth daubed with sweet-scented oil, no doubt to press to his royal nose if the stink became too unpleasant, but at the moment he did not seem bothered.

'I was bored with all the scribe-talk and priest-talk,' Prince Utsef went on. 'But I was bored in the village, too. There are no nice gardens, or bath-pools, or anything.'

'Well, we are poor, humble people, my Prince.'

'Do you have dancers? Tumblers and acrobats? Music? Games?'

'I'm sure there will be music and dancing tonight at the feast.'

He made a face, and turned the shabti around to inspect it from all sides. 'It looks like a little farmer,' he said. 'Harvesting grain.'

'Yes, my Prince.'

'Do you have others?'

She unwrapped more and showed him. 'This one carries wood, and this one here is a stone-cutter, and a brick-maker, and a painter. I will put with each man a shabti to match his trade and profession.'

'Even the mud-people?'

'Mud-people?'

'The mud-people, the slaves.'

'Oh,' Sakhmet said. 'Yes, my Prince. Even the slaves.'

'Why?'

'The shabti will follow the souls of the dead into the next world. When they are needed to do work, they may send the shabti instead. That is what it means, shabti, one who answers when called upon. The shabti will do the work for them, while their souls rest at their ease in the kingdom of Osiris.'

He considered that, smooth brow furrowing, full lower lip poking out. He looked at the little farmer again.

'No,' he said.

'No, my prince?' echoed Sakhmet, perplexed.

'I said, no!' He hurled the shabti to the ground. Again, it landed unharmed in the loose dirt, but then Prince Utsef stomped on it and it crunched under the leather sole of his sandal.

Sakhmet stifled a cry, as if it had been her brittle body under his foot and not one sculpted of clay.

'They should *not* be allowed to do no work!' the prince said. Another stomp cracked the shabti into several chunks.

'But … it is for the afterlife'…'

'They did not do their work in *this* life!'

'They died…'

'They died without finishing *my* father's tomb. For that, they should be rewarded? They should be lazy?' His kohl-outlined eyes narrowed. 'I say, no! *I* will be Pharaoh, and *I* say, *no!*'

He rushed at Sakhmet and shoved her with all his strength. Which might not have been much when he *was* just a child, but she was caught off-guard and kneeling, and her frail old frame went over like a bundle of twigs. Pain flared in her hip and shoulder. Her breath escaped in a grunt; her next gasp drew dust into her lungs and she started to cough.

Through a watering veil of tears, she saw the young prince turn his anger on her carrying-basket. He dumped it over, scattering its contents.

'Are these for them, too?' he shouted, kicking at the figurines. 'Fruit trees and fish? Songbirds to sing for them? Animals to hunt?'

Still coughing, choking on dust, Sakhmet reached for the shabti. Prince Utsef brought his heel down on the back of her hand. Bones snapped. She tried to scream but could not. At his next kick, she felt ribs give with a dry and weary kind of creak.

Voices and commotion surrounded them. Hamun-Ra's sons scrambling up from the trench of the dead, the nurse and guard running over with their wine-skin forgotten. Hamun-Ra himself emerging from the Beautiful House.

Prince Utsef jumped up and down, breaking shabti into pieces. It must have hurt, like jumping on rocks would have, and some of the clay shards gouged his feet so they bled, but he did not stop.

'*I* say they work *forever*!'

Had she thought him splendid, beautiful and perfect?

He was hideous now, his chubby face monstrous in its twisted, hateful sneer.

Sakhmet forced herself to her knees again, cradling her broken hand to her chest. 'Leave them alone!'

The little prince stuck out his tongue and made a rude noise. He raised his sandal over another shabti.

Her withered palm struck his fat cheek with a loud, stinging slap.

It was, in that moment, hard to say who among them was the most shocked, the onlookers, Prince Utsef or Sakhmet herself.

His mouth dropped open. The side of his face bloomed red. His kohl-outlined eyes brimmed with tears.

'Sefi!' squealed the nurse.

A white flash of pain burst in her head, the guard's spear-butt hitting her a fierce blow just above the ear. Sakhmet fell sprawling again. Hip, ribs, shoulder, all her old bones and joints screamed. The horizon tilted, the world spun, as if Nut and Geb rolled, sky and earth changing places. Dizziness whirled a dust storm in her mind. She was aware of everyone speaking, yelling at once, but only one word and one voice were of distinct utterance.

'Death!' the young prince commanded. Just as his mother had done.

Hamun-Ra's protests went ignored.

The guard reversed his spear and plunged the sharp copper point into Sakhmet's back. She both heard and felt the metal grate against her spine.

Then she felt nothing, though she saw her own hands continuing to scrabble in the dirt, the broken one like a crippled beetle, groping for the clay and wood fragments of the shabti. She pawed at them, gathering them to her. Many were sprinkled with grains of sand stuck in Prince Utsef's blood, which the shards of clay had cut from his feet.

She lifted her gaze to the boy. She managed a smile.

Her wizened fingers pressed the pieces together.

'When *you* call upon them,' she said, in a thin whisper, 'the shabti will not answer. And when the dead call upon these which you have ruined, the one who will answer, my little Prince, is *you*.'

With that, she let her ka-spirit fly, swift on its wings. Its talons snatched at Utsef like a falcon hooking a fish from a stream.

He collapsed as if boneless. His wide eyes stared, emptily, into hers. Something stirred in the hollowness behind his red-tinted full lips.

Sakhmet's last breath rose dark in her throat, issuing forth with a cold, oily hiss.

Her ba-spirit swarmed over his, engulfing it as they both died: and she carried his soul, screeching, into the Hours of the Night.

KRAVOLITZ

Tom Johnstone

'When shall we three meet again?' we used to say.
Then it was a joke. Now it seems a little macabre.

I

They used to call us Charlie's Angels, which still used to crop up on television quite a bit back then. The few that liked us did anyway. The rest called us the Three Witches. Still, we didn't care what the bouffant-haired princesses thought, with their pearls glimmering under their turned up shirt collars and turned up noses.

The saying, 'two's company, three's a crowd', didn't really apply to us, though sometimes our friendship could be a little stormy. Now there are just two of us left, and I don't see that much of Phina. I try and visit her as much as I can, but I am very busy, I keep telling myself.

I know what you're thinking: perhaps I make myself busy to avoid doing so, to avoid thinking about why she's in there. It's a place of white-washed walls and ordered calm, where quietly brutal guards escort patients and their visitors from room to room, and regular medication controls levels of Dopamine and Serotonin with benign strictness. The nurses are quite friendly, in a guarded sort of way, but the guards are more like prison officers and refuse to return eye-contact or smiles. Perhaps they believe that to do so would show weakness in front of the patients. Perhaps they nurse a grudge against visitors for naively offering kindness to these danger-ous beasts.

Phina hardly seems a danger now, except perhaps to her-self. For the most part, she just seems lost, confused, a little puzzled.

Funny that, because it was a puzzle that started it all.

II

Rubik's Cubes were all the rage that year at our school.

Just like Phina to go one better, of course. But then Seraphina Ilyana Belosselskya-Belozerskya was never one to follow the well-trodden path. She was the only one out of our little trio that boarded. Emily Blunkett and I were both middle class local girls who attended the school by day on its assisted places scheme, so I suppose that made her the odd one out. We all had to put up with that in some way at one time or another. For example, I was the only one of the three that preferred the Arts to Mathematics and Science. Also, I never got to play Seraphina's strange game, unlike Emily. At the time I was thoroughly peeved at this, at being excluded as I saw it. I've since thought I may have been the lucky one. Emily, on the other hand…

Ah, yes, Emily, poor Emily. She has the dubious distinction of being the only one of the three of us who's no longer alive.

We were all odd though in our way, or at least, Emily and I liked to think so. But neither of us were as odd as Seraphina. The whispers around school were that she was some sort of Russian aristocrat, whose family had fled the October Revolution in 1917. She certainly had enough airs and graces to feed the rumours. We never saw her parents, weren't even sure if she had any. When school broke up, she would leave for London in a black Daimler with tinted windows. There, she informed us, a firm of solicitors administered the various engagements and functions she attended. We never saw her during the school holidays, and whenever the two of us met up in those times, it was all rather awkward, as if the shadow of her absence cursed our interaction. Our parents would orchestrate meetings that were, I remember, horribly stilted.

I suppose they couldn't be any more uncomfortable than these infrequent visits to Phina. If only I could make eye contact. That was impossible behind the dark glasses she always wears now. Where is the tall, elegant girl I once

knew, with blue eyes as pale as her porcelain skin beneath
that severe coal-black fringe? Her hair is dry and papery
now: cobweb-grey threads that twist with crazed electricity
around her head. Her skin's still pale, almost white enough
to match the walls of this place, yet blotchy and pouchy.
And as for her eyes, perhaps it's for the best that I can't see
them after all.

How could someone change so much?

The doctors say the dramatic weight-gain is a side
effect of the medication: Clotramiazole, Haliperidole,
Methyldopa, I'm not sure which; one of the anti-psychotics.
It's difficult to keep track when they change them so often.
She used to be so preoccupied with her weight at school,
as girls of that age often are. Now she doesn't seem to care.
Perhaps that's a side effect of the drugs too. If she could just
see herself...

I'm sitting opposite her at a table in the visitors' room,
thinking about those things, about the game I never played,
when suddenly she says:

'I've still got it you know. The game. The puzzle. The
Kravolitz.'

She says it with a startling clarity. These flashes of insight
amid the blind fog she inhabits give the impression that she's
got some kind of clairvoyant ability. I remember the time
she said something that seemed to indicate that she knew
details about how my divorce was playing out that only I
could know. Maybe it was a lucky guess. Maybe this was
one too, like a stage psychic's hunch. I wonder if she's playing me. Shakespeare taught me that madness can be a kind
of performance. Maybe it's just that most of the time she
seems so vague and unfocussed, that when she says something that makes any sense it seems more significant than it
is. After all, the game was probably on her mind as much as
it was on mine. It's been her obsession since we left school.

'It's in a drawer by my bed,' she continues in low, con-
spiratorial tones. And she checks over her shoulder to see
if the guard outside the door is listening before going on:
'They don't let me have any glass, knives, even spoons in my
room. But *that* they've let me keep, all these years. The most
dangerous thing of all. Still, it's reset itself, like it always does

when it's claimed another soul. But if someone else were to find it, and were able to play it...'

She's just rambling again now, about the delusion she's held onto all these years, the one that's gradually become more real to her than anyone else: that the Kravolitz can steal your soul. Of course, she used to say this at school, and we kind of believed her in a way, despite the scepticism adolescents tend to affect, trying to appear 'cool'. It was a game we played together. Or maybe she played us. It was a ghost story she told us around the campfire, metaphorically speaking. About how a man with two extra fingers on each hand designed and built the first one, the seventh son of a seventh son. That's why it was divided into twenty eight segments.

She kept on about it for years before we actually saw the thing.

The way I remember it, on the first day of the autumn term in the sixth form, she came back from London with a little book bound in worn, black leather. I wondered if it was a jotter to write down lists of those that had slighted her. But she said it was an instruction manual, handed down 'through generations of my family', for a game 'like no other'. So she said in that rather portentous way of hers. She spent a lot of her time poring over it that day, and whenever I tried to peek over her shoulder she would slam it shut and fix her pale blue stare on me, allowing me only a brief glance that was unsettling and fascinating in equal measure.

Later, I saw her and Emily, laughing and joking over the book. I walked off, trembling with rage and humiliation, before they saw me.

It was typical of her of course, trying to play one of us off against the other. She got like that sometimes. Whichever one of us was the gooseberry du jour would have to take it on the chin, until such a time as we were all equal again, or she favoured the other one. I know I said the clichés about trios didn't apply to us; I just never said it was easy.

Later, as we walked home, Emily started gently mocking her benefactor. She was good like that. It didn't fool me, but it did console me a little.

'Apparently you need to be a mathematical genius even to look at the plans,' she confided. 'I promised not to breathe a word of it to you of course. I couldn't understand a word of it. All in Russian. At least, I think it was Russian. And full of these diagrams that made my head spin. But if it can do all the things she reckons, why didn't her great grand parents or whatever they were use it on the Commies?'

'Maybe it wouldn't be any use,' I replied. 'After all, they don't have souls to steal, have they?'

We both laughed at that, though I was still fuming inside about seeing the two of them earlier.

'Yeah, my grandpa says it's the Evil Empire. Better turn right here, or we'll bump into the girls from Oakham Senior…'

Emily liked to think of herself as the street-wise one, and would mention at every opportunity how her parents were humble shop-keepers who had saved every penny they earned to make up the shortfall in her school fees left by the bursary. It was actually quite a large shop, financed in part by her grandfather; a Harrogate toy and novelty wholesaler. She was a good sort though, petite and freckly, with mousey brown hair, though in hindsight it seems she had a sneaky side. If I was feeling uncharitable, I might have said she was a little dull; a blank slate for Phina to write on. I was feeling uncharitable that day, and would do for many others after that. But I didn't say anything. I don't think either of us said much of any interest for the rest of the walk home.

The fact is, while we both rubbed along well enough, we only really came alive in the pale blue light of Phina's gaze. Phina made sure of that.

The next day at school there was no sign of the little black book. Emily and I looked at each other, then to Phina. She returned our enquiring looks with guileless blandness.

'So, Rebecca, have you any new music to tell me of?' she asked. 'What was the band you mentioned last time: The Thrashing… Moses?'

'Throwing Muses,' I laughed.

Phina knew my tastes ran to the more outré, in contrast with Emily, who thought she was being incredibly avant-garde listening to Soft Cell.

'And you, Emily,' Phina continued. 'Have you anything you wish to tell me?'

The girl did a little double take, and blushed. I could tell what she was thinking. Did Phina somehow know of her conversation with me on the way home from school?

'Er, no. Not really,' she mumbled. 'Nothing at all.'

'Ah, Emily, your life is as uneventful as ever,' Phina replied with a cold smile, then she sighed, as if she knew what we had both been thinking all along. 'I suppose you're both wondering what has happened to the instruction manual for the Kravolitz.' It was the first time we had heard the name. 'Don't worry.' She went on. 'It is in safe hands. Actually, Mr Callaghan has it.'

Mr Ted Callaghan was the Craft Design and Technology master. For reasons I still find hard to fathom, he kept an autobiography of Enoch Powell on his desk. I often wondered how this helped him instruct us in the manufacture of dovetail joints. One thing was certain: he held Seraphina Ilyana Belosselskya-Belozerskya in high regard. It was well-known around the school that he thought teaching carpentry to girls was a waste of time. At the beginning of each of his lessons, he would stand before us in his paint-flecked blue workshop-coat, his long, lugubrious face crowned with a shock of equally paint-flecked white hair, and tell us so in no uncertain terms. As the Head Teacher's progressive ideals instructed him otherwise - and Mr Callaghan remained one of the tiny minority of male staff members - he always stuck out like a sore thumb; battered by one of his own hammers.

Perhaps it was Phina's complete lack of interest in the finer points of these 'masculine' arts that he found so appealing. Or maybe, with her White Russian background, he looked upon her with near religious awe. Whatever the reason, she seemed to have some kind of hold over him, possibly similar in nature to the influence she exerted over Emily and me. She began boasting that he was using all his spare time to construct the artefact according to the specifications in the little black book. It took him several weeks to complete, by which time the half-term break was drawing near.

Emily and I were in attendance when the handover took place. Mr Callaghan looked more gaunt than usual as he opened the door to his Nissen hut, gazing at Phina with smitten deference, glancing at me and Emily with ill-concealed distaste. There was something else there in his seedy, jaded old eyes; something haunted. He looked like a shell-shocked war veteran, with the pencils in the left-hand breast pocket of his blue workshop coat as his tarnished medals.

'Poor Mr Callaghan, you look tired,' said Phina in a softly soothing voice. 'He's been working through the night to finish my Kravolitz,' she told us. Her voice hardened almost imperceptibly as she asked him: 'You have finished it?'

Slowly he reached inside the pocket of his workshop coat, and handed her the strangest object I've ever set eyes on.

It was hard to imagine it forming any kind of recognisable shape. It was all angles, random and irregular. Euclidean geometry seemed to have gone into retreat. It consisted of what seemed like hundreds of fragments of polished wood, joined together by who knew what system of tiny springs and hinges.

'I tested it as well, Miss Seraphina,' he murmured in a kind of low croak, nothing like his usual harsh, hectoring tone. 'It took me all night to solve the puzzle, but as you can see, it's reset itself now. Not sure how. Must have been the springs…'

'Thank you, Mr Callaghan,' she replied, and then with effortless condescension, she added: 'Or may I call you Ted?'

He said nothing, only gave a little bowing nod of the head. His grey face assumed a pinkish tinge: God help him, he was blushing!

Emily and I exchanged glances, smirking at her boldness and his reaction.

'Well, Ted, you should not have been the first to try the Kravolitz. It should have been me. But I forgive you. You were just making sure it was in working order, yes?'

Again, the CDT teacher nodded pathetically.

'Now you may rest.'

As she said this, she stretched out her impeccably manicured hand. For an awful moment, it looked as if he would bend his head and kiss it. Instead he meekly dropped the odd toy into it. Then she ambled slowly away from the Nissen hut, turning it around in her hands, me and Emily following closely in her wake. Emily's eyes were fixed doggedly on the puzzle.

Later, I saw them deep in earnest conversation in the senior common room, the toy lying between them. Emily's hand moved close to the thing, and then Phina grabbed it away from her. As they carried on discussing whatever it was they were discussing, Phina's hand remained firmly attached to it. And so did Emily's eyes. I had never seen them so passionately captivated by anything or anyone, except by Seraphina of course.

I could see why. Emily was in the running for 'A/S' Level Maths, and its perverse geometry must have been a source of deep fascination for her. For my part, I had contrived to dismiss the whole Kravolitz business from my mind. It was obvious that the other two were excluding me, thick as thieves as they were; so I wasn't going to give Seraphina the satisfaction of showing any interest in the thing.

Everything changed when it went missing.

It was the last day of term, and I was in the library, reading a story by Alexander Pushkin: 'The Queen of Spades'. Emily had managed to get permission to leave school early for the half-term break, because her parents were driving to Harrogate to visit her grandfather. When I saw Phina come in, I wondered if she was going to mention her illustrious family again. The last time she saw me reading it, she had hinted that one of her forebears was the inspiration for the wicked old Countess in the story. Perhaps the Comte de Saint Germain had been some kind of influence on the mysterious puzzle Phina had procured.

It was the whereabouts of her artefact that was on her mind, however.

'Have you seen it?' she demanded, looking at the table I was leaning on, as if she suspected me of concealing it under my library book.

'Seen what?' I replied, with deliberate obtuseness.

'The Kravolitz!' she hissed. 'Where is it? Have you got it?'

'Phina, what would *I* be doing with it?' I replied, with heavily sardonic emphasis. 'I really couldn't be less interested in your little toy…'

I turned back to my book, but she slapped it down on the table. The echo it made in the silent room drew the librarian's severe gaze. I noticed that Phina had abandoned her usual coy decorum and the rather affected Russian speech patterns I'd always suspected concealed a demure Home Counties accent.

'Toy!' she raged, her pale eyes flashing. 'The Kravolitz isn't a toy, Rebecca. Haven't you heard what happened to Mr Callaghan?'

Slowly I shook my head. I had sensed an odd atmosphere around the school, muttered conversations between members of staff, and police officers wandering around, but I'd been too caught up in my own angst to take much notice; as we often are at that age.

'An accident. A terrible accident. That's what the head mistress said. He lost control of the circular saw in the work-shop. It took his head clean off…'

A vision formed in my head of a paint-flecked white-haired head inclined on a work bench, seedy old eyes watching indifferently as a whizzing blade whirled towards his scrawny, turkey neck…

I was aware of her studying my reaction. It also struck me that she had seemed more distressed by the loss of her trinket than by her admirer's demise.

'I don't think it was an accident, Rebecca.' By now she was whispering, her face close and confidential, the melodrama of her story restoring her Russian accent and phrasing. 'I think that he took his own life, because he had stared into the Beautiful Face. That is what Kravolitz means. Short for Krasivoye Litzo. Krasivoye: beautiful. Litzo: face. That is what you see when you solve the puzzle.'

'Why would seeing that have made him--?'

'I don't know. It's a sort of Russian joke. I have never seen it. Never mind that: I must find it before it falls into the wrong hands!'

'Yes, well, like I said, I haven't got it. Are you sure Emily hasn't borrowed it?'

'Borrowed it? Where is she, Rebecca?'

Then we both remembered that she'd left early for Harrogate.

III

I've often wondered what had possessed Emily to spirit the thing away with her. In my more fanciful moments I've even thought that the answer might have been Phina herself.

Had she noticed the covetous way Emily had gazed at it, and deliberately left it somewhere where she knew the poor girl might find it? I've often wondered if what happened afterward was Phina's way of punishing Emily for telling me about the book behind her back, or daring to think that she, mousey little Emily Blunkett, was worthy of staring into the eyes of the Kravolitz. Phina had implied that this was like staring into the eyes of Medusa, or a visual analogue of the Mandrake's scream. I can't really believe she planned things this way. She seemed as distraught as anyone about what happened.

From what I heard, screaming was what Emily was doing when they cut her from the wreckage of her parents' car; not killed outright like they were. I think she just wanted to show it to her grandfather in Harrogate, who I imagine might have been very interested in seeing it; perhaps even developing it for manufacture. She knew Phina would never have allowed this, so on an impulse, she took it. At least that's what I thought at the time. Except that she never made it as far as Harrogate.

She was still screaming when they admitted her to theatre to amputate her leg. Not about the pain. Screaming about the face she saw; the eyes, the eyes and their terrible, cruel beauty. This is what I heard, anyway. I never heard it from Emily herself of course. She didn't make it out of theatre. Complications to do with the general anaesthetic, they said.

Of the Kravolitz, there was no trace. Everyone assumed it must either have been lost in the wreckage, or else have flown out of the window on impact to land among the whispering trees and scrub bordering the motorway hard shoulder.

Sometimes, in my more uncharitable moments, I wonder if this was why Phina was so distraught about the accident.

IV

The atmosphere when school reconvened was naturally sombre, and Phina and I began to see less and less of each other as I knuckled down to 'A' levels and tried not to think about what had happened. It's always been the way I cope with trauma, throwing myself into work or some other all-consuming but ultimately empty activity. It's how I got through the divorce, for example. It's what enables me to put off visiting Phina in the acute ward.

And that was how I began to put an increasing distance between her and me during that last year at school. We drifted out of each other's lives, until I was left wondering if we'd ever really known each other at all. To be honest, I can't even truly recall quite when she left. It was a bit like that during the final term: more and more girls leaving to become debutantes or whatever it was they did. This was different though. We had been close at one point : sort of. The three-way thing hadn't always worked, and grief had not brought the two survivors together. Rather it seemed to widen the gap between us. Looking at her now, I often wonder if she ever existed at all, the Phina I knew then, that is.

After my undistinguished career as an undergraduate, I carried on drifting, this time into marriage, to a TV producer called Martin. I had been married to him for about three years when Phina washed up on our door step.

She had been wandering the country, scouring all the antique shops and flea markets she could find, in search of her precious Kravolitz. It was a different version of Phina that knocked on our door that day. Her blue eyes looked paler than ever framed by livid eye-liner as black as her hair. Her skin looked paler than ever too. She looked as if she hadn't been sleeping properly. How she had tracked me down to this address? I wondered. She had her ways, she said vaguely, then asked me if I was going to invite her in. Martin was hovering uncertainly behind me, and raised no objection when I ushered her across the threshold.

I asked her what she'd been up to, and she mentioned some work designing games, computer games, an emerging new industry then, again all rather vague. She soon started rambling about game theory, and Martin seemed to wake up suddenly: apparently he had heard of it through the media circles he moved in. Over the bottle of wine he opened, she said she was researching a book.

'It's about rare toys and trinkets,' she smiled, 'and their influence on the imagination.'

'What, like Chinese puzzle boxes: that sort of thing?' he prompted, his eyes eager.

'That sort of thing,' she replied airily. 'I used to have this wonderful doll's house,' she continued, her eyes dreamy. 'It was so real I used to think that the people in it were alive somewhere, in a larger but identical house.'

'Like in that Robert Aickman story,' he grinned. I hadn't seen him so animated in months.

'Robert Aickman?' she queried.

'Oh, an author Martin likes. I've read him too. He is rather good.'

She didn't even glance my way. Neither of them did. I was the one that introduced him to Aickman, as if anyone cared.

'They sold my dolls' house in the end.'

'Really? I think something like that happened in the Aickman story. And then there's that one about the king who has a toy maker build a life-size, life-like replica of him, a kind of clockwork automaton. Then the real king dies…'

'Is that by this… Robert Aickman of yours, Martin?'

She was putting on her irritatingly coy voice again, but for all her affected girlishness, she seemed a faded image; a shop-worn doll of her teenage self.

'Oh no, that's by Gerald Kersh,' he laughed.

'I should write this down for my book. Toys are so fascinating. Those Chinese puzzle boxes… You can imagine a whole universe crouching inside them. I wanted to do a chapter on them. That's why I so wanted to find again the Kravolitz. For my research.'

I could see Martin making as if to refill Phina's empty glass, so I said:

'This book of yours. Do you have a publisher for it?'

Martin's forearm was frozen in the act of lifting the wine bottle, at the harshness I'd only half intended to put into my voice. Phina's limpid blue stare met mine. Noticing the offered bottle, she shielded her nearly empty glass with her pale hand.

'No, thank you, Martin. It is very kind of you, but I must drive. I am going this afternoon to pursue another lead in my research.'

She rose from the table, and made for the door, leaving

me wondering as I have often done since: was she really hunting the Kravolitz for her book, or had she dreamed up the book as a pretext in her quest for it?

V

I suppose the scene I found that evening was inevitable. I had arrived home prematurely from whatever meaningless project I was using at the time to fill the loveless, workless, childless vacuum of my married life. The empty wine bottles on the table. The moans from the bedroom.

I say 'loveless' yet it can't have been entirely so, otherwise I wouldn't have been at all upset by what happened. Which I undoubtedly was. Jettisoning Martin from the stricken ship of my heart was surprisingly painless.

It may sound cold, but what was I supposed to do when I walked into the marital bedroom and Seraphina Ilyana Belosselskya-Belozerskya lifted Martin's face from her twitching loins like Salome offering up the head of John the Baptist on a plate? Break down in tears? Or was shooting both of them in the head with a twelve bore shot gun the done thing in these situations?

No, I quietly and efficiently began to pack Martin's suitcase, while Phina made futile protests that it was just sex that Martin and I were made for each other, and should never be parted.

'Great,' I muttered. 'From scarlet woman to marriage guidance counsellor in zero seconds…'

While she was making these impassioned speeches on behalf of our marriage, I never heard a peep of agreement from Martin, who just sat there, a skinny arm dabbing at his mouth with the corner of a sheet. And all I could think was: *three years, and he's never once given* me *oral pleasure*.

Then I went out into the garden and pruned the Hydrangea with such recklessness that I pushed my face too close to the razor sharp point of a Yucca leaf; horribly injuring my eye. Phina appeared then, fully dressed by now, as I was clutching my streaming face.

'Rebecca,' she began.

'I've hurt my eye,' I replied through clenched teeth.

'I know you are weeping, Rebecca. There is no need to hide it.'

'No, I've really hurt my eye!'

It was only a tiny injury, but it was excruciatingly painful. I'd never held with the notion that emotional or spiritual torment is worse than physical pain, or that agonies of the body can distract the mind from the soul's anguish. It had never been my experience at any rate. And that day did nothing to change that view. Perhaps I've never experienced either to a sufficient degree to know. Or perhaps I've never allowed myself to surrender to the more metaphysical kind of suffering in the way some seem to do. All I know is, after the pain of that superficial ocular abrasion, I can't imagine what drove Phina to do to herself what she later did.

What she did right then was drive me to the eye hospital. As she helped me into her car, I couldn't see any sign of Martin. Either he had left already or he was just cowering inside. It was difficult to see with my injured eye gushing with fluids. In any case, when I got back from the hospital, he'd gone.

In the car, before she pulled out of our driveway, I said: 'I'm sure you know how fatuous it is to say sorry in these situations, so don't.'

'Of course,' she replied.

'So why, Phina? Why us? Why him? I mean he's hardly Don Juan…'

'Your husband is actually rather a considerate lover, Rebecca.'

'I've only just found out today: it's a side my *ex*-husband has only ever shown to you, it would seem.'

'Anyway, as to why… I don't know why. Maybe it was…'

'Jesus!' I cut her off. 'My eye is streaming. Tissues in the glove compartment?'

Before she could answer, or elaborate on her feeble explanation, I fumbled for the catch and opened it. I should add that one of my eyes is slightly weaker than the other, and it was the stronger one I had hurt. Perhaps it was a mercy, for in the dim light inside the compartment I could just make out the blurred impression of a saturnine, wooden face suffused with a lambent glow.

'Don't look at it, Rebecca,' cried Phina, 'I thought it had reset itself!'

She slammed the glove compartment, and in the closing gap, to my impaired vision the face seemed to *move*, to twitch and distort.

'It is resetting itself now, but I never meant for you to see *that*, Rebecca.'

'I can barely see anything,' I snapped, rather testily. Then, a few minutes later, as we drove along the main road to the hospital, I asked 'So where did you find it in the end?'

'Oh, a funny little junk shop in Abingdon run by a retired civil engineer. He said one of the workers discovered it when they were cutting back the scrub during an upgrade of the hard shoulder. A notorious accident black spot, he said. That was why they were widening the road there. It seemed like destiny that I should find it after visiting you: I so wanted to celebrate it with you! But when I got to your house, you were out…'

'So you decided to celebrate with Martin instead.'

'Please, Rebecca, let me explain. I never thought of myself as a scarlet woman, more an experimental theologian. And when I finally found the Kravolitz I so wanted to play the game. I hadn't had the chance in all those years since Emily… since she bought it. I think she must have solved it all those years ago in the car. That's the reason why her father crashed the car, not the road being too narrow. Well, it may have been part of the reason. I don't believe it would have happened if she hadn't gone off her head and distracted him. I think it's why Ted … why Mr Callaghan lost his head too. He was the only other person to have played the game. At the time, it seemed as if every nonentity had played it apart from me!'

This last outburst sounded almost bitter. I dabbed at my wounded eye to make it seem as if the gasp I'd just let out was a reaction to the pain, rather than to her insouciant contempt for two people she seemed to see as her minions.

'Some people just can't face what it shows you about yourself!' It was almost a cry of protest. 'Like Emily. Like Mr Callaghan. I thought I could. I thought I was stronger.' What was this? Humility? 'The man in the shop said he had never tried to solve it. So I was the first person to have played in all that time. I sat in the car for three hours, absorbed in its mysteries. When I came to myself, I felt a little… odd. I needed company. I so wanted to see you. The Krasivoye Litzo is a harsh task master, Rebecca. It demands certain sacrifices. It says you must kill yourself, or the better part of yourself. I thought I was strong enough, but when I came to your house and you weren't there. Martin was, and I could see he wanted me. I needed comfort. I suppose I wasn't as strong as I thought I was…'

'Thank you,' I said, drily. We were approaching the hospital.

'But your eye…'

'I can manage from here. No need to wait. I can get a taxi home.'

I undid the seat belt, forcing her to pull over. Stumbling along the pavement towards the hospital, half blind, I thought about what she'd just said. An admission of weakness, alongside breath-taking arrogance: she'd seduced my husband, destroyed my marriage, not because she'd particularly wanted him, but because she could. And not once had she said 'sorry'. I know I'd told her not to bother, but surely she didn't really think I'd meant it!

Still the same old Phina after all then. And that strange phrase she'd used about Emily: 'she bought it'. Either it was inappropriately callous slang for dying that sat oddly with her affected Russian accent, or she meant that she had literally *sold* the puzzle to the ill-fated girl.

It did seem more likely when I thought about it than Emily just spiriting it away without consent, though everything had appeared to indicate this at the time. Part of the Legend of Seraphina Ilyana Belosselskya-Belozerskya was the story that her family had fallen upon hard times, lands confiscated by the Bolsheviks, etc. So it was always a struggle for them to keep up appearances and continue in the manner to which they were accustomed. It did not seem inconceivable that Phina had sold the valuable toy to Emily to further this aim, perhaps even to help pay for her school fees. Maybe Emily's toy magnate grandfather had financed the deal, possibly handsomely given his political sympathies.

This is all just speculation, from someone who was very much out of the loop at the time. On the other hand, it's a preferable scenario to the possible one where Phina allowed her to purloin it knowing full well what would happen, in revenge for her presumption. This possibility is as terrible as it is unlikely, though the first scenario does still beg the question: given how dangerous she has repeatedly implied it is to the unwary, would Phina really have countenanced the manufacture and mass marketing of the Kravolitz?

Perhaps she would, if she were the diabolically amoral creature I sometimes think she was, in my more uncharitable moments.

VI

On the way to visit Phina, I have to drive along the stretch of motorway where the crash happened. Maybe that's why I put off the visits. Or it could just be another excuse. There are kites that circle overhead on that stretch of road, prehistoric-looking birds of prey, reintroduced in recent years to the woodlands on either side of the motorway. I wonder if they hover in wait for human road-kill. I could imagine them swooping down when the Blunketts 'bought it', to use Phina's unfortunate phrase.

I keep expecting to see a maimed, mousey figure darting around the scrub. Perhaps if I had the Kravolitz…

Surely I don't buy into the legend Seraphina's spun around her lost toy, the powers she attributes to this thing of wood and wire and tiny, coiled springs. And even if I did, she's hardly made it a very enticing proposition. On one visit she compared it to staring into the Abyss:

'You might look away, but then you see it in everything. From then on you are as one whose eyes have become accustomed to the dark, so that you begin to see the shapes moving in the shadows.'

VII

I think she's harmless now, too drugged up to the eyeballs in the white-washed walls of ordered calm to pose a threat to herself or anyone else.

I say eyeballs…

She did it with a spoon. It was quite a shock when she first removed her dark glasses to show me what she had done. She explained that they had to go, because they were evil. Those pallid, blue orbs were responsible 'for hurting Emily and poor Mr Callaghan. Yes, and for hurting you and Martin, Rebecca.'

In that way, she's still the same Seraphina Ilyana Belosselskya-Belozerskya of old, still grossly over-estimating her power over others. But she also blamed the Kravolitz, both for the trail of destruction she believed she'd left throughout these peoples' lives, and for her horrifying act of self-mutilation.

'It changes the way you see things, Rebecca,' she said on one visit. 'It shows you the intense beauty of some things in life, and the grotesque ugliness of others. Both extremes are more than most souls can bear. The face shows you these things, Rebecca.'

She still has a gift for the beautiful turn of phrase, though she's lost her own physical charms, buried under mounds of flesh in plain, baggy clothing like a convict's uniform; strange to hear such eloquence from this lumpen, lethargic, creature, half-asleep with her medication.

Was she still the same Phina, I wondered, even devoid of her beauty, even without those limpid blue eyes? She went on:

'You see, its name is only partly a joke. Its face is indeed beautiful. But it is the terrible, wanton cruelty in that face that makes it so deeply ugly. In the case of weak souls like Ted's or Emily's, the effect is almost immediate. In my case, it has taken far longer for me to feel its full effects. It held up a dark mirror to my soul, and trapped it there. Now I can no longer bear to look into a mirror of any kind.'

What she had done had certainly made sure that could not happen, yet surely the lack of fresh visual stimuli just trapped her with the memories of all her misdeeds? And I am sure there are many. Some years after we parted company at the eye hospital, I heard that she'd drifted into a squat in Brighton. I'm not sure what she got up to there; I imagine it involved a good deal of staring into the Abyss. She subsequently admitted herself voluntarily to Millview

Hospital, where she soon found herself sectioned after they made the mistake of allowing her a metal spoon to eat with.

The eye doctor sent me home with antibiotic eye drops and codeine. For a few days, I thought my good eye was going to be permanently damaged. It seems like nothing compared to Phina's condition. How like her to go one better. Ever the alpha female.

That sounds unforgivably callous I know. I can only imagine what she went through to go to such extremes, what she's going through now. I've only ever experienced light eye damage, after all, so I can only guess what it's like to lose both eyes. Not to mention all the other mental anguish she can boast.

There I go again. I can't seem to talk or think about this whole sorry affair without accusing poor Phina of spiritual one-upmanship, as if she's putting it all on to justify all the liberties she's taken.

Then I think of returning from the eye hospital in the taxi to an empty house. Martin had wasted no time in making himself scarce. I'd never known him so proactive. Our marriage might have been a whitened sepulchre, a gutted shell, but maybe we could have used that empty frame to rebuild it. Should I have tried to make it work, forgive him, or at least given him another chance, put him on probation for the one lapse? Had Phina dragged me into her world of uncompromising, romantic extremes? That's what made me so livid about her behaviour. Not sleeping with my husband: such a silly turn of phrase, as if they just lay down side by side and had a few minutes' cat nap. No, it was this idea she always put about that her torment was so epic and dreadful and incomprehensible to us hidebound mere mortals that such things were bound to happen to poor little her. It left you feeling as if you were made of baser stuff if you weren't getting up to the kinds of things she did. Especially if she made a point of not inviting you to join in.

Like with her toy. It's probably just an upmarket Rubik's Cube. All her hyperbole's left me wondering what all the fuss is about.

The doctor talked a lot about displacement: 'Seraphina feels guilt for the way she has behaved to others. The guilt has become so intense and unbearable that she has displaced it onto an object. A remarkable object, but an object none-theless. An object can be put away, discarded, removed, even destroyed. Guilt cannot be dealt with so easily. When that displacement failed, she instead targeted a part of herself she could blame and objectify.'

He's wrong. She may have discarded, removed, destroyed her eyes, but she hasn't done the same with the Kravolitz. She's just put it away, somewhere within easy reach. She just told me.

Is she playing me? Surely not. After all, she's lost her glamour now, her bulk jammed into a chair, her eyeless face framed by electrical hair. She's got no hold over me now.

So why am I looking over her shoulder at the guard out-side the glass-panelled door, wondering how many are on duty in the corridor, how easy it would be to sneak into her room and rummage in the drawer of her bedside table?

Why am I still wondering what all the fuss is about?

If I don't play the game, I'll never know.

NO PLACE OF HONOUR

A. R. Aston

The world died as you neared the Yucca Thorns. The trees grew gnarled and leafless, the grass and fruits and flowers vanished. All colour and vitality retreated, bleeding away into the lowland regions below.

Few folk ventured this far upland, but the Band of Sessian Cutress was a different story entirely. Her force was stronger than most others in the valleys below; fifty warriors, men and women in their prime, with a well-stocked baggage train of serfs and merchants and other, less savoury camp followers. Sessian had made sure to raid the Narrocmen before the journey to the Yucca Thorns; their larders were fat and their menfolk soft. Some of the Narroc captives walked with the cattle at the back. Most wept openly, while others bore masks of hatred for the war band which had captured them. Sessian paid them little heed in either case.

They said the Yucca mountain passes crawled with bandits, but she had seen none so far on their journey. They likely feared the dozen horsemen who rode on either flank of the march, scoped rifles scanning the high-sided cliffs for any sign of the ravaged ones. Sessian had a dozen rifles; relics, ancient yet deadly as they were in the forgotten days of their creation. New rifles were noisy and crude, but not so these ancestral weapons. She rode at the head on her red charger barded with silver coins, carried a relic bi-barrel shotter in her belt, and a revolver, which only enhanced her deadly reputation. Of course, she didn't use them often; shells were rarer than gold flecks in this age. She favoured her basket-hilt dagger in a fight. No reloading, just the cut and slash of the up-close kill. Still, her advanced weapons made her and her war band a nightmare for the ravaged born, the sickly reavers who were said to roam Yucca, ever hungry for an easy kill.

The pebbled path soon vanished in the foothills, and the horses neighed in misery as they were forced to trot over uneven, hard surfaces. The wind picked up here too. It was bitter and Sessian could almost taste the corpse stench drifting down from up high. The clouds themselves girdled the upper reaches, and already she could see fog rolling down them like a suffocating blanket. Soon, the way ahead would be invisible. She had no desire to get lost in choking fog; not while on the cursed mountain.

Sessian turned to the dark rider to her right. 'Haast. Ride ahead. Need a path, and a camp,' she grunted.

Haast, her half-uncle, was a scout of many years; his face painted black and white, with crow feathers woven into his grey mane, and a crossbow stowed across his back. Haast nodded without another word, before he kicked the side of his swift black mare. His dark shape vanished into the mist ahead, dissolving like a wisp. Though it didn't reach her battle-worn features, Sessian smiled as she considered uncle Haast. He had seconded Sessian when her husband-king Gorl had been challenged by her for the mantle of War Chief of the Band. Gorl Cutress would have had the Tribe Carls drag her from her tent and beat her to death. But with Sessian's uncle supporting her, she was granted a personal duel with Gorl. The duel had been fierce and gruelling, but in the end, her blade was the swifter. When Gorl was finished bleeding, kneeling in the dust with ropes of intestines spilled over his lap, she had made him look her in the eyes before finishing him off. She spared a glance towards the grim-faced warriors behind her, clad in their looted armour painted in the red heraldry of the Mistress of the Dagger.

She knew that they wore their markings grudgingly the further she led them from the fertile lowland plains, the greater the risk of them turning. One false step and they would depose her. She could probably kill any one of them in trial-combat, but not all together. She suspected Olif the rifle bearer, lean and hungry for advancement, was plotting something amongst his fellows, but what form his malcontentment would take, she didn't know. Her only hope was to find what she was looking for up here.

Yucca, the cursed mountain. Ever since she was a girl, people spoke of the dark magic which lingered around this grim ascent;

'Invisible demons. They cut a man's thread without him ever feeling it. You sicken and die, and never see them coming.'

'In ancient days, a necromancer cursed the mountain, when the king of Yucca slew his beloved. 'As you deny me a family, so I rob you of all your children, now and in the ever-after,' the necromancer said, and so the Yuccamen fell; for their mothers and daughters became barren and childless.'

'The bear and the eagle had a war when the mount was Edin. But so loud was their ruckus, they woke the dragon Nukh from his slumber 'neath the hills. He rose up and breathed his poison across the mount. Eagle and bear together died when the forest shrivelled and Edin was destroyed.'

'When God was killed by the dragon Nukh, his crown of thorns fell from his head and crashed to Yucca, and killed everything there forever after.'

'The King of the World died, and his tomb was set into the mountain Yucca, and his infinite treasure were buried with him, marked by the stone thorns and guarded by the ravager plague.'

There were endless tales, each one sworn to be gospel by some shaman or holy whisperer. Sessian did not believe most of them; yet they couldn't *all* be wrong. The tales told of ancient weapons and bountiful treasures. If her war band managed to capture these weapons, they could rule the valley and the lands stretching out beyond it. They would be safe forever from predation by the City-Kings and their Patriot-Crawlers.

Two days, and the acrid fog descended. Directions meant little. Five riders fell from the cliff where the fog clung close.

Three days in, and dead birds strewed the path before them like fallen leaves, whose sodden corpses squelched beneath the horses' hooves. The pass was too narrow to camp on so that they ate from the food slung across the cat-tle's backs. Their slaves ate the fallen birds.

Five days in, the prisoners began to sicken. Too weak to walk, they were dragged, mewling and defecating, behind the cow sleds.

Belhiem had called these events an omen, and had tried to leave with half the war band. Sessian had shot him where he stood. The man looked perversely comical as he pawed helpless at the neat hole in his forehead, before he col-lapsed; face first, into the insipid Yuccan soil. No one else challenged her. Olif and Freda stared at her with eyes alight with disgust, but they knew better than to speak out when Sessian's blood was up.

On the sixth day, Haast returned with word of a wide plateau in the foothills, where the fog was less thick and cloying, and the air less rancid. But that was not all he brought with him. There were two men bound by their hands, tied to his saddle.

One was a young man, no more than nineteen years. The pale-skinned lad was clad only in a pair of loose canvas hose tied with cord. His chest was hairless and smooth, his tus-sled blond hair fell pleasingly across his handsome features. The boy looked terrified as he caught Sessian's fiery gaze. She supposed the sight of a six foot warrior woman with a headdress of horns, and eyes painted a gleaming red must have made him think a demoness had come to devour him.

The second figure was old. His thin limbs were twisted and knotted as Yucca's trees. His flesh was as pale as the boy's, but with the unpleasant pallor of the sickly and wrong. He was covered in markings and tattoos, coiling script etched into his flesh in dozens of old tongues and dialects. His long nails were black like eagle talons, his eyes grey and hard. The revenant wore a mangy hide cloak, from which dangled dozens of fetishes, tied there by sinews and twine. He had little hair, save for a few stray strands of grey clinging to his mottled eggshell skull, and an unkempt beard. When the ancient appraised her fearsome counte-nance, his expression seemed quietly amused

'Crossing the plateau, I came across these two, making spells, messing in entrails and chanting. The boy drew steel against me. Brave but stupid,' Haast said, gesturing to the new dirk sheathed in his belt. 'The elder came with no tumult.'

Sessian hopped down from her saddle and approached the diminutive old alchemist. Even dismounted she loomed over him. He held her gaze with a friendly smile, showing brown teeth set into oozing gums.

'Who are you? What are you on the mountain for?' she growled.

'The magick is strong here. The Capitali thought this place most valuable. Selt is myself, and this one is Talf, acolyte of mine six years,' he replied, his voice a low croak, like a desiccated toad.

Gently, she placed a hand on his shoulder. 'You come for the magick? Then you know the Yucca Thorns,' she replied.

Selt nodded slowly, his horrid grin widening. 'I know it, though it is hidden. No maps show it, for no maps *want* to know it. The knowledge of it flees from the truth because the Nukh, that old wyrm, is so terrible it coils and whispers and kills. It robs the future to slay the present. So my old master said, so it was so in his day,' Selt giggled, spitting a blob of brown phlegm into the grass as he spoke, before taking a bite from some slimy fungus in a pouch at his belt.

Sessian grabbed him by the throat. It felt weak beneath her fingers, she could break it easily; even clenching her fingers slightly was enough to drive the air from the sorcerer's windpipe. 'No games with me, ravaged man. You will show us where.'

'I don't know where... Not yet. I can divine it for you, with my materials. I need my materials, from my tent,' he croaked weakly.

Sessian sneered before she released him. 'We head to the plateau. Your hut is there then so will we be.'

They made camp beneath the looming mountain fastness.

As night fell, camp fires bathed the place in flickering orange light. Two warriors guarded the alchemist's mud-caked tent. Smoke and steam of different colours rose from the hole in its roof and door flaps like the breath of a sleeping dragon.

Sessian had Talf brought to her once her tent had been

set. Fortunately, the boy was more than willing to accommodate her desires, and press himself against her firm flesh. It was much better when there was consensus. Congress at knifepoint held no pleasure for her.

As they languished on her bed of animal skins, by the heat of the hearth fire, she turned to the boy. 'Do you speak Capitali?'

He nodded. 'I speak a little. Selt taught it me. What do y... sorry...' he began, before remembering his place.

'No no, say it clear,' she replied, stroking his cheek tenderly. Smooth, unscarred; this boy had led a sheltered life, which was surprising.

'What do you want... in the Yucca Thorns?'

She chuckled, reaching out to take a gulp from her flagon. 'Same as most I reckon; power, to protect ourselves in this dark time.'

Talf nodded quietly.

'And why is Selt here?'

'He tells me little; just chatter about Nukh and the magick. I mix the potions and fetch the water. He talks to himself more than me most days,' Talf sighed. 'We came here from far Kel-Fornia. This place is important. Dark majestik he says.'

'Why are you his? You don't sound like you want the dark majestik, do you?' she asked, placing her other hand upon his thigh.

'He saved me, as a child. Raised me up and cured my ailments. He protected me from the bad ones.'

'And who are the bad ones?' she whispered in his ear.

He smiled as he turned his face to hers. 'You are, of course.'

She laughed uproariously. 'That I am.'

Talf walked beside Sessian's horse as they continued their march the next day.

Selt led them, seated upon a mule, alongside a great weight of scrolls, tomes, jars and pouches filled with all manner of chemicals. Samples of birds, frogs, bats and various bugs were collected in tubs and bottles. Sticks of smoking incense and otherwise drifted from him as he trotted ahead of the band.

They travelled up and down the mountainside for many hours. Selt held a two-pronged divining branch before him, etched with runes of power. Bells were rung, and many wordless chants spilled from his filthy, bearded mouth. He would periodically call a halt to the formation, fill a basin with brackish water, and place a needle on its surface, watching eagerly as it turned upon the dark fluid.

Finally, toward the end of a full day's trekking, silhouetted against the blazing orange sunset, Sessian saw the object of her journey; the Thorns of Yucca.

They were horrible, uneven things, even at this distance; clusters of barbs jutted from them as they coiled in upon themselves like the enclosing folds of a Kraken's grasp. The narrow pass ahead of them zigzagged between the forbidding stone blocks barring the way. They were forced to travel in single file. Selt's mule first, followed by Sessian and Talf, then Haast and the rest. The blocks were too regular to be natural. This was a tomb, or a city or a maze. Something built by other humans in other times.

No one spoke. Beyond the stones, a ring of desolation a hundred yards deep encircled the thorny mound. There no grass grew, no bird sang, nor even the casual chirp of bugs. The silence here was oppression and despair.

This close, the thorns were revealed to be thirty foot stone spires, covered in spines as long as a man was tall, arranged as if they were clambering over one another to reach the darkening sky.

Sessian's horse whinnied and flinched away from the thorns; its sound deafening in the silence, as it echoed around the valley. She dismounted carefully, patting her mare to reassure her. But Sessian's soothing words sounded hollow in her ears; inwardly, she felt a profound dread, a feeling she had never believed she was capable of. Her men and women peered around the blocks and the towers, holding their axes and swords close.

Selt slid down from his mule and sank to his knees, arms raised in exultation. He whispered and mumbled in a foreign tongue.

'He is thanking Nukh for his guidance,' Talf explained,

by Sessian's side. She nodded and shoved him aside with a dismissive grunt. She felt protective of the young man; it would be a shame if he died here. But she hid her concern in front of her riders.

As she approached Selt, something crunched underfoot.

Bones. Scattered about the base of the thorns; all manner of bones, animal and human. There were skulls too. She looked to the sky, and watched as the sun was speared by a thousand black barbs and dragged beneath the horizon, leaving only the clawing talons of Yucca to pollute the sky with their presence.

Whoever had built Yucca, Capitali or Quarantian, they wanted no one to enter here; ever.

To Sessian that said something was worth guarding long after the extinction of their culture. Though it chilled her blood, she knew she could not leave.

'We make camp. Tomorrow is digging. The Capitali tomb is here,' she called out.

'This is a cursed place. Only death lives here,' one of her men, Olif replied.

'Olif is on the right knowledge. I can feel the wyrd. Evil places shouldn't be defiled,' Freda added, her sisters nodding darkly at her words. There was a murmur of agreement amongst some of the riders. Haast snarled.

'You are oathbound, you scum! If your warlord demands this place is dug, it is dug!'

Further muttered threats and curses rippled through the ranks. Haast made to draw his machete, before Sessian raised her hand.

'If you have loyalty to this tribe, to this band, you will stay. I will not hold you here. This is a dark place. Those who wish to may go. Freedom is yours. Take it. But you take no slaves with you. And when we come down this mountain, you and yours will be our enemies. And you will suffer. '

Olif rode up, slinging his rifle over his shoulder as he spat at her feet. 'Your threat is nothing. You won't come down the hill again, usurper red-bitch!'

And with that, Olif, Freda and two dozen others turned their horses around and left, through the winding entrance they had entered from.

The camp that night was as near silent as the hills that surrounded them. The thorns seemed to writhe in the flickering firelight, casting strange, elongated shadows.

Selt's fire had a green flame, which flickered as he added more of his mystic spice and powders, decades in the procuring. But it was worth it, for in their crystalline particles lurked the word of Nukh. Smoke coiled about him, dense and serpentine. He blinked and saw faces, roiling in the tumult, silent as everything else. He breathed in the fumes as he bit down on more of his foraged mushrooms, and supped Nukh's nectar from his drinking skin.

'This is a revelation space. Manifestly Assured Destruction; madness. Divine profanity; I bring offerings to your altar, *Nukh*, the spirit of the new, clear winter,' Selt giggled.

'Talf is a traitor,' another voice said, deeper than the wellspring of the ocean, deeper than sound; impossible yet real. 'His sentence will be the same as the sacrifices.'

The new voice came from the smoke that billowed from Selt's own maw, circling back around to face him. It was a dragon with a human face and a lamprey's jaws, circular and grasping. Nukh, manifested. The voice echoed in only his head, like a whisper and roar at once.

'No, Talf knows his role. He's a strong one. Nukh will touch him last, and before then, he will return,' Selt argued.

'Selt is a hopeful one,' a second voice hissed, oozing from the blood-filled mushroom crushed between his long claws for hands. The ooze congealed into a mouth, which wetly continued. 'This is a holy place. Talf knows this is your realm. You found it; the magick belongs with Selt. The red marauder is a thief.'

The walls of his tent were becoming stone, and the thorns pushed through slowly, each wound causing the canvas to bleed and drool.

Selt leaned back, letting the blood pool in his mouth and mat upon his beard. He grinned, breathing green smoke from his flared nostrils.

The clamour of picks breaking rocks robbed the thorns of their morbid silence, but the sense of dread refused to leave

Sessian's mind as time wore on. She'd ordered six or seven test holes in and around the thorns. If there was a tomb there, she would find it. With fewer men, the work took longer. The serfs were still ill from eating the birds, and they only seemed to get sicker the more they worked with their flat wooden paddles. The guards she posted had to watch closely to ensure the same number of serfs went in as came out.

Sessian had the bedraggled warlock Selt confined to his vile little hovel, two guards outside at all times. She trusted Selt not at all. His vile glee was wrong. Yet, wasn't that what she should be feeling? She had her prize, and she was sure, if she could just dig deep enough, the power of the Yuccamen would be hers.

On the fifth day of digging Talf had found a stone podium at the centre of the thorn structure. There was a message carved into the black stone several times over that took him quite a while to decipher. Yet eventually, he succeeded and took it to Sessian, his sparkling eyes full of pride in his own cleverness.

'The old-culture talks through the stone. They are talking at you,' he breathed. 'They are warning tomb-breakers.'

Sessian raised an eyebrow. 'What are they saying?'

Talf shook his head. 'Some of their words I do not know because… But I've got close to what they said.'

'Then tell me.'

And so he drew the hide he had scrawled the message on from his belt, and he read it all at once;

> *'This place is a message… one of many messages…*
> *heed us! Sending this message to you was important*
> *to us. We were once a powerful culture.*
>
> *This is no place of honour. No site of a great*
> *victory or triumph. Nothing of value lies here.*
> *What lies here is dangerous and repulsive to us.*
> *This message is a warning, an omen.*
>
> *There is danger in this place, which increases*
> *towards a centre. The centre is here. A thing of*
> *dread, beneath us.*
>
> *The danger remains, in your time as in ours.*
> *The danger scourges flesh, and it will kill.*

> *The danger is a form of fire, energy, spreading out.*
>
> *If you disturb this place, the danger will be unleashed. You must shun this place, and leave nothing living here. Nothing.'*

Sessian listened quietly, before she took the parchment from Talf's hand.

'We must leave my majesty. The Yuccamen-'

'... Are dead; why should I heed their words?'

'But Sessian, what will we tell the others? We must do something!'

Talf gasped as Sessian's hand shot out, grasping his throat. 'The Yuccas lie to protect their treasures. Tomb-builders always lie. No curse will keep me out. One word and I will take your manhood, and then your eyes. We understand, yes?' she hissed in his face, her sharpened teeth and blazing eyes turning the boy even paler than normal.

All he could do was weakly nod, before she cast him to the floor.

She pressed a shovel into his hand and set him to work the very next day.

The passage into the depths was arduous and slow. Underground was threaded with tough black firestone, which the picks could not break. They had to burrow between the blocks, creating a crude labyrinth beneath the hateful thorns. It was hot work that became hotter as they descended.

Sessian worked in the pits beside her war band, wielding her pick like a battle club, cracking rocks as she would crack skulls; ripping the rubble out with her hands; frantic and furious.

The Yuccamen had to be lying. She could not consider the alternative, for that path led only to an ignominious demise at the end of her tribe's vengeful spears.

So she kept on digging.

Nukh breathed into his mind, and Selt opened his arms wide to accommodate the coiling spirit of the world-ending snake.

Through the splits and openings in his tent, Selt watched his captors struggling and vomiting in the dust when they thought no one could see. The barbarian queen's slaves were dying. Serfs went down into the holes; piles of hairless, living corpses came back up.

Their food carts looked empty now; hollow and drained as the faces of the warrior woman's thugs. Nukh had his corrosive fangs in them now.

'This is the moment. The benediction comes. My servants rise up, to consume the living tribute. Feed me Selty boy. Feed me them all.'

It was the voice again; thunderous now, rattling the tent with its black tongue.

The canvas walls of his tent were coated in excrement, mixed with his many powders and oils. But also, he gathered the hot grey dust brought up from the mine on boots and cloaks. The salt of god, the doorway for the hosts of Nukh. Night fell once again, leaving only the camp fires as illumination.

Now was his time.

He pressed a wick into his green-flecked fire, and watched the flames reproduce, from the source to the greasy candle in his talon-like clutches. The childish flame flickered and danced upon the wick, blackening the twine wherever it touched.

Selt set out a jar of potion that was as pungent and opaque as septic pond water; its fumes clung to the nostrils and burned the back of his throat. But he was not finished. He scratched bloody runes into his face with his hooked dagger, and mashed holy unguents and paste into the opened wounds. Fever-heat shuddered through his system like ice water, but the hurt was good. Hurt was cleansing.

'My soul is of the dragon! Come and hear me roar!' he screamed at the top of his lungs, before imbibing a mouthful of his distilled broth.

The guards, daubed in ochre and wreathed with bones, rushed into the hovel, saw-toothed clubs raised. Selt spoke the words of power, spewing his dragon's brew. The candle's flame was kindled by the fluid as it was spat over it.

Hell sprang from his mouth, and his guards shrieked. .

The blossoming fire caught them both in the face, igniting their beards and leather tunics. They dropped their weapons as they pawed at their ruined forms.

Selt's dagger, the dragon's claw, coated in the most gloriously venomous of perfumes, pierced the first guard beneath his ribcage. Hot as the fire that scorched the man's eyes, the blade's toxin did its work. While one died, the other staggered away, ripping through the hovel with his bare hands. Flame spread, streaming from the warrior's face and consuming the canvas with hungry alacrity.

Selt watched this carnival with tears in his jaundiced eyes. The world, again, would burn with Nukh's clear fire. So said the texts, and thus it was manifest.

Sessian awoke with a blade in her hand.

Smoke. It drifted from the open flap of her tent, along with the muffled shouts of her brethren, and the flickering orange of a wayward pyre.

She wasted no time, snatching up her pistol without a thought. Outside, the stench of the smoke was riper, and the sounds clearer. The smell of bodies burning; was like the plague pits of Wall-Streeter Witch pyres. But there was something else, hidden in the scent. Selt's necromantic powders.

The camp was ablaze, green-tinged smoke embracing the site like a leprous lover. Tents were funeral pyres, and the thorns seemed to press in ever closer. She thought, amidst the madness, she could see bodies impaled upon the lower branches of the slender stone spires; men screaming, howling, and thrashing in their death throes. Sessian rushed forwards, weapons drawn, but to what end? Where was her enemy? Selt's tent was burning like the rest, and there was no sign of him.

An axe swung for the back of her head, and would have taken it off her shoulders had she not instinctively twisted away; opening her foe's belly with her basket-hilted blade. Another foe rose up, screeching mad sermons from its toothless mouth. She thrust her pistol, barrel-first, into its jaws, and split its head. The pale, hairless thing slumped backwards, its broken rifle slipping from nerveless fingers.

More pale devils loped from the smoke. Sessian fired

again, but the shot went wide. A club sent her pistol spinning from her grasp. Quick as thought, she dragged her twin-barrel from her belt, and cratered the chest of another slavering ravage-born with both barrels. The weapon spent she tossed it aside. Her dagger punched through the heart of the another foe as her left hand shot out to deliver a vicious punch into the slobbering maw of a third. She took the club of the first foe she slew. Weapon in each hand, she waded into combat, each sweep of her arms gifting another monster its mortal wound. A hissing bald woman pummelled her defensive guard with the stock of a shotter. Only a stamp kick to the thigh gave the pallid, degenerate she-beast pause; time enough to stave in her skull with a well-timed overhead strike. Her knife slid into the gut of another pale demon, but there it stuck fast. The thing twisted away from her, dragging the dagger from her grip.

Sessian swayed backwards to avoid another attack, gulping down a lungful of the noxious smoke. Blinking away fresh waves of the narcotic corruption, she took her club in two hands.

Another loose rabble of creatures scuttled towards her, vomiting and clawing at their own eyes, blindly scrambling towards her. She couldn't circle around them, so instead she backed away towards the stone thicket, giving herself space. Even these mindless monsters were wary of approaching the landscape of thorns.

Had Selt's demented ghouls worked together, Sessian would have surely perished, but the screaming devils hacked at each other as readily as they assaulted her. Those that fell were set upon by their fellows. Their ribcages were pried open, and black organs of the dead were consumed by the living, who wept as they devoured their misshapen kin.

Sessian retreated through the thorns, drunkenly lurching to avoid getting transfixed upon the lethally-sharp construction. But the spines of Yucca would not be denied. They contracted around her, enfolding her like a fly trap's treacherous leaves. Stone points stabbed down at her and all she could do was dive aside; no blade would turn these inhuman weapons aside.

Somewhere above her, perching atop the living thorns, she saw the greenish flames coalescing before her bloodshot eyes. Wings of conflagration swept out from a serpent made of living Fire. Whorls of smoke curled from it like an inverted halo. Just as soon as the image appeared, then it was gone.

On hands and knees, Sessian fled the din of battle and the screeching of demonic things that cavorted, exulting in the carnage being wrought. Eventually, through the demented nest of barbs, the sound died away, the smoke becoming a mere wisp on the air; an insidious, greenish phantom.

Sessian crawled towards that, ignoring the barbs as they tore at her hair and tunic. Her hair came away easily, in great chunks each time.

This was the heart of the Yucca monument, and at the centre of this hateful landscape stood a plinth crowned with a simple symbol; three trapezoids, surrounding a central circle

It looked like a winged angel, rendered in its simplest form, or perhaps a dragon's horn and muzzle; it was Nukh the destroyer.

Sessian only cared about whose blood it was that drenched it. Talf sat in the dirt, back propped against the stone cylinder. He whimpered as he clutched his belly, hopelessly trying to stuff his intestines back into his abdomen, blood trickling between his frantic fingers.

Selt held a curved blade in his right hand, whilst his left gently stroked the dying boy's hair. He cooed and giggled as his surrogate son died and only when Talf shivered and went still did he turn to Sessian.

'Nukh is the end of the world. He was the end of the Yuccans; he was the end of Talf's. So he'll be the end of the Barbarian devil Cutress, yes! Talf tried to tell me this is no place of honour; he claimed the plinth was warning. Heresy. He was wrong. This *is* a place of honour, honour to the ravager, to deadness.'

Sessian rose, her club in hand and her teeth clenched. Imbrued with the ichors of a dozen and more slain enemies, she looked every inch the red-handed war goddess.

'This place is mine. I've killed your allies, I will kill you, and I will strangle Nukh himself if I get my prize!' Sessian snarled defiantly.

Selt laughed in her face. Hysterical, he leapt at her, his

blade flashing in the gloom. Sessian knew the fiend had poisons, and she treated his blade like a viper's mouth. Selt swung the blade without finesse, but instead possessed an animalist mania. His blade darted back and forth in a frenzy of motion. It was not enough. His last stroke was clumsy. It left him exposed.

Sessian brought her club down, hard, shattering his wrist. The old man yelped. She smashed the club into his side with a dull thud, driving the air from his lungs. An overhead strike shattered his collarbone with a crunch. A third blow crashed into his knee, forcing the old man to an agonised kneeling position. Finally, she smashed the flat edge of the club into his face. His jaw came away, and he spewed blood across the dusty ground.

Sessian grabbed his head, tilting it back to look her in the eyes. 'Where is my prize?' she spat. 'You came here from far to the west. You knew there was something here. Tell me and I kill you quick. Deny me? Then slow.'

Selt chuckled wetly from his ruined mouth. 'Prize? Your prize ish thish!' he gestured with his functional hand towards Talf's corpse. 'Nukh ish death. Thish ish his gift. Thish ish his sacrifice. Deadness ish all he knows and you gave it gladly.'

Selt continued to gurgle and cackle, until Sessian snapped his neck, and left him to rot beside his murdered boy.

The sun was rising when she finally made her away out of the thorny entanglement. The last traces of the narcotic fugue had passed, but she still felt a sickness deep inside. *It was a dreadful malady, a soul sickness, perhaps*? she thought.

In the cold grey light of dawn, the camp was a very different place. Ash and charcoal littered the dead place. Her serfs were all dead. Most of her warriors were dead also. Not merely dead but mutilated; butchered like beasts.

She knew then why the sickness grew inside her. There were none of the pale monsters amongst the fallen. Her own warriors' bodies now appeared pallid in their turn, but all these corpses were... human.

She found Haast, laying where he fell, with Sessian's basket-hilted dagger protruding from his belly like a conqueror's flag.

Her eyes were raw from the smoke, and she was too dehydrated to cry out. Sessian saw one of her warriors raise her own pistol toward her. There was no honour in this death. There had been honour in none of this, she cursed wearily. There was a phrase; a fragment of a psalm of some ancient wise man. His words came to her now, unbidden, as if she was desperate for her end to somehow be profound, and not ignoble and pointless as everything else she'd done here on this lonely, dead mountain.

'I am become deat-' she began, before the bullet drove all thoughts from her mind.

THIS BLESSED UNION

Adrian Tchaikovsky

'Cheer up, brother! Is that long face fit for a man about to meet his intended?' Duke Malmer of Daine boomed cheerfully.

'Screw you,' was Ralpe's response to that.

Malmer laughed hugely. 'Really? One wedding and you'll be rightful lord of Tyrenan! What's so terrible?'

'And the reason you're not marrying her yourself is…?'

'Because *my* eventual spouse will be clean and accomplished and housetrained!'

'Quite.' Ralpe scanned the forest edge sourly. Malmer, his elder brother, had been his tormentor since they were children. Little had changed.

'You don't even like women,' Malmer pointed out inexorably. 'Just marry the feral bitch and you can see all the pretty boys you like on the side.'

'How delicately you put it.'

'You're not going to make a scene, are you?' Malmer asked him. 'I mean, this is for the family, right? The family and the duchy? You want what's best for-'

'Yes, yes, all right. What's keeping her?'

Malmer shrugged. 'Probably they had to take her for walkies or something. Probably she's left her spoor on every tree on the way here from the deep forest.'

Nineteen years before, the widower duke of Tyrenan had died in battle, leaving his kingdom to his newborn daughter and her ambitious uncle. Nature had taken its course, and soon enough the uncle was on the throne, wearing the circlet and conducting the ongoing war with the other seven duchies that had lasted well over a century, and showed no signs of stopping.

The new king had stopped short of direct kin slaying, when it came to disposing of his inconvenient infant niece.

Instead, being a man of traditional habits, he had ordered the babe taken into the deeps of the forest that stood at the centre of the eight duchies, and had her left there. Apparently that somehow made it better.

He had proved unpopular with the fractious populace of Tyrenan, that ambitious uncle – both for his usurping and the grand scale of his predatory hedonism. After almost two decades of rebellion and unrest, he had been found hanging in his own chambers, and by that time nobody cared enough to mount much of an investigation. That had left Tyrenan to the ambitions of the other duchies and the unravelling chaos that came with lack of government.

Except... persistent rumour amongst the peasantry said that the girl had not died, but somehow lived and grown to maturity within the forest. For a long time, persistent rumour could stick it in its ear, as far as Malmer and Ralpe were concerned, because everyone knew that the deep, *deep* forest was deadly. Grown men, experienced hunters, whole platoons of troops had vanished into its venomous darkness, never to be seen again. There were wolves, they said, and bears, and the wolves and bears lived short and terrified lives because there was far, far worse.

And yet the rumours kept coming back, of a girl seen within the trees, a human child where no human ought to be, and, as the years went by, not a child but a woman.

And then there had been contact: the girl had come to a village of loggers and hunters at the forest fringe in Daine, or they had trapped her somehow. Those who saw her said she bore the features of the old Tyrenese royal family. Forest rumour became a duchy-wide obsession. She was the heir that the people of Tyrenan would accept.

Malmer had wasted no time in sending for his studious younger brother. For too long Ralpe had closeted himself with his books and the more muscular members of his personal staff. It was time Malmer's junior sibling dipped his wick for the greater glory of the family. For generations the eight duchies had struggled against each other, borders shifting back and forth, fire and the sword sweeping the land. If Daine and Tyrenan could be united, then abruptly the world would know a power great enough to crush the others one by one and end the war.

And, Ralpe thought, perhaps it would not be so very terrible being Duke of Tyrenan. At least he could keep a decent library.

Then there was a disturbance from the forest fringe. A handful of the locals, woodcutters and charcoal burners and the like, came skittering out, and for a moment Ralpe thought there must be some monster about to make its appearance. They said the deep woods were full of them. The wretches were forming two shaky lines, though, a bridal path down which he would finally see his intended. The escort of soldiers and advisors the brothers had brought with them shifted and shuffled, ready for trouble.

And then *she* stepped from the shadows of the trees, and a change passed over all who saw her, like a summer wind.

Hunchbacked, Ralpe had predicted; wall-eyed, disfigured, bow-legged. Filthy, of course, her hair matted and tangled – and probably all over her body. The woman he looked on now was none of these things. She was beautiful. She stood tall, clothed in a gown of gossamer silk that clung to the rich contours of her body. She wore a crown of ivy, and a chain of foxgloves gave imperial splendour to her throat. Her eyes were green like the sun on the leaves, her skin pale as birch bark.

And she *was* heir to Tyrenan. Ralpe and Malmer had both guessed that the feral foundling of the woods was just some wild brat of the right age, a coincidence that Daine could exploit to press its claim to the vacant throne of its neighbour. Ralpe had seen portraits of the late Tyrenese royal family, though. The woman before them was a younger and more radiant version of the last duchess. She was the real thing. He would not have put so much as a bent penny on it.

He stepped forwards, mouth opening to recite the portentous words that his brother had written for him, about unions and destinies and bloodlines and the like. Before the first word could clear his lips, Malmer had virtually shouldered him aside.

'My lady, last blood of the ancient and noble house of Tyrenan!' the Duke of Daine declared passionately. 'I bid you welcome, as your brother in nobility; welcome, as your husband to be!'

The look she turned on Malmer made him stumble, so charged was it with bright mischief.

'I give you thanks.' Her voice made the men there swallow with abruptly dry throats, straighten their backs and puff out their chests. If she had any idea that the identity of her bridegroom had just been switched, she gave no sign of it.

Her name was Candide, she said. On her lips, in her voice, it was the most beautiful name in the world.

Ralpe spent the month leading up to the wedding in a state of constant nail-biting anxiety, waiting for things to fall apart.

That he was no longer the groom was, frankly, no great concern to him. The dukedom of Tyrenan was a burden he could live without, and for various reasons – that were the stuff of ribald and mildly insulting songs in most taverns – a nubile young wife was not high on his list of priorities. He was involved, though, even against his will. Now Malmer had dragged him into this, Ralpe found that the success of the union, the possibility of Daine-Tyrenan bringing a much-needed order to the eight duchies, was something he was invested in. Except every day it seemed that the wedding would be off and everything would fall apart.

It was not the Tyrenese. He and Malmer had anticipated meeting a lot of resistance there, despite the clear provenance of their new duchess. After all, they would still have to swallow a Dainish duke.

But Candide had spoken to them, and they had loved her. She had passed amongst them, meeting the barons and lords, and Ralpe had seen something in their eyes that was part adoration and part pure lust. And when she had asked them to accept Malmer as their duke, they could not refuse her.

There had been resistance within Daine, too. Many there held old grudges against the Tyrenese. Ralpe had heard rumours of all manner of plots, and heard many openly expressed opinions that were little short of treason. The Tyrenese witch, they said, had ensorcelled their duke.

And she had gone to these men, these old soldiers and

scheming statesmen, and she had spoken softly to them, and met with them in private, and smoothed away their concerns. Now she had no stronger supporters than those who had once spoken against her.

In fact it was this very success that set Ralpe to biting his nails and waiting for the inevitable explosion. There were a lot of rumours flying around the duchy concerning Candide, and many of them focused on just how well she was getting on with various members of the court. Calumny, of course; scurrilous lies, except Ralpe had seen the way men looked at her – and most especially he had seen the way they looked at her after she had met with them behind closed doors. There was a yearning there that was almost unhealthy. Not a longing for something denied them, but a longing for a second bite of a particular cherry.

And Malmer never shared. That was Ralpe's abiding memory of childhood. If Malmer had the faintest whiff that his bride to be had been generous in her affections, he would fly into a rage. He would order executions. He would…

Except he didn't. Ralpe held his breath and waited, but the moment of disaster never quite came. When Malmer was with Candide he was besotted, utterly infatuated. When she spoke, he listened, and it sometimes seemed he listened to nobody else. Certainly he had little time for his brother, or the actual logistics of the wedding.

For Ralpe, this was a marked improvement. Before the betrothal, his elder brother had made it a fond pastime of his bored moments to force Ralpe to dance attendance on him, to mock Ralpe about his predilections for study (and his other predilections), and to generally continue the bullying habits of their younger years. Malmer obsessed with his bride to the exclusion of all else was no bad thing, in Ralpe's estimation.

And so the wedding went ahead, and without a hitch. The assassins sent by the other duchies were all apprehended, and even the ambassadors from those same duchies left the ceremony with a wistful look in their eyes, at the majesty of the proceedings, and at the ethereal beauty of the bride.

She made a speech. It had not been part of Ralpe's plan, but who could have stopped her? She spoke about the terrible destruction that the war between the duchies had wreaked: the hardship of the people, the burned forest, the salted earth. With tears of sincerity in her eyes she had expressed her heartfelt wish that her marriage to Malmer, the union of Tyrenan and Daine, would be the first step towards a lasting peace between all the duchies. Even those who stood to lose a great deal from the union seemed moved.

Candide came to Ralpe's study frequently: perhaps once a tenday he would glance up and see her at his door. She, who had the entire courts of two duchies trailing after her like lovelorn swains, seemed fascinated by him.

Now she wandered his cluttered chambers, examining the spines of his books, and the various stones and bones and oddities he had collected. The smile she turned on him, at his question, was that same mischievous expression that had first won over Malmer.

And he could feel it: the magnetism of the woman. She was so perfect a balance of grace and elegance and invitation. No wonder that the men of the court, old and young, wooed her chastely with all the tropes of courtly adoration. No wonder, too, the persistent rumours suggesting that less than chaste things went on behind Malmer's back.

And Malmer didn't seem to know, or else he didn't care. When he came to council meetings, he went mechanically through the business that had once absorbed him. Where before he had been a hothouse of plots against the other duchies - scheming and dealing for the sake of outwitting his opponents – now, he was a quieter, meeker man. His policies were for a longer and less confrontational game, an ideology that Ralpe had gladly embraced. Malmer's passions now were all for his wife. Indeed, he seemed almost sick with her. The eyes he turned on her were like a fever victim's; an addict's. There was almost a fear, Ralpe sometimes thought: a fear of something he was in thrall to and could not escape from.

'How did you live, in the forest?' Ralpe asked her, now. His curiosity had gone leashed long enough.

'Do you know,' Candide said, 'nobody has asked me that question, except you?'

'I have an enquiring mind.' Ralpe raised an eyebrow. 'They say the deep forest is a terrible place, inimical to human life.'

'It is dangerous for those who do not understand it. The same is true for many places,' she told him idly.

'How did you learn language, then? There are no schools in the deepwood, I'd wager.'

'The people of the forest edge, they speak. When they come to hunt, to burn, to cut, they bring their language with them.'

He frowned at her wording. 'But…'

'You are distressed that a child brought up in the wilds can adapt so well to your courts and palaces?' She made such a hurt-looking face that he laughed despite himself.

'I suppose that is what I'm saying, yes.'

Her wicked grin broadened. 'But Lord Ralpe, for all the words in all the world, there is a single language that speaks to all of us, and that we cannot resist.'

'That is a very elegant way to speak of love,' he admitted. Her expression, in the echo of that, seemed almost caught-out, as if that was not what she had meant at all.

'I like you, Lord Ralpe,' she told him. 'I like you because you are a man to whom peace comes naturally, and that is a rare thing in these lands.'

'I have simple and restrained tastes. Which I suppose is also a rare thing.'

'And you work for your brother's cause, now he is committed to unifying the duchies.'

'Considerably more so than when his plan was to sow strife between them,' Ralpe admitted. It was not something he felt he could have said to anyone else.

Her smile was fond. 'Will you ride with me some day, to the forest? I will show you my school and my nursery.'

This sounded like a dangerous invitation, but his curiosity was up and, despite everything, he found it very hard to refuse her.

That conversation with her was a turning point. His eyes

seemed to have been opened to that secret language of hers, written in the faces and the mannerisms of those around him. He found that he had started playing a game: spot those men who had been favoured with the duchess's attentions. Oh, nothing could be proved, and he had no intention of making any accusations, but there was a certain look, now he was searching for it. There was a pallor, as of late nights; there was a redness of eye, a slight shake to the hands. At council meetings and at court, an increasing number of men – and some women – were touched by the same hand, their faces turned towards the same radiant sun. It was a sun they cringed from; a fierce and terrible centre to their cosmos, and yet they could never look away from it for very long.

'Surely the forest is no place for horses,' he suggested.

Candide's grin was back. 'They'll take us part of the way, as will our escort.' She waved at the rabble of servants and soldiers and minor nobles who had ridden out with them. 'And then it will be just you and me, Lord Ralpe.' Beneath the coquetry, there was something new to her manner. Was there a tension, in her? He had never seen her worried by anything. Or was it eagerness, to show him something she had never shown anyone else.

'And what of the beasts and the monsters?' he asked her. 'Everyone knows it is death to set foot in the deep forest.' In truth the thought was very much on his mind but, at the same time, he could not resist the thought of somehow securing safe passage to that place, never before seen by human eyes.

Never before seen, save by Candide. She had come to them from the deep wood, chaperoned by woodsmen and charcoal burners and herb-gatherers. Like a creature of folk tales, she had come. She was the lost scion of royalty, so beautiful and innocent that even the monsters had overcome their savage natures and raised her as their own.

'I speak the language of the deep forest,' she told him.

'It has a language?'

'That same one true language we spoke of, Lord Ralpe. That same language that conquers all living things.'

He raised his eyebrows. 'Forgive me if I say I had not thought the beasts of the deep forest were motivated by love.'

She laughed at him, for that, and then they were touching their heels to their horses' flanks and moving into the shadow of the wood.

It began as a pleasant ride through woodland made open and spacious by the attentions of woodcutters. Polite conversation murmured around them, hangers on at court trying for a smile off the duchess with some choice piece of wit. She favoured them with a look, a word, but all the while she was leading them deeper.

Ralpe felt as though they were travelling back in time, in some strange way. Here, where the trees were that much closer together, was what the wider wood would have looked like before fire and axe had thinned it. Here the trees were old and getting older as they progressed. The signs of human presence were less – no more than the trail they followed and woodsman's marks cut into the trunks. Conversation dwindled and the looks of their attendants grew anxious as the shadow beneath the canopy deepened.

And now they were riding single file, winding in and out between trees that muscled in upon one another, branches interlocked like the limbs of wrestlers, the noonday sun dimmed almost to dusk. Strange things moved in the gloom, to lumber off when the light of lanterns was turned on them. Creatures buzzed in the air and slithered underfoot and cackled amid the branches.

And Candide turned to their followers and said, 'Lord Ralpe and I will continue onwards alone.'

Ralpe saw not a little relief on many faces, but there were still some dutiful enough to protest.

'My lady,' said the captain of their guard, 'from here on in must be the deep forest. That is no safe place for anyone. We should turn back.'

'Captain, of all here, *I* have nothing to fear,' she assured him. 'I am going home, after all. And Lord Ralpe shall fear nothing while he is with me.'

Except you, Ralpe thought, but he said nothing. He felt that he was on the brink of a great secret, and he had always been one for secrets: not the petty secrets of court intrigue, but the grand understanding of what made the world move, which wise men sought always and so seldom found.

They left their mounts with the captain, and she led him deeper, by paths he did not see before they took them, by paths he would not be able to find again, to where the light was smothered green by the leaves above, the air choked grey. She led him between trees so close he had to suck in his belly to squeeze through; she led him over secret dark streams where pallid fish-like things clutched at the water-weed with fingered fins, and through shadowed clearings where the fairy rings of mushrooms stood man-high, and gleamed with their own furtive radiance.

At the last they came to a grove where the trees soared tall enough that their upper branches were lost in a gloom of their own making. In a cathedral-like space lit by the luminous shelves and florets and clutching hands of fungi, sparkling with the glimmering motes that they exhaled into the air, she halted. She turned about; head tilted back, arms outstretched, as though dancing with the forest itself.

'You have come here because you are curious, Lord Ralpe,' she said.

'I have.' There was a leaden stone in his gut from the feeling that he would die there; that the price of his answers would be his life.

'Then tell me this: what are the true lords of the forest?'

He glanced about them: the answer seemed too obvious, but he said it: 'The trees, surely.'

She laughed. 'And yet there are a hundred kinds of gnawing beast that daily crop their leaves and chew their bark and burrow into their wood.'

'Those beasts, then.' He felt he was in a folk tale, the young hero being tested.

'And what of those with fang and claw that make a meal of them – that would make a meal of you, if I allowed it.' Her words peopled the dark between the trees with hungry eyes.

'And if I said *those* beasts?'

She fixed him with a quizzical stare. 'So what will you say?'

'I say that, by your logic, the flea that bites the wolf is the wolf's master.'

Candide laughed delightedly. '*Now* you are thinking. Everything in the forest is a feast for the insects, Lord Ralpe: trees, beasts, living, dead, there is some bug that makes each thing its dining table. And yet they are not the dukes of this duchy. Within the bugs, Lord Ralpe, are worms that live out their lives through the innards of many different creatures in turn. And in the worms, my lord, are a thousand spores, and the spores riddle the worms that consume the bugs that feed on the beasts that browse the trees.'

He swallowed and nodded. 'I see. Your forest is a terrible place of things feasting on other things and being feasted on in turn, from without and from within.'

Her expression arrested him: it was the first time he had seen her look upset.

'Lord Ralpe, this is a world bound together in balance and harmony. This is life that grows as fast as it decays, and so can live eternal. This is what I was brought up to cherish, until they took me from here and sent me to your world. Your world is fire and violence, exploitation, starvation, *division*, the catastrophes unleashed on humans by humans for no reason than that you disagree over who owns a field or a ditch.'

'Or a duchy,' he pointed out.

'It is but a greater field. Would you truly wish to shed so much blood and cut so many trees for no more than that?'

He took a deep breath. 'Malmer would: my brother; your husband.'

She read the rest in his face. 'But not you. I thought I had your measure. My lord, shall we return? Our escort will be worried.'

He thought of what he said when he lay in bed with his chosen lover, an athletic young groom named Helvers.

'The petitioners all complain of her, of course,' Helvers told him. 'Where before it was a matter of greasing the right palm, now their bribes achieve nothing. No merchant, no land-owner can buy preferment any more, not since she came. Now, all the lords think about is her.'

'And you?'

'I think only of you.' Helvers shrugged closer into his

embrace. 'And for that, they would all bribe me to press their cases to you, seeing you as their last hope.'

'It's very different to how they once saw me,' Ralpe observed. 'But you must tell them, there's no joy for them that way. I won't be moved. And you mustn't be bribed.'

Helvers sighed. 'A man could grow rich.'

Ralpe thought only of the dark, dark forest, that consumed itself forever, and of Candide's displeasure.

'Don't be tempted,' he warned. 'It's not worth it.' *I don't want anything to happen to you.*

He was still thinking of what Candide had said when he sat at his brother's next council. He looked from one waxy face to another; their collective attention giving her a seat at their deliberations even thought she was absent. His brother's rictus smile; the general's shaking hands; the chief steward's nervous tic: men possessed by the very thought of the woman in the next room.

There had come, with Candide, a shift in policy in the duchies of Daine and Tyrenan. Where before ambassadors had been met with veiled threats and resurrected grudges, now they encountered overtures of truce and offers to bury old grievances. The more aggressive of them met with the duchess, too, and went away as infatuated as everyone else. Something was spreading outwards from the union of Malmer and his true love – leaching into the soil and the water of the duchy, sprouting in each town, growing in the dark, unregarded places until it was ready to burst forth. It was peace, Ralpe thought; it was justice, spreading from wherever Candide laid her hand, from each footprint she left behind her.

He was not bound to her by his longings, as were those who had – why try to hide it? – shared her bed. Still, he found he was a little in love with her, nonetheless. He was enamoured of the effect, while the rest all lusted for the cause.

It was a week later that he was woken past midnight by someone rapping at his chamber door. He jack-knifed up, reaching for the dagger he kept by his bed. *Assassins!* he thought, as though they would have knocked. Ralpe had always feared assassins – sent from other duchies, sent by his brother, or just hired by magnates from the court who felt his proclivities brought shame upon his family.

Someone stirred in the bed beside him, a comforting weight. *Helvers.* And wasn't it strange how those proclivities of his didn't seem to matter much, now, so that he could be in the company of one man most days, without fearing the old censure? It was as though the great and the good had other things on their minds…

For a moment he just listened: no wide-scale panic, no sound of fire or battle, just that knock and a man's voice hissing his name.

He rolled himself out of bed, slipping a robe on and tucking the dagger inside it just in case.

Ralpe did not recognise the man there, some slightly shabby-looking servant. The message the man had come bearing was enough to get Ralpe dressed and hurrying into the ducal palace as swiftly as he could manage, though. The court physician needed to see him urgently.

The court physician was a decade older than Ralpe, thin-faced and with a distinct air of authority. He was to be found down in the cool cellars where he kept his specimens and his operating theatre. The air there was heavy with perfume underlain with the scent of corruption, a sure sign that he had been hard at work. When no live patients braved his clutches, the man was known to hone his skills by investigating the internal configurations of the dead. Sure enough, on the table before him, a suspiciously human shape was shrouded by a cloth.

The physician was usually a man of frosty, detached manner. Right now, he seemed positively grim, as though the next corpse on the slab would be his own.

'Get out,' he told his man, and then nodded sharply to Ralpe. 'Thank you for coming at such short notice, my lord. This is a matter that needs urgent attention at the highest level.'

Ralpe gave him a crooked look. 'Then you have the wrong brother. Malmer's the duke, remember?' A sudden thought struck him and he recoiled from the shrouded cadaver. 'Or…?'

'No, not that,' although the physician sounded strained enough that it might have been. 'But it's hard to hold your brother's attention these days. He is often… preoccupied.'

Ralpe had to concede that point. *And who would have thought the duchy would be such a brighter place now that Malmer is not obsessing about growing its influence? Or his own influence…* His brother made so much more congenial a groom than he had a bachelor. 'So tell me, doctor. What's worth getting the duke's brother up past midnight? Have you learned how to raise the dead?'

His jovial tone fell into the physician's expression and sank without a ripple. 'Lord Sae fell from his horse while hunting. His horse came down atop him. His injuries were severe. All they could think of was to bring him to me, of course.'

Ralpe winced at the thought of the dying nobleman spending his last hours jolting across the countryside in a cart at the hands of panicking servants. Sae was the army's third most senior officer, and he had been out hunting, no doubt, because abruptly the duchy seemed to need far less input from men like him. 'I take it he's dead, then.'

The physician nodded at the laden table with a single nervous jerk of his head.

Ralpe put a hand to his brow. 'Then he would be just as dead in the morning, doctor. This could have waited-'

'No, my lord, it could not,' the physician snapped at him. 'I need to show you the body.'

Ralpe wanted to walk out, then. He would very much like to have left, thinking only that the man's personal hobbies had at last grown beyond his ability to keep them private. There was a dreadful intensity to the physician, though; a tension that gripped every line of him.

'Show me.' Even saying the words, Ralpe knew that he would be happier remaining ignorant, but here he was, being the responsible brother in Malmer's absence. 'What's so important?'

The physician stripped the cloth back from the corpse's face, revealing the bluish, pallid features of Lord Sae. So far, so dead, but the shroud was pulled further and further down, showing flesh that was mottled black with bruising, an arm that had been shattered when the horse came down on it.

Sae's chest and stomach were mutilated, but Ralpe had been a spectator at the doctor's demonstrations before. What looked like the excesses of a knife-wielding maniac were just the man's professional ministrations.

'So, with Lord Sae dead of his injuries, you decided to do a little prying,' he observed.

A defensive gleam flickered in the physician's eyes. 'A perfectly serviceable cadaver…' he started.

'Save it. Show me.' Ralpe steeled himself for the glistening horror that was the truth within all men. Obligingly, the doctor folded back the flaps of Sae's skin, opening him up like a window. It was a window on a different world, though, a horror quite unlike the one Ralpe had expected.

Some parts of the tableau were still moving, albeit sluggishly. There was a lot of clutter in there, but not the right clutter, not Sae's expected innards. Right then, all those slimy tubes and lumps and sacs that were the common plumbing of humanity would have been a welcome sight. But it was gone, it was all gone. What filled Sae up was a riotous growth of bile yellow and faintly luminous green, a flourishing tangle of fronds and gills and fruiting bodies amidst which were the feebly twitching bodies of round-shelled, crablike insects. The bugs clustered like festering sores under the ribcage or clung to the exposed inner membranes of Sae's skin. Most were still and dead, and some had already sprouted out into little fungal florets of their own, little budding fingers prying their way between the creatures' chitin to unfurl into the air. *And in the bugs, the worms; and in the worms, the spores…*

'Where's the…' Ralpe got out hoarsely. 'Where's the rest of him?' There was no sign of all the organs that made up a man, just this fecund, seething mass of growth.

'Gone,' the physician said hollowly. 'Eaten away. This was all that was inside him. My lord, what do we *do?* Sae was walking, talking, everything like a living man, with *this* within him. Anyone else could be infected with the same contagion.'

For a long, long while, Ralpe forced himself to stare at

the festering excrescence that had consumed Lord Sae from within. He let every detail of it assault his senses, seeing it slowly evolving, decomposing and recomposing even as he watched.

He thought about the way the duchy had changed since the wedding. He thought about the dark heart of the forest, and what Candide had said there. He thought about the future that had been slowly growing within the duchy, and what it promised.

And Ralpe was a man who dearly loved his peace and quiet.

'You're right, something must be done,' he told the physician. 'And it is true my brother has been... distracted of late. But this must be raised at the highest level.' He looked the doctor in the eye; he owed the man that. 'You must bring this to the duchess immediately. Go straight to her; tell no-one else. She will be very interested to know what you have discovered.'

Later, he stood with her upon a balcony, overlooking the grounds of the ducal palace. If he squinted, he could imagine that he saw a branching network spreading out from them, hidden invisibly in the air, the earth, the people.

'Will you take everyone, in the end?' Ralpe asked quietly.

'Why should we need to?' Candide gave him that mischievous smile – despite all he knew about her, he still felt that expression was something truly of hers, that outer skin of her that was human. 'The spores influence the worms, the worms influence the bugs, the bugs influence the leaders, those men and women whom we have touched and loved. And those leaders shall guide the rest. We do not need to reach into the heart of every farmer and herdsman.'

He could not stop himself from shuddering slightly, at the thought of how very literal she was being. 'And... how long will they last, like that?' He thought of his brother, surely rotten to the core with Candide's love by now. But then there had never been much fraternal affection between Ralpe and Malmer, before.

'As long as any fleeting human life would last,' Candide told him carelessly. 'Longer, most likely. I am a jealous lover.

I will not permit my darlings to share their affections with the cancers and frailties that human life is subject to. And they do not know. They think they are themselves, and free. They cannot know what agents tweak the thoughts within their minds.' Only with him did she speak like this. Only he had understood the truth, and yet was trusted enough to remain free. He thought, sometimes, that was the sole reason for her forbearance: she valued having someone to talk to who was not simply another *her*. With Malmer, with the rest, it would be as though she spoke to her reflection in a glass.

'We have watched you for so long, as you ate into our forest,' she said softly. 'As your need for war tore up our trees for bow staves, burned them for charcoal. We have watched all your little duchies fight and fight, every state, every lord out for himself. You place such emphasis on individual destiny and greed and ambition, and so you are divided, and proud of your division, no matter the cost. But enough is enough, Lord Ralpe. The forest has had enough. We will make a union of you all; we shall bind you all together. There shall be balance and harmony at last. There shall be peace.'

THE BOOK OF THE GODS

Sam Stone

Lady Arabella Hutchinson lifted the skirt of her wide ball gown and pulled out the gun that was holstered against her thigh. The weapon had been made to her personal specification. Adapted from the old style duelling pistol, the gun now featured a small steam-powered engine linked to several copper tubes, which wrapped around the long thin barrel and connected with the bullet chamber. It was semi-automatic; meaning that the mere squeeze of the trigger instantly loaded a new shot and powered it from the muzzle, saving time, and Arabella's neck, on many occasions.

Arabella shrank back against a large crate as the first mate, closely followed by the Captain came into the gloomy warehouse. The situation had deteriorated far faster than she had expected.

'What's all the commotion about?' demanded the Captain, pulling the first mate up short.

'The crew say the woman cheated at cards and stole their money,' he replied, casting his eyes around the storage area.

'A *woman*?' asked the Captain.

'Yes, sir.'

'Where is she now?'

'I don't know Captain,' said the first mate. 'I left her on deck for just a second, then she was gone.'

Arabella edged forward. She would have been long gone before the obvious dawned on one of the men but she had stayed behind to finalise the documents while the cargo was loaded on the carriage, and her partner in crime, Joseph, spirited it away. The Captain had been detained, which meant that Arabella had been left to her own devices for too long. While she waited she had explored the dock warehouse, hoping to find something of value that she might add to the haul, when she came across a small group of sailors playing poker. She couldn't resist the opportunity to fleece the unsuspecting men. A mistake, she realised, she might not live to regret.

It was their own fault. They shouldn't have assumed I was just 'a girl', she thought. She knew this excuse wouldn't wash if the crew found her stash of money and papers; some of which she had won, others she had taken. When the row started, she had slipped away, hiding right under their noses, even as the sailors scurried around shouting 'thief'. It was not long before she realised that the cry had nothing to do with the small haul she had taken but rather with something else entirely: something large and more valuable.

'Must be the girl,' the boatswain had said to the first mate. 'She's taken my wallet.'

'And mine,' cried another man. After that they all realised they had lost something and so Arabella was also being accused for these other things too. The thought annoyed and intrigued her. She didn't mind being accused for thefts she had committed but was somewhat outraged when the accusations were unfounded.

Why didn't I just leave with Joseph? she thought. *My damn arrogance will be the death of me.* She knew perfectly well why she had stayed. She had secretly been hoping to be discovered. The excitement of escape made the effort of deception so much more thrilling.

The Captain and the first mate moved away from the crate and Arabella sighed softly.She glanced down at the ball gown. Crinoline wasn't the quietest fabric to sneak around in and the large skirt made it difficult to run. Fortunately she had come prepared. She placed the gun down on the floor and, reaching behind her back, she began to unlace the tight corset.

A rustling sound whispered across the warehouse; Arabella paused and listened. She heard the sound of feet running towards her and so she pressed back against the crate and reached for her gun. It would be unfortunate if she had to kill over some stolen cargo and a few pounds, but Arabella would do just that if it meant getting away in one piece. She felt the familiar rush of adrenaline coursing through her veins.

A small group of crewmen ran past her hiding place,

and Arabella held her breath a moment longer. She knew she was too well hidden and they could not know where she was. The space she had squeezed through was tiny, even though behind the crate there was lots of room.

'Captain!'

The Captain reappeared and the first mate ran back to meet him. The two men stopped close to the crate that Arabella was hiding behind.

'The book is missing too, sir,' said the first mate.

'That damned woman!' the Captain hissed. 'Don't let our passenger know until after we find her.'

Interesting, thought Arabella. *What book? And if they think I shouldn't have it, then do I want it?*

Once the men had moved away, Arabella finished her transformation. She pushed the corset, dress and bustle back into the far corner behind one of the other crates. Then she rolled down the legs of the dinner suit trousers she had been wearing under the dress. She opened her carpet bag and pulled out a dinner jacket and shirt and shrugged herself into them. Next she placed a wig and hat on her head and glued on a fake moustache. Finally, she pulled free a bottle of gin, sloshing some of it on her clothes, and took a large swig directly from the bottle. Once the disguise was in place, Arabella squeezed back out from behind the crate and slipped away. She tucked the gun away in the inside pocket of the dinner jacket. She left the carpet bag behind with her dress, neither of these items contained anything that could lead the sailors back to her, and she walked out onto the dock and into the chaos.

Sailors were running back and forth between the ship and the warehouses and few of them noticed the thin, drunken, aristocratic boy who stumbled around, holding a bottle of gin and singing bawdy songs rather badly. As the Captain walked down the gangplank, the boy fell across his path, breathing a blast of gin right into his face. The Captain was a member of the Temperance Society and active supporter of Lyman Beecher, God rest his soul, and he pushed the boy away in disgust.

'Filthy rich,' he muttered as the boy staggered on and away from the port.

Arabella kept up the pretence until she was out of the

dock and back onto the main road. She hailed a Hansom cab and made her way to the rendezvous point.

Her partner, Joseph, resided in the rough part of town. He had a semi-respectable cover as the landlord of 'The Sailor's Rest' and so Arabella arrived there with her disguise still firmly intact because a young man entering the premises would be less noticeable than a woman.

The carriage pulled up, and Arabella paid the driver before making her way around the back of the Inn to the rear entrance. She gave the secret knock, three slow raps, and the heavy lock slid back from the door.

'You took your time,' Joseph said. 'Poker game was it?'

'You know me so well.'

'You'll be the death o' me one day lass,' Joseph laughed.

He sat down at the fire and picked up his pipe. Arabella smiled at his grumpy bearded face and sat down opposite.

'The strangest thing happened,' she said.

'They figured out you cheated, huh?' Joseph grunted.

'That's what I thought at first, but something else went missing. It seems they had also lost a book, and they believed I'd taken it. I hadn't. This does mean another thief was working the docks tonight.'

'A book? Not really your style,' Joseph commented.

'Not unless it's valuable,' Arabella agreed. 'That is the point I think. This book they wanted must be valuable. There was an awful amount of activity. The whole crew was out looking for me and it. They didn't even realise that they had handed their cargo over to the wrong people. Or at least cared less about that than this book.'

'I see you escaped despite it all,' Joseph said. 'Right enough. No one would believe that disguise hid a lady underneath.'

Arabella smiled and preened. 'That's because they cannot conceive of a woman getting the better of them.'

Joseph took a swig of ale and puffed his pipe. 'Crate's stowed in the usual place,' he said finally. 'Want to open it and have a look?'

'Of course.'

They went down into the tavern basement. Barrels of ale and wine were stowed under the feet of the clients, and so too was an underground escape tunnel into a storage area that smugglers had hollowed out some years before. Arabella led the way by first opening the doorway that was hidden in the front of one of the huge barrels. She and Joseph passed through the crawlspace and out into the tunnel.

The torches were already lit, and so they traversed the narrow passage to the storage room without difficulty. After a few moments Arabella came face to face with her haul for the first time.

The crate dwarfed the small room. It stood taller than Arabella and she had not recalled it looking quite that big on the cart as it was loaded; but then she had been distracted. In fact it looked like the same crate she had hidden behind in the warehouse, although she knew this couldn't be the case.

'We brought it in through the sewers,' Joseph said. 'It was heavy. Damned thing. Took three men to pull it through.'

'I can imagine,' Arabella said.

She walked around the crate, excitement colouring her cheeks. She noted the lettering that covered the box was in a language that she had never seen before. There were several customs' stamps too. This crate had been as far as Tasmania, and had passed through several European ports before finally reaching its destination in London.

'Let's open it then,' Arabella said, removing the masculine dinner jacket, which she threw casually onto the floor.

Joseph came forward with a crowbar and they eased the front off the crate. Straw and sawdust tumbled out and Arabella reached inside to brush the packing away from the statue. As she did so, her hand caught on a protruding nail and she yelped. The nail had torn a deep cut across the palm of her hand and blood already tarnished the straw. She took out a handkerchief and wrapped it around the wound and then, taking more care, she pulled back the straw to reveal the face of the statue.

It was hideous. Joseph took a sharp breath behind her, 'What is that thing?'

'An ancient god,' Arabella said. 'Worshipped by the Aztecs I believe. The statue was found when it washed up in Australia. Luckily for us a Colonel in the British Army thought it would make a good trophy for the Queen.'

'But how did you know about it?' asked Joseph.

Arabella laughed. 'The way that I know about anything. I have sources. In this instance it was a rather helpful sailor, who was very, very put out that his Captain wouldn't let the crew drink on their shore leave.'

Joseph eyed the statue suspiciously and Arabella reached her bandaged hand forward to examine the demon figure's carved fangs. It had the face of a wolf, and yet the body was that of a naked man.

'What does this say?' asked Joseph pointing to the writing on the side of the crate.

'I don't know,' Arabella said.

'It doesn't look like a god to me. It looks more like a devil,' Joseph said.

Arabella pulled back her hand and realised she had smeared the wolf-like snout with blood. It gave the statue a sinister sneer and the blood streaked its fangs as though it had just made a kill.

'I agree it is grotesque. But this, my dear friend, might just be our ticket out of the city,' Arabella said.

'I'll make some discrete enquiries with our sailor friend tomorrow,' Arabella said, after they re-nailed the front onto the crate. 'I have to meet up with him to complete the payment now that we have the goods. Maybe he'll know about this book they were so keen to find. Perhaps it is connected to the statue.'

Athos crept along the gangplank and off the ship. By midnight the search had been called off and the sailor was free to retrieve the book from its hiding place. Everyone had assumed that Arabella had taken it. Athos had set her up well. After all, who needed an old and cumbersome statue, when an ancient grimoire would pay so much more and was easier to steal?

Athos recalled how often he had seen the book left out on the writing desk. The Captain had been so casual about its safety, never suspecting that members of his crew might understand what the book was.

The most interesting thing of all though, was the civilian passenger, a Mrs Constance Stirling, who owned the book; even though the Captain kept it in his cabin. Stirling slept in the cabin above Athos, and the sailor had soon learnt that the woman talked in her sleep. The narrow space between him and the ceiling had always felt confined and claustrophobic, but unlike the other sailors who shared his small room, he was in a prime position to make out the words behind the passenger's mumblings. Athos was for once pleased that he slept in the top bunk.

Athos discovered that Stirling was distressed and fearful; her dreams filled with unmentionable horrors. And gradually Athos began to understand how some of that was because of the book. She feared its content. In her sleep she often cried out, 'Don't read it! Never read from the grimoire!'

Athos realised that an equally susceptible collector might perhaps be led to believe that the book really did contain some power, and part with good money to own it. Athos himself did not believe in such things, even though he knew people who claimed to have witnessed supernatural happenings. Ghost stories were common among the sailors, and so were tales of beautiful seductive sirens. Athos had never seen anything on land or sea that couldn't be easily explained by some natural cause. He only believed in what he could see with his own eyes and Athos knew that words could not hold magic. They were just words, even when people set such store in them.

Athos slithered along the dock to a heap of empty barrels that were stacked high against the warehouse building. He reached behind them and retrieved the book. It was wrapped in an old sack and Athos hugged it to his chest and slipped away from the docks, never to return.

The next morning, Arabella ate breakfast with her parents. She was the model daughter, dressed neatly in a brown velvet skirt, jacket, a white ruffle blouse and a subtle bustle. Her hair was tied up and she looked like someone who would make the ideal governess, except that a lady in her position didn't have to work.

'Good heavens!' said Lord Hutchinson. 'Sailor found dead in house of ill-repute! How the devil can they justify putting that story into a respectable newspaper?'

Arabella said nothing. She was used to her father's outbursts and she didn't agree that the newspaper was respectable at all. She knew far too much about the editor's other line of work and the backhanders he took to write stories that suited the sensibilities of the empire. It was all propaganda. The story did interest her however because of her recent scrape at the docks. It seemed an unlikely coincidence. She wondered if she knew the sailor in question. She waited for her father to discard the paper before subtly retrieving it and went back to her room to read the piece.

A sailor had indeed died in a brothel and Arabella knew the place well. She had arranged to meet Athos there later that day. From the description of the dead sailor she strongly suspected that her useful contact would be of no further use.

'I'm just going out to the Mission to visit the sick, Mother,' Arabella said as she walked into the drawing room. She was carrying a wicker basket and a jar of cook's homemade damson jam peeked out from under a piece of muslin.

'You're such a kind girl, Arabella,' her mother said but she didn't look up from her embroidery. Arabella left the room and headed out.

In the family carriage, Arabella pushed aside the jars of jam, block of cheese and the small jug of sloe gin. She was already wearing her thigh holster and gun; her automatic crossbow and spare arrows, bullets and gunpowder cartridges were hidden in the bottom of the basket. She covered the weapons just as the carriage pulled in at the Saint Christopher's mission building.

'Come back for me at five,' Arabella instructed her driver and she turned and walked up the steps of the mission.

Inside, Arabella passed the sick, disabled and helpless that the mission helped every day. She felt no remorse. Her money helped these people, especially the extra revenue she and Joseph brought in from their nightly excursions. Helping the mission was her justification for being involved with Joseph's band of thieves, though Arabella would have done what she did regardless. She was addicted to the adventure. It made her feel strong and powerful. She resented how women, with the exception of the Queen, were considered to be so fragile and weak. The money she earned paid for her gadgets and gave her the life she wished to live: albeit secret.

Through the back door another carriage waited. This one was driven by one of Joseph's men. Arabella climbed inside and found Joseph waiting for her.

'I think my contact is dead,' she said. 'The sailor found at The Red Room?'

'Nasty stuff. The word is he died badly.'

'Get me into the morgue. I need to see the body.'

A few greased palms later and Arabella and Joseph were looking down at the dead body of Athos. His face was twisted and distorted with the agony of his death.

'What killed him?' Arabella asked. She could barely keep her face and voice bland.

'Animal attack,' the mortuary assistant said. He was a man in his late forties, with greased back hair. There were several splashes on the front of his apron, which Arabella took delight in observing to be blood in varying stages of freshness. Some of the stains were a dark brown, others still vibrant red.

'Animal? But how?'

The assistant pulled back the cloth covering the body and Arabella and Joseph saw the victim's naked, ripped stomach. He looked as though something had tried to eat him from the inside out.

'Innards, what's left of 'em, are over there,' the assistant said.

Arabella placed her handkerchief over her mouth and nose and feigned disgust while really it hid her smile. Her eyes followed the assistant's hand and she saw a bowl containing the remains of Athos' guts resting on a weighing scale. The blood and gore intrigued her. Death was, after all, the ultimate adventure.

'Most of his intestines were eaten,' said the assistant and his cruel eyes scrutinised Arabella for signs of nausea. She pretended to find his words distasteful.

'Oh my! How dreadful. I do feel terribly ill at such a horrid thought,' she said.

'Didn't anyone hear or see anything?' Joseph asked the assistant, pressing a pound note into his hand.

'I overheard the police inspector say that the doxies there

said they heard nuffin'. You'd fink someone would have though. Apparently the room was covered in 'is blood.'

Joseph released the note and the assistant hurriedly placed it in his pocket.

'There's more for you if you hear anything else,' said Joseph.

The assistant nodded. Arabella and Joseph left but they weren't sure what to make of the death.

'Perhaps one of the whores has a dog,' Arabella suggested. 'Maybe Athos stepped out of line with one of the girls, the dog attacked and they are covering it up.'

Joseph shook his head. 'Never heard of a dog being at The Red Room, but then I'm not in the habit of visiting the place.'

'Well it was just a thought,' said Arabella.

They returned to the mission and as Arabella let herself back in the rear entrance, Peter, one of the helpers, greeted her.

'This arrived for you a few hours ago,' Peter said holding out a parcel made up of brown paper and string.

Arabella took the package. It wasn't unusual for one of her contacts to send things to the mission even though she hadn't been expecting anything. Her eyes narrowed as she looked at the package.

'Who brought it?'

'Street urchin.'

Arabella took the parcel into the mission office. The old nun who worked there nodded but said nothing as Arabella headed towards the back room. The nun was used to the lady being around. Arabella closed the door and sat down at the desk. This was technically her office. She paid rent for the space, and gave the mission so much money that her use of the room was never questioned.

She placed the parcel on her desk and reached into the top drawer to retrieve the letter opener. Arabella then carefully cut the string and the paper slipped away to reveal a large, thick leather bound book. Arabella stared at the book cover. She couldn't understand the writing at all that covered the front. It was just like the scrawled letters that had been on the outside of the crate containing the wolf god statue.

That was enough to make her realise that they were indeed connected.

'The book,' she murmured. 'But who sent you to me?'

Her mind flew back to the planned meeting with Athos. Had he taken this from the ship and sent it to her before his death? It seemed likely. She turned the book over, checking the back. There were symbols carved into the animal skin.

'What's so special about you then?'

On the spine she discovered a faded word. It was too difficult to decipher. Whereas on the opposite side, the pages were held together by a strap that wrapped around from the back to the front keeping the book closed. It held some kind of spring lock. Arabella examined the mechanism. It looked like a glass fronted pocket watch had been submerged into the cover. She turned what she thought to be the winder but nothing happened. The device seemed to be broken or jammed. She picked up the letter opener and probed the lock with the silver knife point. At that moment the watch cover sprang open.

'Ouch,' Arabella remembered the sharp gash she had received from the night before as a hard piece of metal scraped against the cut, reopening the wound. A drop of blood fell on the lock. The cogs began to turn and instead of the ticking she might have expected, the sound of music box notes playing an unfamiliar melody echoed through the room. The lock sprang open.

The book fell open and Arabella looked at a page of illustrations and words, none of which were familiar. The shapes began to move and form into English words and she realised she could read it. The picture formed into a half man, half beast: a direct facsimile of the statue.

It's a poem, she thought. 'No. A spell.'

The words formed on her tongue, her mouth opened and the language, strange and ancient poured from her lips. It burnt like liquid flame. Sharp and yet still intangible, she read the words but their meaning and sound dissipated as each one was spoken.

Arabella felt a dark horror eating away at her soul. In her mind's eye she saw an ancient resting place, a sarcophagus surrounded by hideous statues. Malformed humans, monstrous insects, creatures from the sea, and there was the wolf: a large animal head on a human male body. She found herself lying at the statue's feet, felt its claw-like hand stroke her hair. Then, Arabella did something she had never done: she screamed. A terror-filled cry that released her very soul from the cage of its human form.

Arabella woke. Her cheek was pressed against the animal skin cover of the book. She raised her head and looked around the room. For the first time she noticed how decayed the office was. A dark green mould grew around the window frame and up over the ceiling. Arabella blinked. The lamps were lit yet her eyes felt dull and sluggish. It was as though she had brought the darkness from her dream out into her world. She tried to retain some remnants of what she had been dreaming but could only conjure up the image of a room and the vague shapes of statues.

It's this book! She thought. *The words inside made me* … Her mind stumbled and she glanced down at the desk trying to remember the thread her thoughts refused to find.

The book was closed again and no matter how much she fiddled with the lock it refused to budge. She didn't remember feeling tired, or settling to sleep, but when she looked outside she saw that the day had rapidly passed into evening and she realised she must have just drifted off and imagined opening the book.

Even now the images and words evaded her. If only she could remember! In the dream, she was sure, they must have had clarity, but despite every effort to recall them her mind wouldn't obey.

She felt tired and drained. As though she had been doing anything else other than sleep. *That will serve me right for not getting home early last night.*

Her driver should have come for her hours ago. Arabella pulled her watch out of her waistcoat pocket but it had stopped. She rewound it and saw the second hand start its sweep.

She picked up the book and re-wrapped it in the paper, then, holding it against her chest, she opened the office door.

'Sister Mary?' Arabella said. 'Do you know what time ...'

Her voice trailed off as the outer office was strangely dark and quiet. Sister Mary wasn't there. Arabella frowned and walked out into the mission looking for the staff and nuns.

The lamps were lit but the building seemed empty. Maybe there had been some emergency and everyone had left, forgetting that she was still in the office. This scenario seemed more and more likely as Arabella wandered from room to room, finding them all empty. Even the sick were missing, the covers thrown back as though they had left their beds in a great hurry.

As she drew closer to one of the sick beds she saw the stain of a body, left to rot in one place until the flesh had disintegrated, becoming a vile sludge of fluids. For a moment she couldn't understand what she was seeing. She hurried from bed to bed seeing similar stains: evidence that people had been there and had died in a hideous manner. It all seemed too horrible. The mission now appeared to be a charnel house allowing the patients to die and rot away for years. Arabella backed out of the ward then turned and ran from the mission.

Outside, the world was unfamiliar. The city seemed to have fallen into decay. She looked up at the mission and watched as the roof began to slowly cave in, the building walls sagged and the heavy marble steps melted like snow in the sun.

I'm still sleeping, she thought. It was the only explanation for her bizarre surroundings. She pinched her arm but the pain was real and so was the hunger she felt deep inside the pit of her stomach. It was the appetite of the impoverished and it burnt into her like the flames of hell. Arabella had never known such pain. She doubled up, holding her stomach, and retched bile onto the cobbles. This was one adventure she could not enjoy. The ending seemed far too uncertain.

An hour later she stumbled down the empty streets fighting her way back to her home, and possible safety. The houses on either side of the road began to disintegrate as she passed by. The street pooled into muddy water and Arabella waded through it until she reached the steps of her parents' home. The house looked as desolate as the streets, but she ran up the steps – they remained sturdy beneath her feet – and as she reached the top the door opened for her.

'Miss Arabella,' said the butler. 'Your parents are waiting for you in the drawing room.'

She stumbled inside, her muddy velvet skirt clung to her legs, tripping her as she fell forward.

'Miss Arabella!' said the butler. He helped her to her feet and stared down at her dishevelled clothing. 'What happened, Miss?'

Arabella looked around the hallway. All appeared to be normal. She looked back towards the door and the butler hurriedly closed it.

'Can I help you Miss?' he asked.

Arabella narrowed her eyes. Through the stained glass panel beside the door, the world was colourful and light again. The streets were normal and the murky night had changed back to the afternoon daylight that she had expected to see when she woke in the mission.

'Please tell my parents that I don't feel well,' Arabella said, and hurried up the stairs to her room.

In her bedroom Arabella hid the strange book under her pillow before stripping off her clothes and wrapping herself in a robe. Her mother entered the room without knocking, and by then Arabella was sitting in the armchair by the window. She watched the street for signs of change but the world moved on as it always had. For the first time she felt truly afraid and it was not enjoyable.

'My dear, are you are ill? Do you wish me to send for the doctor?'

'No mother,' Arabella said. 'I'd prefer to rest first. I'm sure I will feel much better tomorrow.'

Her mother didn't appear to notice the muddy clothes piled on the carpet beside Arabella's bed.

'Very well, rest up and I'll have some food sent up to you.'

A few moments later a tray of food was brought up. Arabella devoured the soup and bread and asked for more. She drank a pitcher full of water and afterwards she felt the liquid squeezing through her body, watering down her veins with the coldness of death. The emptiness and pain remained like a dull ache. She felt no joy in the world.

Through the window she observed that the street outside remained the same. After some hours the night slowly drew in and eventually Arabella climbed into bed and slept.

Her dreams were haunted by statues. A squid-like monster reached out its tentacle arm and stroked her face, while a ghost-like blur dissolved into a foggy mass of poisonous gas. She choked on the fumes as the creature passed through and around her. Then there was the wolf, rearing and twitching as it contorted and turned. The creature ended up as a despicable half human, half animal and it sniffed around her until she crawled away, hiding behind crooked tombstones.

In the morning Arabella felt the darkness gathering around her eyes. If she closed one eye she could see her home rapidly turning into the decayed and rotted shell of the crypt in her dream. If she closed the other eye then all seemed well. With both eyes open she felt the coldness of one world fighting against the warmth of the other. It was a battle that raged whether she was awake or asleep.

She refused to join her parents for breakfast or lunch, accepting the tray of food which was sent up for her, and by afternoon she had demolished a full cooked breakfast, a ham and cheese platter with pickles and bread and she was settling down to afternoon tea of cucumber sandwiches, spotted dick, jam and clotted cream when a messenger arrived with an urgent note from Joseph.

> *Miss Arabella,*
> *I urgently write to tell you the statue is gone!*
> *Yours*
> *Joseph*

'Tell him I'll be over as soon as I can be. I haven't been feeling myself today,' Arabella explained.

When the messenger had gone, Arabella dressed carefully, ensuring that all her weapons were in place. She had a feeling she might need them. Part of her didn't want to go out, but she knew she must.

Maybe I have lost my nerve? she thought. The idea seemed absurd yet entirely possible.

'Arabella, you are not to go out today,' her mother said

when she saw her in the hallway with the wicker basket. 'You've done quite enough for the poor this week. What if you've caught some dreadful disease?'

'I'm fine mother. There are many starving children relying on me.'

It took some time but she finally persuaded her mother to let her leave and outside Arabella told the coach driver to take her straight to The Sailor's Rest. The man said nothing, and she couldn't tell if he was curious because he was bundled up in his heavy coat, a huge scarf wrapped around his neck and face and his hat was pulled down over his eyes.

Joseph was down in the basement when she arrived. Arabella felt nervous as she crawled through the secret passageway into the storage room. Though her hallucinations had stopped after her third meal she still felt strange. She did not want to feel that cold wind, or see the beams of the building cave in around her. The crawl space filled her with unnameable dread but still she forced herself onwards.

'What happened?' she asked as she reached the storage room.

'One minute the thing was there, then it was gone. I've had the men search every inch of the cellars and sewers but they found nothing. I don't know how the thief got in so quietly and took the statue,' Joseph explained.

'This is very odd indeed. When did you notice it gone?'

'This morning. But it could have been taken at anytime after yesterday afternoon.'

Arabella climbed back into her waiting carriage, giving instruction to return home. Then she opened the wicker basket. Her weapons were there, but so too was the book. Arabella didn't recall placing it inside the basket. She rubbed her eyes and sat back while the carriage drove through the streets.

She felt ill again. It was as though someone had placed a curse on her. She thought back to her lucid and terrible dreams, and how these had all occurred after they had acquired the statue, and, more tellingly, the book. Even since it had come into her possession, Arabella had felt wrong.

The carriage came to an abrupt halt. Arabella looked out and discovered that they had stopped at the docklands.

'Driver! What are we doing here? I said you were to take me home.'

When she got no response, Arabella opened the door and looked out. The driver's seat was empty, but for the coachman's scarf and hat. She looked around. The dock was unusually quiet. Several cargo ships were tied up along the massive harbour, but no sign of life.

She retrieved her crossbow and patted her leg to reassure herself that the gun was still attached to her thigh. Then she prepped the crossbow. It was small and easy to fire, with a trigger mechanism. She draped the basket, still containing the book, over her free arm and walked down the dock to look for her driver. He would be reprimanded for this.

She saw the ship that had brought the crate, with none of the activity she might have expected on board. There was no one on the deck at all. The ship appeared to be as deserted as the rest of the port.

This is like the dream I had in the mission. Only, Arabella was sure now that it had been no dream.

At the warehouse Arabella placed the crossbow down and removed the book from the basket. She unwrapped it and held the leather skin against her chest. Things had gone wrong since she had opened and read from it but how could she reverse that? She left the basket on the floor, retrieving her crossbow as she clutched the book against her chest with the other arm.

The warehouse was cold and deserted and smelt of fish. There was no group of sailors enjoying their game. There was no Captain screaming of theft. Only a circle of crates stood in the middle of the otherwise empty space. Arabella noted a coffin at the centre. She walked around it, looking suspiciously at the peculiar markings on its surface and at the daunting and varied shapes of the others that surrounded it.

Then she noted the obvious gap; a space in the circle of the same shape and size as the crate she and Joseph had taken.

'You have the book,' said a voice behind her.

Arabella turned, bringing the crossbow up on instinct while she firmly clasped the book against her chest.

It was a woman she had not seen before, wearing the heavy coat of her driver. She removed the coat and threw it aside to reveal a red velvet dress. She shook her hair free of the driver's hat and it fell long, silver over her shoulders. She was striking to look at but not young. Perhaps in her fifties but was full of all of the vitality of the young.

'Who are you?' Arabella asked.

'A guardian,' she said. 'I keep the Ancient Ones safely in their own realm.'

'You talk in riddles ….'

'You opened the book and now one of them is free,' said the woman.

Arabella shook her head. 'No. I couldn't open it.'

The woman smiled. 'My dear Lady Arabella the book opened for you, and you read from it, and it brought you to me.'

Arabella felt fear then. A real terror that what the woman said was true. She recalled the sarcophagus and glanced at the central crate.

'It's just a book,' she denied shaking her head. 'I had a dream, that's all.'

'It's a grimoire and it holds the secrets to a universe that you couldn't possibly imagine. You didn't dream it. The *Fenrir* is free and he terrorises your city even as we speak.'

'If that is true… then what can be done?'

The woman's smile widened. 'The only solution is sacrifice. The Ancient One will not return until he can take a soul back with him.'

The woman entered the circle and Arabella stepped back.

'Sacrifice? Look— who are you?'

'My name is Constance Stirling. I am the keeper of the book. I didn't realise that the ship I travelled on was also carrying a certain crate. In a way I should have seen the signs. I was suffering from disturbed sleep, I foolishly allowed the Captain to examine the exterior of the book. It was as though I had lost my judgement.'

'I don't know what you're talking about. But this book… I suppose it is valuable?' Arabella said.

'What price can be put on the life of humanity?' Stirling replied.

Outside, a cold wind picked up. Arabella felt its icy tendrils slipping along her spine. She was afraid, but unwilling to give the book to Stirling. Even though she now really believed it had brought her bad luck.

Stirling had been slowly edging forward and was now at the other end of the centre crate.

'Tell me something?' Arabella said. 'Is this—a sarcophagus?'

Stirling smiled. 'You dreamed of a temple, the statues positioned around you, this shape in the centre?'

Arabella nodded but her mouth was so dry she suddenly couldn't answer. How could Stirling know this if she didn't speak the truth?

'And the buildings around you decayed, did they not?'

'Yes,' she gasped.

'People disintegrated into vile puddles?'

It was as though Stirling could read her thoughts.

'This will happen if the Wolf is not returned to his cage. The Ancient Ones will rule the Earth and the people will die to satisfy their sick lusts.'

Stirling's eyes gleamed and Arabella saw again the dead and empty streets. She felt the world turning to mud and filth around her and she knew that Stirling told the truth.

'Already they convene,' Stirling said. 'Look around you. You have brought the others here.'

'I didn't,' Arabella protested. Never before had she been so out of her depth. She believed Stirling but still had to deny her part in the madness. 'I didn't take the book. It was sent to me. How was I to know what it was?'

Stirling smiled again and it was not a kind expression. 'My dear, do you know how many souls there are in Hell who cry out their innocence? Crimes against humanity, be they by accident or by intent, still bear the same punishment. The only way to salvage this is to sacrifice yourself for the good of all.'

It slowly began to dawn on Arabella that Stirling was suggesting that she die for her mistake.

'You're insane,' she said, raising the crossbow to point at Stirling. 'I'm leaving. Don't try to stop me. I'm not above using this on you. You wouldn't be the first person I've killed.'

Arabella backed away from Stirling and circled the sarcophagus as she made her way back to the warehouse door.

She turned around only when she thought Stirling wasn't following her, but found herself not in the warehouse at all, but back in the temple of her dream.

'Set us free,' a voice hissed. 'Open the book and read.'

She turned back to the room. The crates were gone; in their place she saw the monsters. They surrounded her, touching, tasting and stroking her skin and hair with their vile appendages.

'I can't…' Arabella said backing away until she was pressed against the hard wall.

'You freed our brother,' murmured another of the creatures, this one, a huge and monstrous snake with a female head and pendulous breasts. It reminded her of the mythological Medusa except that her hair wasn't composed of snakes but glistening tentacles and they reached for her like loving arms. Another creature, the most monstrous of all, had the sex organs of both man and woman. The penis writhed and twisted as though alive, and the vagina opened and closed like some horrendous greedy mouth. Another of the creatures was mist, formless and yet suggestive of the most terrifying nightmares, while one was nothing more than a vile ichor, dripping greenish black all over the marble slabs of the tomb, and then pooling and collecting, driven by some hellish intelligence.

Arabella was suddenly pulled back. The temple fell away as her crossbow was yanked from her fingers and she found herself lying Stirling's feet. She was back in the warehouse; the crates had moved and were closer now to the one standing in the centre. She shuddered as the vision hung in the air between them.

'They are drawing you into their realm,' Stirling explained. 'It is only a matter of time before they persuade you to set them free.'

'They are horrible. Vile. I could never let them into this world.'

'Don't you understand? They have a direct pathway to you now and they will torture you until you give in.

Arabella, these things know our deepest and darkest fears. They will use that against you. You won't be able to resist. No one can.' Stirling said.

'But you…?'

'I have never opened the book,' she explained. 'And I never would.'

Stirling's steady gaze met hers. 'I'm so sorry,' she said.

'What for?'

'This.'

Stirling lifted the crossbow but Arabella dived out of its path just seconds before the arrow fired. She was on her feet, grabbing for the weapon with her right hand; the fingers of her free hand clawed at Stirling. She scratched at the other woman's face, leaving bloody furrows on her cheek below the eye. Her desperate fight was useless. As the second bolt loaded automatically Stirling pulled the trigger and the arrow fired between them straight into the book still clasped against Arabella's heart.

The arrow pierced the cover, penetrated the sheets beneath and buried itself deep into Arabella's chest. She sank to the floor, a look of astonishment on her face.

Her blood and bone began to dissolve into the book. She shuddered as her body twisted, her skin merging with the dried leather cover. Stirling watched as the markings faded from the book and then return as Arabella's twisted body warped, becoming part of the book, as so many sacrifices had before her.

Arabella tried to scream, but her breath was taken from her, and with the sound of snapping bone and tearing sinew, she ceased to exist, being absorbed totally into the grimoire.

Stirling looked at the book on the floor. It seemed so innocuous, so harmless. She then retrieved a pair of leather gloves from her pocket. Her hair was no longer silver, but had become a deep chestnut. Her face no longer had the aspect of a mature woman, but appeared to be no older than mid-twenties. The youthful spring was well and truly back into her step. She turned and looked at the crates.

The Wolf God was back in its place and Stirling smiled sadly.

Behind the central crate, Stirling picked up the carpet bag that Arabella had left behind on her previous visit. She placed the book inside then turned and walked out of the building.

Now that she had the grimoire, Stirling knew that she had to travel once more, far away from the crates and their monstrous contents. They would follow her; perhaps once again, one of them would catch her in a moment of weakness. Stirling was only human after all and the Captain of the ship had been most attractive and persuasive. But then, at least there could always be more sacrifices to undo the lapse. And to give her back her youth whenever she needed it.

In an ancient tomb in an unknown place Lady Arabella Hutchinson lay at the feet of the Wolf. His claw-like hand stroked her hair as the tentacled arm of another monstrosity burned furrows into the pale skin of her legs. She screamed. It was the deep terror-filled cry of someone who had finally lost her soul and her mind.

HOW TO BE THE PERFECT HOUSEWIFE

Chloë Yates

Being a good wife is not easy. Being a perfect wife is nearly impossible, but that doesn't mean you shouldn't try. Every husband has dreams of a good wife; by following our helpful tips, you can make his come true.

The tangled aroma of roasting vegetables twisted through the air in a welcoming rush. Kitty let the oven door slam back into place, smiling at the satisfying clunk it made. Kitty was a good wife. Prided herself on it. She certainly tried hard enough to please her husband, had done ever since she'd met him. They were happy. She had made sure of it. He never needed to lift a finger at home; she took care of everything except the Man tasks, but they didn't count. He couldn't fail to be happy with life when he stepped through the door after a long day at work, whether or not he happened to be three hours late, whether or not he'd been drinking whiskey or chasing trollops...

Silly goose. She was standing there wool gathering while she had goodness-knows-what on her hands from emptying the bin. Honestly, what was she thinking? This was no time to be away with the fairies. With a shake of her head, she crossed the kitchen to the sink and dipped her hands into the warm soapy water.

The bubbles were red. Staring down into the sink Kitty wondered at that. It was troublingly hard to think. She felt more tired than she had ever felt in her life. It was like a weight in her soul. It seemed like she'd been on the go non-stop since forever ago and now she was paying the price. She ignored the empty strip of anti-psychotics on the counter beside her. She didn't need them and they weren't for thinking about now.

Shaking the bubbles, red or otherwise, from her hands and the inertia from her shoulders, Kitty grabbed a dishcloth. It was warm from where she'd taken the roasting vegetables out of the oven a few moments before. The hiss and spit from the frying pan reminded her that the steaks were probably well and truly sealed and, after wiping her wet fingers with the warm fabric, she deftly flipped the sizzling meat into the roasting tray.

Always have dinner ready. Plan ahead because having a meal on the table when your husband comes home from a hard day at the office is an essential part of welcoming him home.

Once the tray was back in the oven, Kitty turned her attention to the stock bubbling merrily on the stove. She always liked to have plenty to hand and this batch was going to be a doozy. She poked at the bones with a wooden spoon and did her best to give the thickening gloop a hearty stir, all the time smiling happily. She loved cooking, loved preparing meals for her husband. The way to a man's heart was, as everyone knew, through his stomach. Maybe she should have made haggis from that bitch's… Kitty took a deep breath. It wouldn't do to lose her focus now. She'd come such a long way already.

Keep noise to a minimum. Time it so that the washing machine has finished its cycle, the dishwasher is not rumbling and never allow the vacuum cleaner to be anywhere but in a cupboard when the man of the house is home.

There was still a lot to do. The stain in the hallway would have to be attended to; scarlet rivulets were already making a break for the Persian rug in the living room and that simply would not do. Then there were the walls. Kitty sighed. She hadn't meant to make such a mess, but needs must when the devil drives. It had been so satisfying. Closing her eyes, she remembered another pair, wide with terror, lips moving to make the incessant music of pleas for mercy, pale skin, trembling hands. It was all a memory now, but it had been a luxury like no other. Better than sex, that was for sure. The swift pinch of a blade point against, into, quivering flesh, the promise of something more, something deeper, more revealing. Kitty opened her eyes. She was losing herself again and there were chores to be done.

Heading for the utility room at the back of the kitchen, she ticked off what she would need in her mind; bucket, mop, scrubbing brush, bleach…

> *Ensure the children are quiet, that they have*
> *clean hands and faces and their hair is combed.*
> *Their father does not want to be greeted by filthy*
> *unkempt little terrors.*

The children. She'd forgotten all about them. Honestly, she'd forget her head if it wasn't screwed on. That's what her Mother used to tell her, over and over, each time punctuated with a hearty thwack of the paddle against the back of her legs. Merciless, but she had learned the lesson well. All the lessons. Each one more cruel, more calculated to demolish than the last. Whining about it was not going to get her chores done any quicker, however, and she had forgotten, hadn't she? Forgotten like the simpleton she was. Well, time to remedy that.

'Children! I'm coming. I hope you've washed your hands and faces.'

> *Take one last look around to make sure the house*
> *is spick-and-span. Gather up any clutter and run*
> *a duster over the tables, sideboards, windowsills*
> *et cetera. Your husband should feel as though he is*
> *returning to a haven, not a war zone.*

That was the children attended to. Honestly, those boys were just like their father. Always running her to the edge of patience, misbehaving with that endearing glint of roguishness in their eyes: irritating, irritating little shits. She had to teach them a lesson, just as her mother had taught her. With any lesson, however, there was often a resultant mess and, darn it all, she was already behind schedule. She was finding it hard to think again; things kept reshuffling in her mind like a dodgy spine on a potholed road. If she didn't start getting it together, didn't regain order over everything, smooth it all out, she was soon going to… The sound of the stock boiling over snapped her out of it. Now she really was in a fix.

Kitty sprinted for the hob, grabbing for the knob and yelped as the hot overspill splashed and spat at her skin. She turned the temperature down and grabbed a tea towel, heaving the large pot onto a dormant burner. Bloody woman. She was still more trouble than she was worth. Well, as long as she was tasty, that's all that mattered now.

> *Before your man arrives home, take a few minutes*
> *to refresh your make up, fix your hair, and change*
> *your clothes if need be. Ensure you are nice and*
> *relaxed when he comes through the door. Be ready*
> *to give him a lift with a smile as you greet him.*

It was time for the jacket. She'd worked on it all afternoon when she should have been cleaning. The old Singer was the only thing she'd inherited from her mother - the only thing other than the psychosis and the piquerism - and was still in perfect working order. She took good care of it, just as mother had beaten into her. It still hemmed seams like a dream, creating a beautiful jacket for her out of… That old saying "silk purse out of a pig's ear" might be deemed appropriate. Kitty chuckled. That woman, - the pigwhorebitch - had learned the hard way. Learned that she, Kitty Darling, was not someone to be messed with, that her family unit was not something anyone else would be allowed to endanger. Not anyone. Least of all some filthy, blowjobbing disease trap…

Kitty drew in a long breath. Her hands were shaking. The empty pill strips laughed at her from beside the sink, the light twinkling mockingly on the metallic material; mocking *her*. She hated to be mocked. Hated it. Hatedithatedithatedit…

The rage.

A moment of panic flashed through her, but even as she scrabbled to stop it, she felt it bubble over at last.

It shot through her veins, zinging up into her brain like

a champion pinball, making it throb. She raked her hands across her face, trying to scrape it out. Red lines scored her skin, but she couldn't stop, not until it was gone. Still it pulsed in her head, her thoughts scattering.

The sound of a key in the front door lock punched through her mania. She'd been anticipating it for hours and now that it had come, she wasn't ready. Goddammit, why did nothing ever work out right? Something always went wrong, something out of her control, something infu-ri-fucking-ating. Fury screeched through her, more potent than ever, those redundant pill packets not mocking her anymore. She felt the terror of the world around her as she stopped making a mess of her face. She felt it tremble at what she was becoming, had become.

As the key turned in the lock, seconds became minutes, became hours. Time elasticised with Kitty as she felt the change finally come over her, punching away the Kitty she'd tried so hard to be, so yearned to be. She'd felt its touch before but never its full force. She'd fought it for so long but every cell, every atom, was infused with red-hot anger, *righteous* anger. How dare he? How dare he do this to her? How dare he…

'Darling? What on earth happened? Where…'

Although the fury governed her now, she knew what she had to do. There was a kind of calm in the eye of its storm. Kitty stepped from the shadows, the cast iron pan in her hand.

'Welcome home, darling.'

'What the hell…?'

The sound of human skull crunching beneath cast iron echoed around the hallway and the man fell with a splash into the scarlet lake at his feet. Kitty looked down at her shoes and wondered how she was ever going to get the stains out.

> *Greet him with his favourite drink and make sure that he is comfortable. If he wants to take a nap before dinner, make sure his pillow is plumped and offer to remove his shoes. It is your job to ensure he is relaxed and can unwind unimpeded from his day.*

Vodka, rocks. Just how he liked it. Kitty was sure he'd be awake by now. She'd had to help him to bed, of course. Silly man had practically worked himself into a stupor. The bedside lamp cast a soft glow across the supine form of the man on the bed and as she stood in the doorway Kitty sighed at the perfection of his beloved face… except for the blood trickling from the wound just above his hairline. Why did she always have to focus on the details when they weren't important? She'd drive herself mad with them one day. Now was not the time, she needed to stay calm.

'Are you awake, darling?' She kept her voice low, soothing, as she crossed the room to sit on the bed beside him. When he didn't reply, she raised it slightly but made sure not to overdo it, just.

'Kit-Kitty?' His voice was groggy, hoarse. He didn't sound like himself at all. She'd already said it; the poor dear had been working too hard. Well now, wasn't it her job to make sure he relaxed? And wouldn't she do just that, even if it killed him?

'Of course it's Kitty, darling. I've brought your drink.'

'Untie me, Kitty. Please.' The panic in his plea was like a slap in the face. She didn't like it. She didn't like it at all. The heat of the fury prickled at the base of her skull, rolled in the pit of her stomach. No. She wouldn't let it take over again. She had a plan and if you could say one thing about Kitty Darling it was that she stuck to her plans. In the end.

> *Do not subject him to complaints and problems.*
> *He has most likely had a hard day and anything*
> *you have to say will probably be inconsequential*
> *in comparison. Be considerate and attentive, let*
> *him talk to you and not the other way around.*
> *However, your husband is not clairvoyant. If you*
> *want something from him, ask for it, but make*
> *sure you keep your tone positive and never accusa-*
> *tory. Whatever you do, never let anger take over.*

It was tricky, staying calm, but Kitty had had a lot of practice. Once upon a time, she had constantly been at the mercy of the fury - the cold white rooms, the hypodermics, the placating smiles and 'hush nows' of Dr Tish as he felt her up beneath her gown - but she had learned to keep it in its place. She had.

Deep breaths. The mindfulness book had said to go back into her breathing if she was having trouble focusing - Dr Tish had said the same thing, but for something quite different. She thought it was fair to say she was having some trouble focusing.

Deep breath in, two three four, deep breath out, two three four, and repeat.

Better.

Now. The jacket.

Luckily the other woman - that bitchwhoreskank - was quite a bit bigger than Kitty, so she'd been able to nip and tuck the garment to suit her frame, but it had still been a bugger to get into. Kitty looked at herself in the mirror. She admired her handiwork for a moment, allowing herself just a touch of pride. She'd always been good with her hands. Even when mother had broken every one of her fingers after she'd stolen an apple from the bowl that sat on the kitchen table in the farmhouse they'd lived in - she'd not eaten for days, days, she'd been so young, so hungry, so frightened, always so frightened - they had healed well and only ached when the cold weather came. There she was again, going all goopy at herself. It was time for dinner. She didn't want those steaks overcooking now, did she?

The jacket took a bit of getting used to but, as she made her way back into the kitchen, she was glad she'd made the effort. The look on his face when he saw her was priceless. He clearly hadn't failed to notice it, to realise what it was made from. Her talent as a seamstress was probably one of the reasons he'd married her.

He was sat at the head of the table, just as he should be, and the two boys were pinned to their chairs. It had taken her a bloody age, but pinned they were. Their bowing heads were the only oversight she'd made, making the tableau a little less than she had hoped for, but she had to suck it up for now. Hopefully they would come round before their dinner got cold.

Ensure the cutlery and glassware are sparkling

*clean. Your napkin always goes in your lap. Never
lick your fingers and never ask who you're eating.*

The table was set. The tablecloth was gingham. Perfect red and white check. Kitty smoothed the cloth across the table before taking a step back to admire her work. It was perfect, of course. Perfect. How she liked perfect. She felt much better now things were going according to plan again. Calmer. Clearer. Happy.

As Kitty looked around at her family, she wondered if she'd ever felt so at peace before. There might only be four of them, but they were a perfect family. One day, maybe, they'd have a little girl. She'd always wanted a girl.

'Let's eat.' Picking up her knife and fork, Kitty began digging into the meal in front of her, her left elbow sticking occasionally in the jacket's sleeve. She'd have to take another look at the stitching after dinner. Steak with roasted potatoes, pumpkin, courgette and onions with the delicious gravy she'd made from the stock on the stove. It smelled divine. Closing her eyes, she savoured the meat as she chewed. The meat was succulent and tasty; its juices sliding decadently down her throat. It was cooked to perfection. She had surpassed herself this…

No one else was eating.

'Your food will get cold.' Neither of the children replied, they sat in silence, refusing to pick up their knives and forks. Well, if they didn't eat what she put in front of them they would go without. He was no better. Sitting opposite her, staring at her, the expression on his face one of… no, this was intolerable. She would fix this.

Scraping her chair back, Kitty stood up and walked around the table. She picked up his knife and fork and cut a large piece of meat for him. Blowing on it gently, she raised it to his mouth. He flinched away, keeping it firmly shut. Kitty pushed it against his - bastard, ingrate - closed lips a second time. And a third. Then stabbed him in the mouth with the fork when he still refused to permit her entry. He yelled in surprise and pain but the fork sticking out of his face muffled the sound. Blood trickled from the wound she'd made and Kitty fought the urge to lick his face. That sort of thing was for the bedroom, not the dining table.

'Now look what you made me do. Eat up or I'll find another way to get it all inside you.' Kitty pulled the fork back out, ignoring his whimpering, and waited. Slowly, he opened his mouth and, smiling, Kitty popped the fork between his lips. 'Chew.' He was clumsy but obedient. She liked that. She liked it a lot, but she couldn't stand there feeding him like a baby - snivelling baby, snot running out of his nose. He might be her husband but she needed (oh how she needed) to eat too. Decision made, she swiftly, with the occasional sticking of her left elbow, cut up his dinner into manageable pieces and used the steak knife to slice through the gaffa tape binding him to his chair on one side. Just one hand. She popped the knife into the pocket of her apron - she didn't want any accidents - and put the fork into the hand she had freed, wrapping his stiff fingers around the handle. Returning to her seat, enjoying the unusual meaty shuck of the jacket's fabric as she sat, she was pleased to see him digging - picking - at his vegetables.

> *Never overdo it on the wine. A glass or two is*
> *acceptable but you should always keep in mind that*
> *no man likes a drunk Wendy for a wife. There is*
> *also the washing up to consider. You're not going*
> *to get that done when you're three sheets to the*
> *wind. Remember, first and foremost, a good wife's*
> *responsibility is to keep her home spick-and-span.*

Maybe working too hard was affecting his appetite - or maybe he ate before he came home, with his friends or per-haps another woman, maybe he hates your cooking, maybe he knows. Kitty decided to go easy on him. She could be magnanimous; the apple might not fall far from the tree, but it did fall and she was *not* her mother. Picking up his plate, she took it to the sink and began scraping the leftovers into the little tub she kept for…

Sharp pain, intense, sudden, pierced the junction of her neck and shoulder. The sweet spot. Kitty dropped the plate onto the counter, the fork skittering after it in a shower of leftovers. She scrabbled at her back, but he stabbed her again before she could stop him. His reflection in the darkened window - she should have seen him, heard him, stupid stupid - above the sink was grim, determined. The children. She'd forgotten - treacherous little shits - about their plates, their cutlery. Without thinking, she thrust her head backwards, right into his perfect, double-crossing face. The crunch of his nose breaking under her skull fired the fury through her even better than the stab of the fork in her neck. She whirled around, one hand grabbing for the carving knife she'd left on the draining board earlier. She jabbed at him, piercing his chest with a smattering of shallow puncture wounds. He was strong though, despite the head injury, despite the fear - or because of it - and, as her damned left elbow caught again, he punched her hard in the stomach, doubling her over, her hand opening reflexively and dropping the knife. Gasping for breath, but not outdone, Kitty bared her teeth and drove them into his thigh, feeling her jaw click hard as she bit down. He screamed so loudly it hurt her ears and then he punched her again, this time in the back. Kitty fell to her knees but she was far from finished. She ground her fingers into the soft flesh at the side of his knee, pinching hard - she was glad she'd cut the bitches hands off now - watching as his leg buckled beneath him. When his face came into view, she head-butted him again, the crimson bloom of his blood splashing across her face. She licked her lips as he fell backwards, the salty taste almost as good as her gravy. Maybe it was for the kitchen, after all.

'Did you enjoy her, you cheating fuck?' She snarled at him, not waiting for an answer. 'Was she tasty? Everything you ever wanted?' He groaned in pain and confusion, on his back - just how the whore liked him - his hands flailing defensively, helplessly. 'I made sure to add a lot of pepper to her tasteless backside. Ha!' Even in his stupor, she could see he heard her, his bloody face clenching helplessly, his eyes wide with shock, as though this one depravity was the final straw, the snap of his sanity. His kids unconscious - dead, Kitty, dead - and pinned to a table, his whore's skin draped over her, they were nothing compared to eating human flesh. 'Delicious, wasn't she?' She laughed then, laughed so hard she thought she might never stop. When he punched her in the face, she stopped. She sat down on her bottom with an 'oof' and stared at him. She'd thought she'd broken him, but there he was, scrabbling to his feet and heading for the front door. Stars danced around her head like a sauce panned cartoon character. She blinked several times. Shaking her head was not an option just yet.

'Bitch!' He'd found her little trick then. Did he think she was stupid? Of course she'd locked the door. Thrown the key away. Banged in some nails. No one was getting out. No one. Clinging to the kitchen cabinet, she hoisted herself unsteadily to her feet. She pulled the cleaver from where it sat on its magnetic strip above the sink and followed him. He was trying for the windows, of course. Standing on one of her beautiful cream sofas with his feet all bloody from the lake on the hallway floor. He'd ruined her plans by arriving home early so she couldn't finish her tidying up and now he was ruining her sofa with his selfish sticky feet. Sticky sticky feet. Oh, he was going to get a lesson, all right, and it was going to be more than sticky.

A shriek tore from her throat as she sprinted at him, cleaver waving in her hand above her head, ready to chop into him wherever she could. He slipped just before she got to him, his sticky - sticky sticky - feet offending her yet again. The cleaver sank into her beautiful cream sofa and she had to pull it out with both hands. He was away from her by then, running for the back door. Kitty was, not for the first time, over his disobedience. Right. Over. It. She chased after him, catching him as he realised that door was locked too. She sank the cleaver into his shoulder with a battle cry that shook the walls. He tried to shake her off, but she let go of the heavy knife and climbed onto his back, clawing at him, sinking her teeth into his flesh wherever she could. He thrashed around, trying to dislodge her, but Kitty was tenacious, Kitty was strong, and Kitty was not giving up. She kept her hold on him despite that tricky left elbow even as he backed into the kitchen wall, wrapped her legs around him and squeezed hard.

'Don't fret, lover,' her breath was coming in short harsh gasps, but she kept talking, 'all this can be explained, sorted out, we can…'

'You killed my fucking wife!' Kitty saw red. How fucking dare he?

'*I'm* your wife, you ungrateful piss stain!' She snarled the words as she pressed harder with her thighs.

'You made me eat her. That thing… that thing you're… you're wearing her. Oh god! It's touching me!' His voice cracked and he whimpered, the sound making Kitty's patience slip a notch. Slip a few notches, truth be told, but by then it didn't need any help.

How. Dare. He?

'Just because you were fucking her, doesn't make her your wife. I'm your wife. Your only wife, your love. Say it! Say it or I'll make you regret being born, you cheating shit! *Say it!*'

'My wife? No, please. You're not my wife, Kitty.' He sounded out of breath, or was he less sure of himself now, battling to persuade her away from his deceit? 'You're not my wife. I'm sorry. We shouldn't have slept together, I know that.'

'You made me promises, vows, you said you…'

'I shouldn't have done it. I'm sorry, I'm so sorry, so fucking sorry…' His pitiful litany went on and on. He was pathetic. She'd done all this for him and this was all he had? All he could give her at the last?

Red fury filled her with a vengeance. Gritting her teeth, she angled her head so she could look down into his treacherous face.

'You lying bastard, you'd say anything, wouldn't you? I. Am. Your. Wife. Say it!'

'You're our au… our au pair.'

> *Two blond children, boys, swinging happily on the back garden set. Two smiling faces looking up at her, asking her for ice cream. Twin boys. Twin blond boys. Four glassy eyes as she looked down into their dead faces. Her boys. Her boys. They were hers –*

'Please Kitty, please!'

Kitty realised how tightly she was grasping him around the neck, the throat. She was strangling him and he was gasping for air now. This man. This man who denied her. What right had he… *two blond children, eyes like a summer sky; 'Kitty, Kitty, push us some more before Mummy gets home, please, Kitty!'…*

Kitty shut her eyes against the unwelcome memory. She would not be seduced by his words. Would not. She tightened her hold, relishing the feel of his strain for breath, tasting his imminent death on her tongue like a sugar cube.

She enjoyed it too much, it slackened her concentration, and he took advantage - they always do in the end - elbowing her in the stomach and hoisting her with her own petard by smacking the back of his head into her face. He missed the nose but caught her cheek hard. Her grip fell away and as she fell to the floor he stepped back from her, grabbing one of the kitchen chairs and throwing it hard against the kitchen window. The chair bounced off and they both watched - gormless rubberneckers - as it arced back at him. He stepped away before it could hit him, reached for another chair, but the stockpot was already in Kitty's hands. She could be quick, quicker than lightning, quicker than that bitch's knickers hitting the floor. Then the liquid was cascading over him, his whore's (his wife's!) head tumbling out with it, hitting him in the solar plexus like a fist, bowing him forward. He screamed again when he saw what had done it, but this time there was something broken, something feral about the sound. He stood there screaming, eyes wide and staring at the skinned head as it rolled aimlessly on the floor, screaming and screaming and screaming. Kitty would have laughed but… she was so tired now… she needed to finish this. It had all gone so horribly wrong, despite her careful planning, despite her attention to detail. How she wished it had turned out differently. How she wished… but if wishes were horses, as her mother used to say, beggars would ride. In truth, it was simple. She needed to decide. Keep him or kill him?

It was no decision at all, not really.

Carefully, Kitty placed the wig she had made on her head, pulling it firmly - that bitch's scalp was big and she'd had to pad it right out - down over her own hair, fiddled with it until it sat just right and then checked her make up. The red scratches and burgeoning bruises on her face were hidden beneath a thick layer of foundation. She decided she looked a bit like Marilyn Monroe. She'd always wanted to go blonde and now she'd had the balls to do it. She smiled at her reflection. After a moment of rightly earned admiration, she turned, grabbing the holdall from the sofa (ignoring the sticky sticky stains) and the car keys.

The body of her dead husband - employer, lover - had made her cry at first, but she was over that now. She'd mistaken him for the love of her life, for her destiny. He hadn't been, he had been a wicked lying cheat instead. So she had killed him and he had deserved it, but now what? Her life was nothing without Him, without The One. Kitty knew what she had to do. It would complete the circle and she would be with her family again, in another place - deepest darkest Hell, you snivelling bitch - and they would be happy again. She just had to find them. That was her purpose, her mission. Her family were out there. She knew it. She just had to take it back from whichever bitch had stolen it from her.

A perfect wife knows her place. Perfectly.

RED RIBBONS

Stephanie Burgis

'I can help you forget.'

That was the first thing she told me. Thérèse Mondoval, her golden hair unpowdered, her eyes like polished ebony... no, like the night itself.

And I, only two weeks out of convent school, trembling with confusion and desire.

I'd fled the ballroom and the Duc my parents had chosen for me, with his hot, groping hands and his contemptuous eyes. I ran until the candlelight and noise were all far behind me, and then I flung myself against the corridor wall and sobbed for my poor, broken illusions.

And then she stepped out of the darkness before me and spoke, and my life changed forever.

'Forget,' she breathed into my ear.

Her voice was as intoxicating as champagne, drawing me in; her slim hands, deliciously cool as she tilted back my chin. Her pink, plump lips curved into a smile.

Oh, Thérèse...

I would have fought a whole army to find her again. Clawing my way out of a mere grave, seven days later, was no effort.

Not when I found her waiting for me, her face softening with delight. She reached out, touched my cheek. I saw tears sparkle like diamonds in her eyes.

'You see? Now isn't this better?'

'Annette Davenant,' Thérèse pronounced, when she chose my newest name this year. 'Your father was English, no doubt a great lord in the North, and your mother...'

'Died for love when he abandoned her for a pickled herring!' I concluded, and blew a raspberry on her bare shoulder.

'You rascal!'

We were lying in each other's arms in our favourite resting place, a spacious, ornate tomb left abandoned when its family turned emigré to flee the Revolution and the bloody Terror that had overtaken the world outside. Snow piled against the outer walls of the tomb, and starving wolves prowled around the outskirts of Paris, but inside, we were free, and the chill of the air was nothing to either of us.

Thérèse pushed me over and landed on top, her hair falling around me like a shimmering, golden veil. 'Silence, ninny!' she ordered. 'I am being perfectly serious. We're going to introduce ourselves to high society.'

'I already was introduced, ten years ago. I didn't care for it.'

'I remember. You tried to throw yourself at a fool of a Duc, as I recall.'

'My lost love...' I sighed wistfully. 'Ah, what could have been, had not cruel Fate parted us.'

Thérèse narrowed her black eyes at me. 'You almost make me wish he had not met Madame la Guillotine.'

'Why? So you could return me to him with your deepest apologies?'

'No. So that I could bite him.' She nipped me instead, her teeth grazing my throat enticingly but not breaking the skin. That was Thérèse to the essence. I wriggled against her, trying to pull her closer, but she pulled back.

'Not yet,' she said. 'Not until you've agreed to my scheme.'

'Don't I always, in the end?' I sighed. 'Well? If there is such a thing as high society left anywhere in Paris...'

'Oh, now you're just being sulky. You know perfectly well, now that our greatly esteemed Thermidorian leaders have saved all of France from the horrors of the Terror, out of the pure, unblemished goodness of their mercenary little hearts...'

I rolled my eyes. 'Yes?'

'Anyone may join modern high society,' Thérèse said smugly. 'If only they have money, a touch of style, and... if they happen to be women...'

I shook my head in resignation. 'What are you planning?'

Thérèse's eyes sparkled. 'I can hardly wait to see you in a dampened dress.'

We made a grand entrance to the ball that night. Thérèse had found us both fashionably thin Indian muslin dresses, á la merveilleuse, and only the slightest application of water was necessary to make them cling to our figures quite as closely as the most shocking new styles demanded.

But Thérèse, of course, was not one to skimp on the water needed.

'If I were still alive, I would freeze to death,' I whispered to her as we entered the ballroom and struck a carefully careless pose.

'Citoyenne Annette Davenant and Citoyenne Thérèse Lacombe!' the master of ceremonies boomed obligingly behind us.

Public balls were the order of the day, and tickets--like everything from lives to armies, in our grand new, Thermidorian Paris--were available to anyone with the money to purchase them. And Thérèse had been insistent: it was this particular ball, tonight, and none other, that we must attend. As usual, she hadn't bothered to explain her reasoning, turning away all my questions with quips and distractions; and as always, in the end, I had sighed and laughed and agreed to everything she wanted, not even caring that I did not understand.

The tall ostrich plumes in Thérèse's hair bobbed as she smirked at me behind her fan. 'If you were still alive, you would have died of boredom years ago.'

'Without you, you mean? My, what a fine impression you have of my inner resources.' I spoke lightly, but the words rang strangely flat in my own ears.

It was the damned ballroom that did it to me. It was the first time I'd entered a room like this since my own miserable début ten years before; since I'd met Thérèse and she'd rescued me. I swallowed down sudden sickness.

'Thérèse,' I began, in an urgent undertone.

But she spoke over me, looking out across the sea of dancers and mingling crowds before us. Her eyes narrowed; I could have sworn she was looking for someone in particular. 'I have so much faith in your inner resources, my dear, that I'll dare to leave you to them. Shall we meet again in two hours? They should be serving supper by then.'

'I'm not...'

'I'm sure we can both eat our fill before then, somehow,' Thérèse said demurely, and disappeared into the crowd before I could call her back.

I bit back my exasperation. There was no use chasing after her and causing a scene. And she had been right about one thing, at least: I was indeed hungry.

As I strolled through the crowded edges of the room, I passed women in scanty Grecian tunics that skimmed across the tops of their thighs and women with bare breasts or bosoms covered only by shields of massed diamonds. They sighed and cooed and fluttered in turn at lisping dandies with powdered hair cut short in back á la victime; at soldiers with colourful uniforms and dazzled eyes; and, most of all, at the well-dressed, avaricious men who ruled the country now with the soldiers' help. My father would never have recognized a single one of them as a gentleman... but then, the world had changed in the last ten years, and all our definitions with it.

I kept my gaze half-slitted above my fan as I studied their faces and waited to select my dinner.

I found a young soldier from the provinces. Already giddy from the wine and the company, he was determined to prove himself as sophisticated as everyone else around him... and easy to persuade into the snow-covered gardens outside.

'Aren't you cold?' he asked as we stepped out into the darkness.

'Warm me,' I whispered, and pressed myself against him.

He let out a high-pitched laugh; nervousness and excitement combined in his voice, spoiling his attempt at nonchalance. He was very young. 'Could you have conceived of this gaiety only three months ago, Citoyenne? When blood ran through the gutters, and any word taken the wrong way and reported...'

'Shh,' I whispered. He wore a stiff cravat. I wormed my finger inside, working it loose. 'All's well now. The Terror is past.'

I felt him swallow. 'We can't forget, though. Can we? Have you heard of the bals des victimes held at the Hôtel Richelieu? Guests wearing red ribbons around their throats as if they'd been guillotined, jerking their heads when they meet as if... *ah*!'

He wasn't drunk yet, fortunately. His blood tasted fresh and warm, just like him. I left him slumped just inside the back door, where servants would find him soon enough and take him for another hopeless intoxicant, overwhelmed by the manic gaieties of freedom. He wouldn't wake in time to put me in any danger; probably he wouldn't even remember what had happened.

But I felt oddly melancholy as I stepped back into the warm, crowded ballroom. Thérèse was nowhere to be seen; probably she had taken her own meal to another part of the garden, or to one of the corridors upstairs. I had still over an hour to wait before we were due to meet. I ought to look for another meal myself; Thérèse had been right: a public ball such as this, crowded full with healthy, well-fed strangers, was a paradise of choice after years of poor pickings. I started forward...

And a hand closed over my arm. 'Annette de Rocheval, as I live and breathe!'

It was the name I'd been born with, twenty-six years ago.

'I can scarcely believe it. I heard you were dead!'

I turned. The woman beside me wore a fashionable blonde wig, cut á la victime. But her round, smiling face...

My heart sank. Henriette. My classmate for seven years at convent school, and one of the kindest, loudest gossips I had ever known.

She twinkled at me beneath her wig. 'Now, don't pretend you don't recognize me! I would have known you anywhere. You haven't changed a bit, have you, you lucky creature? Why, I could swear you were still sixteen. And those unusual eyes I always envied--we used to call them witch's eyes, didn't we? Pure Rocheval.'

'It's Davenant now,' I said. 'How lovely to see you again, Henriette.' She had left the school a month earlier than I, to be married; I struggled for the name. 'And your husband, the Vicomte--ah, that is, Citoyen Marchande?'

Henriette's eyes dropped. 'Madame la Guillotine. My sisters, too. And parents.'

'I am sorry.'

'Oh, we all have our stories, don't we? I was in La Force

myself for a month. It's a badge of honour now, isn't it?' Her laughter was bright and metallic. 'Even my wig--it came from the hair of one of les victimes, that's what made it so valuable. I like to think I might have known her, or even been her friend, years ago. Now she can enjoy herself again with me, when I wear her to these balls.'

'How... sweet.' I wished, so keenly it felt like a lance of pain, to be safely alone with Thérèse in our own quiet tomb, far from this glittering ballroom. I had hated my first ball, indeed, but I began to think it had been no hardship, compared to my second. 'Well, I'm afraid I must really--'

'Oh, no, you mustn't leave now, when I've only just found you again!' Henriette said. 'You must tell me everything! Davenant—you married an Englishman or an American, then? I thought you were betrothed to a Duc. I thought you were dead!' Her face pursed into a frown. 'I'm sure I heard you were dead. And from more than one source. The funeral...'

'You must be thinking of someone else.' I tried to tug away, but her small fingers clung to my arm.

'But I'm sure it was you. Everyone said it was so mysterious-- that you'd been perfectly healthy and then, less than three weeks after you left school...'

'I was ill then, I remember,' I said. 'But the rumours exaggerated. They usually do.'

'But I'm certain...' She trailed off, eyeing me wonderingly.

I gritted my teeth. I was tired, I was unhappy, and I did not wish to kill Henriette Marchande, who had never harmed me in her life. Nothing short of death could silence her; even if I took enough nourishment from her to ensure hours of sleep, she would still wake eventually and remember this conversation and how we had met just before her strange faint. Worse yet, she might even connect it to the mysteries that surrounded my death, and to my unchanged looks; and even if she did not, she would inevitably spread the story until it met someone who knew enough to put all the clues together.

But I did not want to taste Henriette's blood, laced with memories and pain. The mere thought of it made me gag.

'I must go,' I said, and I wrenched my arm away with a force that made her gasp.

The crowd felt suffocating now as I pushed through it, all the jewel-covered, warm-blooded animals around me whirling through their meaningless dances, manic with gaiety but not happiness, no, never that. Happiness did not exist in ballrooms, before the Revolution or afterwards. Happiness only existed in one place I knew of, and I craved it more than blood.

'Thérèse...' I breathed her name as I searched the crowd for her golden hair, her beautiful black eyes, her grin of perfect complicity.

When I glanced back, I saw Henriette in deep conversation with two other women and a man in soldier's uniform. Her brow furrowed in puzzlement as she talked, and the others leaned in close to listen. I clamped down on panic before it could overwhelm me.

I would find Thérèse and we would disappear together. Safe. As always.

That was all that mattered.

I ducked through the door that led to the stairwell. The thin, golden straps of my Grecian sandals bit into my feet as I ran up the stairs.

How long would it take the story to cross the ballroom? How long before it reached someone who knew the legends... or the truth?

The first-floor gallery above the ballroom was brightly lit and filled with embracing couples. *Too public.* I turned back to the stairs, shaking with urgency. How long did I have left?

I should have known better than to leave Henriette untouched and free. No, I had known better, but I hadn't listened to common sense. It had been madness to let sentimentality put us in such danger. Thérèse would never have been so foolish.

Too late now for regrets... or rather, too soon. Once I found Thérèse and we were safe, then I could pour out all my regrets to her alone, and she would laugh and stroke my hair and soothe me, calling me her soft-hearted ninny, *not safe to let out of her sight*, and I would laugh, too, as I agreed with her.

Once I found Thérèse...

I leapt the last two steps onto the second floor landing, in the darkness.

'Thérèse?' I whispered.

And that was when I heard her scream, far below.

Time is the cruellest of all masters.

I was born twenty-six years ago, in my parents' country house outside Paris, and my first sixteen years passed with all the slow placidity of a cow's life, imprisoned in a field she did not choose. Ten years ago, I met Thérèse in a darkened corridor, and I was born again. In all our ten years together, time raced by as quickly and as fluidly as a stream rushing toward a towering waterfall, unknowing of the cataclysm ahead.

But time stopped altogether as I heard Thérèse scream. And as I ran back down the three flights of broad, marble stairs, each step took at least a decade to complete.

I couldn't hear Thérèse anymore.

With each step I prayed. I prayed the Rosary of my girl-hood, and I prayed to anything, anyone else who would listen, until all the words my lips could form were:

Thérèse. Thérèse. Thérèse, please, Thérèse...

I hurtled into the ballroom.

The dancing and the music had stopped.

I couldn't see through the shifting crowds. Shocked whispering and chatter formed a high-pitched whine against my ears.

I pushed my way through, taking in scattered words without meaning.

'...His daughter...'

'She was dead!'

'I saw her move.'

'Her smile--'

'Died seventeen years ago--'

Thérèse.

She was facing me, in her last moment. Her black eyes widened. Restrained by three soldiers, she still shook her head, flattened her hands in a gesture that meant *Go!* even as I lurched forward to save her.

Too late.

The force of the stake was a meaty *thunk!* that resonated in my bones.

Her body fell and lay, unmoving.

I fell to my knees. I couldn't breathe.

The man who'd wielded the stake brushed his hands off and turned to the men around him, all wearing the same finery. He wore a gold medal on his jacket. His face was lined with age, his hair thin and white. But his eyes were a black I'd only seen once before.

'It was the same with her poor mother and both her sisters,' he said. 'You learn the trick of managing them soon enough. I'm only surprised this one had the gall to attend tonight, knowing I would be here with the rest of the new régime.'

'She--' began one of the younger men nearby.

Thérèse's father shook his head. '*It*,' he corrected. 'Oh, it may look like a beautiful woman, gentlemen, but it's no more than a demon beneath the skin.' He began to move away, then stopped. 'Oh, and for safety's sake, it'll still need its head cut off and garlic stuffed in its mouth before it's buried.'

A scream welled up in my throat. My vision blurred. I felt the blood-rage lift me from the ground.

A hand closed around my arm to stop me.

'Annette,' said a voice I knew. 'Annette. You can't help her. Annette.'

I turned around. It was Henriette Marchand, silly Henriette, with her blonde wig and her worried face.

'She was your friend?' Henriette said softly. 'I'm sorry. I can tell she was. I found someone who took care of me, too, when I was in La Force and should have died. But you have to leave her now before someone sees you in such a state and suspects.'

I shook my head. My voice could barely form words. Later, I would wonder at her calmness, and at myself. Now all I could say, like a child, was: 'Thérèse...'

'You can't stop them,' Henriette said. 'You're surrounded by five hundred people, can't you see that? They would have you in seconds, before you could even touch him. How would that help her?'

'I have to--'

'Didn't you learn anything from the Terror?' Henriette

asked. Her face was pale with anger now. 'Do you think I wanted to see my sisters guillotined? Do you think I wanted to become a filthy sans-cullotte's mistress? Do you think I like what I've become? We don't have a choice! You have to survive! That's all that matters anymore.'

I stared at her. Behind me, I heard movement. Henriette gripped both my arms and held my gaze. I heard wet, horrible sounds.

And I let Henriette hold me.

'We've survived,' Henriette said at last, as she let me go. 'Be grateful.'

She turned and walked away through the crowd.

Thérèse never told me about her past. Oh, we made up new histories for her every year, just as we did for me. We called her a Spanish princess, an actress, the lovechild of a nun. But I never asked her for the truth, and she never offered it.

I think I must have believed, somehow, that she had never truly existed before she met me, just as I was only born into myself when I met her.

My Thérèse.

That boy in the gardens--he was right. Gaiety can mask our losses, but it can never heal them.

'I can help you forget,' she told me, our first night.

But she never forgot her own past, did she? We only pretended, together, that it had never happened, in our own private, glittering bal des victimes, where nothing in the past could be allowed to matter, and we could feel no pain. And it was that pretence that killed her in the end.

'Citoyenne Davenant,' the secretary calls. He's kept me prisoner in this waiting room for hours--just one of the many unimportant supplicants waiting to see one of the most powerful men in new, Thermidorian Paris, to buy favours, laws, armies... and lives.

As I step into Thérèse's father's private office, I raise the dark veil I wore over my face to protect myself from sunlight on the long walk here.

I look into his black eyes, not yet widening with fear, and I see only Thérèse.

'I will never forget,' I tell him. 'Never.'

A CHANGE OF LEADERSHIP

Jonathan Ward

It had been raining for the last half-hour: the clouds thick enough that the moon and stars were blotted out entirely. Fortunately, there was enough light cast by the lanterns hung at irregular intervals along the street below for Jayla to be able to see what was going on. She swept her gaze along there now. Persistent rain was turning the already-saturated road of packed earth into more of a quagmire than it had already been, and sluggish rivulets of mud could be seen oozing along the base of the long, high wall that formed the right-hand side of the street and the very edge of the city. On the other side of the wall there was nothing but a long drop off a sheer cliff to jagged rocks far below, and as a result this section of the city wall was not permanently guarded.

The buildings along the left side of the street were all abandoned: their inhabitants had fled when the palace at the summit of the city had first been razed. Many across the city had done the same during that dark period, although most of them had returned now that repairs on the newly-renamed Drake's Roost had been completed. While some form of order had been restored, the population was still well below the peak found during Bask rule. All this combined with the bad weather meant that there were unlikely to be any witnesses to what they were going to do tonight. Conditions could hardly be more ideal, which was some consolation for the fact that Jayla was getting completely soaked.

She pushed such thoughts out of her head and focussed on the here and now. From her position lying prone at the edge of a roof halfway down the street she could see the connecting road winding away deeper into the city. That road *was* occupied and a custodian patrol passed along it once an hour, every hour, with idiotic predictability. By her estimation they were a few minutes late, and she felt the knot of tension inside her twist itself a little tighter. It was possible that the bad weather had kept them indoors, or perhaps they had changed their route, or...

There.

The faint, bobbing light of their lanterns was just visible as they rounded a corner and started down the road. Within half a minute they would have passed the junction and moved on: the time to act was now. Jayla allowed herself a few more seconds to make certain of what she was seeing, then she dangled her arm over the edge of the roof and made a quick signal before drawing it up and out of sight once more.

Moments later a woman screamed. Right below her, two figures were locked in a desperate battle. A woman, slim with shoulder-length brown hair, was struggling to pull away from the grip of the burlier man, who was half as tall again as her and far more muscular. She kicked out repeatedly; the man twisted to avoid most of the blows but a raised knee smacked into his groin and he let out a tightly-controlled grunt of pain. He backhanded her across the face, and she staggered against the nearest wall. She screamed again.

Jayla looked round and saw that the twin circles of light had changed direction; now heading towards the fight at rapid speed. Seconds later two custodians, dressed in dark-brown leather uniforms with a black symbol emblazoned across their chests, came into view. Their pace slowed as they drew closer and took in what was happening. Both drew their cudgels from the loops at their belts. The younger of the two stepped forward, closed his hand around the attacking man's arm and yanked him backwards. It was not enough to make him release the woman fully but it did twist him round and throw one arm wide. In the moments before the man recovered his balance the second custodian stepped in and drove the end of his cudgel into the attacker's stomach, driving the air from the man's lungs. He released his grip on the woman and doubled over; his descending head meeting the first custodian's knee coming the other way. The blow flung the attacker backwards, landing hard enough to raise a spray of mud that splattered across the legs of all three of the others.

As the younger custodian crouched down beside the prone man with his cudgel raised, the second moved to where the woman still stood against the wall, eyes wide and mouth agape as she struggled to take in the rapid change in her situation.

'It's alright,' the custodian said, smiling reassuringly. 'We're here to help now. Did he hurt you?'

'No, I-' the woman hesitated, her gaze darting to the fallen man.

'Don't worry,' the older man said. 'He's not going to hurt you again.'

Jayla watched as the woman stepped away from the wall and made eye-contact with her rescuer.

'I know.'

In one fluid movement the woman swept her arm up and around, her clenched fist thumping against the custodian's temple. A puzzled expression briefly formed on his features before she pulled her fist back. The knife she had been clutching in her hand tore itself free and dragged a spray of dark red blood behind it. The man collapsed immediately as if the knife had been the only thing holding him up.

The second custodian began to rise, letting out an incoherent cry of horror and denial. His hand flew to the short sword at his waist, but before he could draw it, he looked down and saw that the 'unconscious' man at his feet had a hand wrapped firmly around his ankle. The attacker swept his arm round and the custodian went over on his back with a squelch of displaced mud. Before he could rise again the woman crouched down and drove her blade through the base of his jaw, up into his brain. The custodian took a few seconds to die: from her vantage point Jayla could hear the man gargling helplessly as irregular sprays of blood frothed from his mouth before he finally expired.

She took a few seconds to scan each end of the street, looking for any sign that someone else had seen or heard what had just happened, her hand resting on the haft of the mace hooked to her belt. Nothing. Even so it would be wise not to linger. Jayla sat up slowly, wincing as her muscles protested after their long period of inactivity. She lowered herself over the edge of the roof, hanging by her hands for a moment before letting go and crouching to absorb the impact as she hit the ground. Mud was flung up by her landing and some of it splattered against her cheek but she ignored it: the rain would wash it away quickly enough.

When Jayla turned the man and the woman were waiting for her. The man looked a little unsteady on his feet but greeted Jayla with a curt nod, which she reciprocated. The woman still had her knife drawn, the blood dripping from its tip being slowly absorbed by the quagmire of mud at their feet.

'Good work, both of you,' Jayla said. 'Let's get moving.'

'Wait a second!' The woman snapped, grabbing hold of Jayla's wrist as she started to turn away. 'You're happy, right? I'm in?'

Jayla looked at the hand for a moment and the woman snatched it away as though Jayla's arm was burning her. Jayla turned her gaze to the body of one of the custodians lying at her feet, her eyes fixing themselves on the symbol emblazoned across the man's chest. It was like a giant hand rendered in black paint: crudely done, but not without a certain artistry. She knew what it meant: just thinking about the message it conveyed made her guts churn with loathing and the urge to kill pulse within her mind.

Six talons: one for each of the clans, all linked together to form the paw of a firedrake. The six clans brought together under the creature's rule: it was intended to signify alliance, unity. Hope.

It was a symbol of oppression and tyranny.

'Yes Leana,' she hissed. 'You're in.'

The tavern was old and showed every day of its age, seemingly held together as much by the half-hearted prayers of its owner as by anything as prosaic as decent building materials. Nobody remembered its name, if it had ever had one to begin with. It was deep within a slum district; its only customers those who were either unaware how heavily watered-down the beer was, who didn't care because they couldn't afford anything else, or those who couldn't risk showing their faces in any other drinking establishment in the city. Since the firedrake had established its dominance over the six clans, the custodians had been cracking down much harder on crime throughout Talscar, but they still avoided the slum unless they had no other choice.

That made it ideal for Jayla's purposes.

Through careful, oh-so-innocently-posed questions over the course of several nights Jayla had learned that the landlord, a Bask clansman, had utterly no respect or loyalty for their new ruler, though he concealed it well. That, coupled with regular payments of silver, had led to Jayla being handed a key to the premises along with the understanding that what went on there at night, while the owner was at home in bed, was none of his concern.

She knocked four times in careful sequence before unlocking the door. The inside of the tavern was barely any brighter than out in the city; the feeble illumination provided by two flickering candles placed on separate tables. A dark mass off to one side was the long slab of oak that served as the bar, with a row of kegs just behind that. The air stank of stale beer, vomit, and the half-rotted straw that covered the floor.

'It's me,' Jayla said, and on the edge of hearing she registered the faint sound of a blade being slipped into its oiled leather scabbard. She glanced around the room and spotted Rae in one corner, mostly concealed by the shadows. She nodded in her direction. The other three sat within the candlelight, and Jayla watched the emotions play across their faces as Leana entered next. Tor came last, closing the door behind him. Jayla sat down at one of the tables and waited for the others to do the same. Once they had, she looked slowly around the room, making eye contact with each person in turn.

'Leana has proven herself,' she said, and a subtle tension went out of their postures. 'She's one of us now.'

'How many, and what clans?' The question came from Rork, a man who seemed to be built of nothing but muscle. He had customised his leather armour heavily to fit him, but even so it still strained to contain all of his bulk. 'Two custodians. Bask and Black Wolves.'

Rork's fat lips curled into a sneer and he looked away. Jayla knew what he was thinking. Talscar was a *Bask* city;

there was a time when only the Bask would have been charged with keeping law and order in their settlement. But the firedrake and his consort cared nothing for the traditions of the people they ruled over: clan affiliation was becoming less and less important in their precious new order.

'Well done, Leana.' That came from Dolan. His expression was a mixture of approval and ill-concealed relief: he had recommended his sister, Leana, be admitted to the group and knew that if Jayla had not approved then she would have ensured that Leana didn't survive to tell anyone about her failure.

'Thanks, Dolan.' Leana paused. 'I'm glad to be here, as long as what my brother said is true. Was he right? Are you going to do something about that bastard creature that's enslaved us all?'

All eyes turned to Jayla, and she felt a thrill of anticipation steal through her. One day her name would go down in history for this. She rose to her feet and rested her clenched fists on the table as she gazed around at her comrades once again.

'You all know what life is like out there now, what it's like all across the land. Before, the Bask ruled and kept order, but now all of us, all of the six clans, are nothing better than slaves. The firedrake killed our leader and his best warriors before it burned down half the palace and built its lair in what remained. The other clans, cowards that they are, submitted to it almost straight away. Only the Bask had the strength to resist for as long as we did. We are going to continue that resistance.'

'You want us to attack the firedrake?' Dolan gasped. Jayla's lip curled in response to the uncertainty in the man's voice. She tried not to let her anger show: perhaps it wasn't cowardice, just confusion. The creature's power was without question.

'No.' She replied, forcing the word out. 'Not yet. We are too few. Many of the Bask in this city are losing sight of what it means to even *be* Bask, much as they would deny it.' The expressions of the others shifted and Jayla pressed on with her argument. 'Some have given up all hope of resisting, and are using despair to excuse their lack of action. Some are too afraid to even try.' Jayla's voice rose now, anger blazing in every syllable spat from between clenched teeth. 'There are even those who argue that life is getting better, that submitting to the will of a *talking beast* has *improved our lives*. They talk about the land being at peace, of bandits in retreat, of improving trade. All empty words to hide their treachery and cowardice.'

She paused, drawing in a deep breath before continuing. 'But as I said, we cannot kill the firedrake. Not yet. What we *can* do is strike at the very heart of its rule, by slaying the one person that it relies on; the woman who betrayed our great leader and doomed us all to slavery. Dana, the fire-drake's consort. The last member of the Rushani clan.'

Jayla watched the expressions of the others change as they took in what she had said and thought through the implica-tions. Some looked excited, others nervous. Rae's expression was impossible to read in the darkness.

'How?' Rork asked. 'It's been tried before but Dana is well-defended and no slouch with a sword.'

Jayla nodded. It was true. Though she hadn't witnessed them herself, there had been at least two attempts made on Dana's life; once within the walls of the city itself and once while she had been travelling between settlements. It was said that Dana herself had killed many of the attackers with great skill, though she wasn't certain how much credibility could be attached to such claims. In each case the survivors had been taken to the Drake's Roost for questioning and had never been heard from again. It was whispered that the firedrake had eaten them alive once it had no further use for them; a rumour that Jayla had no trouble at all believing.

'Their mistake was to strike when she and her guards were at their most alert. We will attack where she thinks that she's safest: inside the palace itself.'

The room erupted into a babble of questions, everyone talking at once and making no effort to hide their scepti-cism. Jayla felt frustration rise inside her and struggled to keep it restrained. 'Enough!'

They all looked round as Rae stepped out of the shadows; one hand on the hilt of her sword and a look of fury on her face.

'Look at yourselves. You're *Bask*, not Mixlan fishwives! Get yourselves under control.'

As the others quietened down and returned to their seats Jayla nodded slightly in silent thanks to Rae. Though she had not known her for long she was once again reminded of how much she valued her support. She was everything a Bask clanswoman should be: loyal, fierce and dedicated.

'I know that you have questions. But I assure you I have planned for everything. I've studied the security and it is tight, just as you would expect. It would take an army to breach the palace by frontal assault, but we're not going to do that.'

'How then?' Leana asked.

'When the palace was built, an escape tunnel was constructed. One exit is in a cave outside of the city. The other end survived the damage caused when the firedrake turned the palace into its lair.'

Now she had them. Their eyes were all fixed on her now, their expressions showing surprise but also a growing acknowledgement that Jayla knew what she was doing; that this *would* work. She revelled in the feeling that blossomed within her; this was just as it should be. And from modest beginnings her support would only grow.

'I know this because I have a man on the inside. A true Bask,' she continued, 'a warrior who has willingly served the usurper to learn what we need to ensure its eventual downfall. We will make our way through the tunnel and at the appointed time, after nightfall tomorrow, when most of the people within the Drake's Roost will be asleep, my contact will open the entrance to the tunnel and allow us inside. He knows where the treacherous Rushani woman sleeps and will lead us there.'

'How will we avoid being spotted by the guards?' That was Cole, the last of the seven conspirators and the oldest by at least a decade. Withdrawn and taciturn at the best of times, the man rarely spoke, but when he did it was always direct and to the point. Jayla respected that.

'Good question, Cole. The warrior is a member of the elite Draconic Guard: charged with the protection of the firedrake itself along with the key people in its so-called government. He will leave uniforms and armour for the seven of us within the tunnel. Wearing that, we will not be challenged. After we slay the traitor, we will escape back through the tunnel and to freedom.'

Jayla paused and looked at each of them in turn, coldly searching for any signs of doubt or duplicity in their expressions. She allowed one hand to rest on the haft of her mace, and knew without looking that Rae would be ready to act as well. If any of them now decided that they wanted out, they would not be allowed to leave the tavern alive. She wondered how many of them had already worked that out.

'Now you know the truth. Do any of you want to back out?'

Nobody moved. Nobody spoke.

Jayla allowed herself a brief, tight smile. 'Good. Try and get some rest, we leave at dawn.'

The pre-dawn air was chilly and Jayla suspected it was going to be another miserable autumn day. On the positive side it wasn't currently raining, though puddles of standing water filled every hollow in the saturated ground, and soon enough their legs were coated by splashes of mud.

As they descended through the city to the main gate they encountered an increasing number of people. Mostly labourers, yawning and chatting amongst themselves as they trudged towards another day of work. Few paid attention to Jayla and her party, perhaps assuming that they were workers just like themselves. Jayla found it grimly amusing and wondered if any of them would remember this in the future; whether they would be inspired by the knowledge that they had walked alongside people who were going to save Talscar.

They joined onto the main road that ran directly to the city entrance and the number of people increased sharply. The noise of conversation was a constant babble in the background. Carts were lined up in rows in front of the gateway ready to carry labourers to the quarry almost twenty miles away.

It was a vast work programme put into place by the fire-drake and its puppet government. According to them, the mined stone would be used to construct tunnels beneath the surface of the city through which excess water could be drained away, as well as being broken up and spread on road surfaces to make it easier to transport goods. It all *sounded* very public-spirited, but Jayla knew the truth behind it. Keeping so many people employed at the quarry would prevent them from having the time to appreciate the fact that they were in reality slaves, regardless of how much they were being paid, and leave them too tired to plot against the firedrake. No amount of so-called *civic improvements* could obscure the reality of what was happening in Talscar.

Despite the early hour the sides of the road were lined with people: mostly traders selling food to those off to work in the quarry or in the fields to the west of the city, though there were more than a few beggars as well. Some stalls were selling clothing or tools, while one or two had other more exotic items that had been gathered from across great distances, if the proclamations of the traders were to be believed. One man, wizened and hunched with straggly grey hair, was even claiming to have genuine firedrake scales for sale, but nobody seemed to be paying much attention. As Jayla walked past the stall she saw why: the *scales* appeared to be little more than uneven pottery plates that had been painted a drab shade of grey. If the old man was particularly unlucky he would end up being paid a visit by a custodian: she couldn't imagine that they would be too impressed by someone trying to sell their ruler's body parts, even if they were fake.

Thinking about custodians made her glance around for any sign of them, doing her best to be casual about it. The last ones she had seen had been on guard by the main gate, though she couldn't see any out here. Her view of the other side of the road was blocked as a cart rumbled by, loaded down with labourers staring blankly at the scenery. When it had moved past it took her a second or two to realise what she was seeing, and when she did she had to fight back the urge to curse out loud. Leana was over there, talking to a man she didn't recognise.

Jayla turned round and saw that the others had stopped as well, most of them looking at her and obviously wondering what the problem was. She jerked her head at Dolan.

'Get over there and bring that idiot back, now!'

His face pale, Dolan nodded rapidly and jogged across the road, cutting in front of another cart and provoking an annoyed shout from its driver. Her jaw clenched as she struggled to control her impatience, Jayla watched as Dolan grabbed hold of his sister's arm, said a few brief words to the person she was speaking to, and started to lead her back. The others were standing around trying to look inconspicuous and failing miserably.

When the two had re-joined the group Jayla turned without speaking and stepped into a gap between two nearby stalls, gesturing for Leana to follow. When Leana came within arm's reach Jayla seized hold of her and dragged the woman close to her. Leana gasped in shock but otherwise remained silent: Dolan stepped forward as if to intervene but Jayla shot him a furious look and he stayed where he was.

'By the gods, what were you *doing*?' Jayla hissed, her grip tightening around her arm. Leana winced but met her gaze without flinching.

'That was my neighbour; I mean mine and Dolan's. We know each other, I had to go and say hello. He would have been curious if I hadn't, might have remembered seeing us all.'

'*You will talk to nobody*,' Jayla growled, forcing each word out through gritted teeth, 'unless *I* say so. This is too important for any fuck-ups. Are we *clear*?'

For a few seconds she stared back at her defiantly, but her expression slowly changed as she looked into her eyes and saw the passion there. Jayla was quite prepared to kill her if she didn't obey, and perhaps she sensed that.

'Alright. Fine.'

Jayla studied her for a few seconds more until she was certain that she understood, then let her go. Without another word she stepped out into the open and gestured for the others to follow her. She started to turn, then hesitated and looked back. Rae was just straightening up from where she was crouched next to one of the many beggars that they had passed; silver glinting within his begging bowl where Jayla was certain that there had been none before. She actually looked embarrassed to be caught in the act, much to Jayla's carefully-concealed amusement. The beggar was staring up at Rae with a look of surprise and gratitude on his grime-encrusted features.

'Let's get moving.'

They followed the road for another half hour before turning east and walking along the edges of fields, with Talscar
always on the northern horizon. They occasionally spotted
labourers at work but ignored them, and if the workers
noticed the party they gave no indication of it. When the
road was no longer visible behind them Jayla led the group
north, following the course of a swift-flowing stream for a
while before walking cross-country in the rough direction of
the capital.

As they drew closer to Talscar the ground sloped steadily
upwards, becoming increasingly rocky, and within an hour
the last of the fields had been left behind. The capital had
been built on a series of hills surrounded on three sides
by sheer cliffs, making it relatively easy to defend against
attacks from anything that didn't fly. The area that they were
walking through, to the south and east of the city, was a
maze of rocky slopes and sheer drops with streams coursing
along narrow valley floors: it would be all too easy to get
lost here. Fortunately Jayla knew where she was going. After
her contact in the Draconic Guard had told her about the
escape tunnel she had journeyed out here by herself to con-
firm that it existed. Even so, she nearly took a wrong turn
on more than one occasion; her need to concentrate not
helped by the fact that she was constantly keeping watch for
signs of custodians. As far as she knew they didn't bother to
patrol out here, but she wasn't certain of that. So much had
changed since Dax had been slain by the firedrake.

It was mid-afternoon by the time they clambered over
the top of a ridge and first saw the cave. It was the only gap
in an otherwise solid and sheer cliff face; wide enough at the
ground for two people to walk abreast, narrowing sharply
the higher she looked until it became little more than a
barely-visible crack in the rock.

'There it is,' Jayla said. 'We've found it.'

'About time,' one of the men muttered, the words carried further than he had intended by the faint but persistent
breeze. Jayla stiffened but decided to ignore it, instead walking swiftly up the slope and into the cave.

The air inside was cool and with the sun obscured by cloud the back of the cave was in almost total darkness. Jayla had left a couple of torches behind a rock when she had last visited, and it took her only a few moments to find and light them. Taking one herself and passing the other back down the line, Jayla walked to the rear of the cave. The flickering light cast by the torch made the shadows leap and dance deceptively and it took her a few seconds to find what she was looking for. The gap was invisible from the cave entrance and narrow enough that she had to turn sideways to squeeze through. She could hear and feel her chest and back scraping against the walls, and had a sudden vision of the unyielding rock snapping together like a mouth and crushing her into a bloody paste. She sucked in her chest as much as she could and squeezed around a hairpin turn, letting out a relieved sigh as the tunnel suddenly expanded and she stumbled into open space.

Jayla moved aside as one by one the others came through; most appearing very relieved to be out in the open again, relatively speaking. There was enough room in the tunnel for them to walk three abreast if they had wanted to, the rock surfaces around them scarred by tool-marks. Rae was the last one through.

'How far?' She asked.

'It's about a half-mile walk,' Jayla replied. 'The other end will be sealed; we'll have to wait there until after midnight when my contact will open it up and let us in. And keep the noise down; sound carries easily in here so I don't want to risk anyone in the palace overhearing us.'

Nobody spoke as they walked up the tunnel, although Jayla suspected that had as much to do with where they were as the order she had given. Outside of the light cast by the torches the darkness was absolute, and the claustrophobic sensation of being entombed within the rock was a hard one to dispel. Even worse was the silence. Outside of the noises that the seven made, and the crackling of the torches, there was no other sound, not even the drip of water. It was incredibly unsettling. She did her best to ignore it by focussing on what they were going to do, and what it would mean for the future of all of them.

After an unknowable amount of time the tunnel came to

an abrupt end. A large square slab, by its shape obviously artificial, blocked off the passageway completely. It had such solidity to it that she would have found it easy to believe that it had been there forever. When Jayla stepped closer she could see evidence of scrape-marks on the walls and floor just around it, and a faint whisper of fresh air was issuing from the minute gap between the base of it and the ground. As she turned the glint of metal caught her eye- the torch-light was reflecting off the chainmail of the Draconic Guard uniforms lying near one of the tunnel walls. Her contact had come through for them.

'Put those on,' she hissed, gesturing to the uniforms and armour. 'Then try and get some rest. And keep quiet.'

The others did as she had ordered, though there was enough grumbling and clinking of chainmail as they tried to sort out which uniforms fitted which person to set Jayla's teeth on edge. Within the close confines of the tunnel even the slightest sound was magnified to the point that it seemed like everyone within the palace must be able to hear everything they were doing. Eventually everyone sorted themselves out and settled down for the long, tense wait.

Jayla took a position at the far end from the slab and sat down against the wall. Wearing the Draconic Guard uniform with the claw symbol emblazoned on it made her feel more than a little uncomfortable, but she knew that was ridiculous. It was simply a means to an end, after all: this was their best chance of getting through the palace and completing their mission without being challenged. And when the news got out that Dana had been slain by men and women wearing those uniforms, it would only undermine the firedrake's grip on power still further. To the ordinary people of the city it would seem that even the fire-drake's elite recognised it for the tyrant it was.

'So what do you think will happen?' Rae's voice jolted Jayla from her thoughts. She had been so deep inside her own head that she hadn't even registered the fact that Rae had sat down next to her.

'When we've killed the woman?'

'Yes.'

'Well, by killing that bitch we'll be taking away the fire-drake's most trusted advisor. We've all heard the rumours of how much it leans on her for counsel, and they make sense. It's a creature that crawled out of a volcano, how much could it possibly understand about the people it's conquered? With her gone it won't know what to do. Its grip will slip and the people will see that. It'll be the beginning of the end.'

'That could cost lives. A lot of them, if the firedrake loses control like you think it will.'

Jayla met Rae's gaze evenly. 'Yes, it probably will. But in the end, we'll be free again. It's worth the cost.'

Rae watched her for a few seconds, her expression unreadable, then nodded sharply and looked away. Jayla settled down to wait again, reflecting on what she had told her. In fact she was utterly certain that people would die. The firedrake was a beast, without its advisor what else could it do but kill? If smouldering bodies in the streets didn't turn the people against it then nothing would. And when that time came, she would be ready to take advantage of it and lead the Bask against the beast.

The touch of a hand on her shoulder awoke Jayla from an uneasy slumber. Her eyes snapped open, her hand flying to the haft of her mace before she even registered what was going on. Rork stood over her, his expression grim. He gestured to the end of the tunnel, and it was then that Jayla registered the faint grinding noise and the increasing level of light. The secret door was opening.

Jayla got to her feet and quickly pushed her way to the front of the group, drawing her mace and tightening her grip around the haft. She felt her pulse quicken as the door continued to open. If there was more than one person on the other side then that would be it, they would have been betrayed. As the gap yawned wider she caught sight of a figure in Draconic Guard uniform clutching a halberd and stiffened, moments later his face became visible and Jayla allowed herself to relax a little.

'Jayla?' The guard's voice was tense, his posture stiff as he saw the seven people waiting in the tunnel. 'Is that you?'

Jayla stepped forward slowly so that her face was visible. 'It's me, Max. Any trouble?'

'No.' The guard paused, darted a nervous look up and down the corridor. 'All of you get in here, quickly.'

Jayla nodded and the others all filed out into the corridor. When they were clear Max pulled a lever set into the wall and the secret door ground shut again. He turned back and glanced at every member of the group in turn, his expression doubtful. His gaze lingered in particular on Rae and Dolan, the only two that had opted to wear the enclosing helms that had been provided with the Draconic Guard uniforms and armour. He was obviously nervous.

'Is Dana in her chambers?' Jayla asked, keen to keep Max focussed on the task at hand.

'Yes. I think so. She hasn't emerged from there for a few weeks, but that's not unusual. There's plenty of food and water, and a direct route from there to the... to the firedrake's lair; they often spend a lot of time planning things.'

Jayla absorbed that for a moment. The fact that Dana hadn't been seen for a while was far from reassuring, but they had come too far to turn back now. She nodded sharply, keen to project an air of authority.

'Lead the way.'

They walked in silence down stone corridors with torches mounted in wall-brackets at regular intervals, passing closed doors without slowing. Jayla heard movement from behind some of them but nobody came out to investigate. Obviously guards patrolling the corridors of the Drake's Roost were a regular occurrence. Hopefully that would get them to where they needed to go without arousing any suspicions.

After a few minutes of walking Max stopped dead as a strange sound echoed down the corridor. At first it sounded like gusts of wind but the noise was too rhythmic, like an immense pair of bellows being worked. When she realised what it was Jayla felt a chill steal through her. It took a few moments for the sound to die away, and only then did the Draconic Guard look round.

'It's alright,' he said, though the expression on his sweat-sheened face suggested otherwise. 'It's gone to hunt. It won't be back for a while.'

'Fantastic,' someone muttered, low enough that Jayla

wasn't sure who had said it, sarcasm dripping from every syllable.

They walked on and after turning a corner were confronted by a set of double doors, one of which stood open. Max paused, and glanced back at them.

'Through the main hall is the quickest way.' He said. 'Her chambers aren't far beyond that. There will be guards, so keep quiet.'

The hall was vast, with twin rows of stone pillars holding the high vaulted ceiling aloft. Once this would have been the place where Dax or one of his representatives received visitors. Jayla remembered a throne standing at the end of the hall, but that had been removed. Where once only icons and symbols of the Bask would have been displayed in here, great banners now hung between the pillars, each displaying one of the symbols of the six clans. The Bask symbol was there too, but to see it relegated to just one among the others filled Jayla with a cold fury. Largest of all was the firedrake's symbol hanging on a banner pinned to the back wall where the throne had once stood: it was a crude and unsubtle illustration of just who had the real power now.

They were halfway through the hall when the door slammed shut behind them. Jayla whirled, at first wondering if it had been blown shut by a draft, but then the rattle of chainmail reached her ears from all around them. From their hiding places behind the banners Draconic Guard stepped out into the open; all in armour with halberds pointing towards them. Rae and the others drew their weapons, several spitting out curses as they recognised what Jayla had already realised. They were outnumbered at least three to one.

They had been betrayed.

Her first thought was that Max was to blame but one look at how the man was shivering, the halberd in his hands visibly trembling as he pointed the weapon at his erstwhile comrades, suggested otherwise. Leana then. Obviously that *neighbour* she had spoken to outside the city was nothing of the sort, the bitch must have-

'Place your weapons on the ground, now!' The shout came from her right, and Jayla turned. Clearly the Draconic Guard's commander, this man was the only one not wearing a helm, and Jayla felt her lip curl as she saw that the com-mander's hair was tied in the Bask fashion. *Traitor.*

'Go fuck yourself,' she spat in response, clutching her mace even tighter. 'We'll never surrender to cowards like you.' The commander rolled his eyes.

'Brave words from a woman coming to murder someone while she slept,' he snapped back. 'Give it up. There's no escape from the Drake's Roost now. There are many of us, and only seven of you.'

Eight, Jayla started to think, then heard someone behind her begin to move. She turned, her mouth falling open as she saw Rae step quickly away from the group, pulling her helm off and shaking her hair free. At the sight of her Max let out a soft *oh gods* and dropped his halberd. The weapon clattered onto the floor but Jayla paid no attention, unable to make sense of what was happening. She had trusted her, she was a loyal Bask, how could she… then she remembered the beggar, the coins Rae had given to him. What else might she have passed on or whispered while Jayla was busy deal-ing with Leana? She had been such a *fool.*

'Is this all of them?' The commander asked. Rae nodded.

'All that Jayla wanted involved. There are probably others that she didn't trust for something like this. So, Brin, did I miss much?'

'Nope. It was pretty dull around here without you.'

Jayla watched all this, taking in the manner in which they spoke, their posture and how the two looked at each other. Then she remembered how Max had reacted when he had seen Rae's face for the first time, and she felt the floor disap-pear from under her.

'You're Dana,' she said numbly.

'I am,' she replied, her expression neutral. 'And you're Jayla. You look a lot like him, you know. Dax. It's a shame he never acknowledged you.'

'Why did you do this?'

Dana shrugged. 'We've known about you for some time, and suspected that someone inside the Draconic Guard was feeding you information. This was the best way to flush him out of hiding.' Nearby Max let out a sob, but Dana kept her eyes fixed on Jayla. 'If you meant why me personally, well. I was bored.'

The Draconic Guard commander snorted, and Dana glared at him for a moment, an expression that he returned in kind. She smiled, and the expression stoked the anger that permanently bubbled deep within Jayla to new heights of fury. Before she knew what she was doing she was lunging forward, lifting her mace and letting out an incoherent roar of pure rage, ignoring the alarmed cries from all around her and the sound of rushing footsteps, only seeing the smug bitch in front of her who-

Dana moved faster than she had thought possible.

In one smooth motion she sidestepped and drew her sword from its scabbard, twisting slightly and swiping out with the blade. Jayla felt a fiery pain across the side of her wrist, the shock of it jolting her hand open. As she fumbled to grasp hold of her mace again she sensed the hilt of Dana's sword come sweeping in towards her temple.

There seemed to be no transition between that moment and the next. Jayla found herself flat on her back, pain blazing through her wrist, the tip of a blade resting against her throat. Dana looked down at her, her expression impassive. Behind her she could hear the clash of arms and a brief, abruptly cut-off gurgle as the Draconic Guard restrained the others. They had followed her willingly and she had led them to their doom.

'It's a shame you don't understand what we're trying to build here,' Dana said. 'You're very much like your father, but I don't know. There might be hope for you yet.'

Jayla snarled up at her in response. 'I'll never be like you. I'll never betray my people and sell them out to a *creature*.'

'My people are dead. Your father saw to that long before you were a twinkle in your whore mother's eye. As for the *creature*, well. Saramanth is a lot smarter than you might think.' She smiled at the look of surprise that Jayla couldn't entirely hide. 'Of *course* she has a name. She might be fearsome but she's no fool; under her rule the land is going to become better for everyone. The changes the city is going through now are only the beginning. She'll be back soon; perhaps she'll be able to persuade you of that.

'And if not?' Dana shrugged. 'Well. She's always hungry.'

The last survivor of the Rushani clan turned and walked away. Jayla snarled and lunged to her feet, but could take no more than a step before Draconic Guard appeared to either side of her and strong hands closed around her arms. Dana and Brin ignored this and walked away together while Jayla was dragged in the opposite direction, past more than one body, spitting curses and crying out that she would get her revenge on her, that her father would be avenged, that Dana would pay for what she had done.

Later on, in the darkness of the dank prison cell into which they had thrown her, Jayla heard the pounding wings of the firedrake as she returned to her lair.

DOWN AT THE LAKE

Jaine Fenn

Dawn already? Cold too: winter's on its way. As I stumble back up the slope to the cottage my feet break through a crust of frost; freezing mud squelches up between my toes, thick and chill and sticky.

There's no smoke coming from the chimney. *Damnit papa, have you let the fire go out again?* A shadow passes over the sun and I shiver; before I can catch it the shiver becomes a shudder, something beyond a mere reaction to the cold.

Even as I wonder where this sensation comes from, it's gone again and all that matters is getting inside, where I can be dry and warm.

The cottage is empty, but I should have expected that. Last night papa was so pumped up with his great victory that he swept out without a word. He must still be over the far side of the lake, gloating. Ah dear, you poor, tragic birdies. Sorry princess, looks like you got your hopes up for nothing. What a shame.

I just wish papa would give me some credit for his triumph. I danced until my feet bled.

Or perhaps he's avoiding me because of what I found out yesterday. How spells work both ways: black needs white and night needs day. It's all about balance. Pay a price – and gain a reward.

There's a lot of crap talked about magic. To hear the villagers prattle on you'd think papa could pull gold coins and fine linen from the very air. If only. You need to start with the right raw materials.

You can't just magic things away either. Which is why, between the fabric, beads, paint and knives papa used to make me look the part, and the crusty plates, cobwebbed corners and unwashed laundry that built up while he was enchanting and I was practising, this particular sorcerer's cottage is a stinking hovel.

I need clothes. Up in my room, I find and pull on a fairly clean kirtle, drab brown but warm and familiar on bare skin. While I fasten my dress I find myself looking at the shapeless frock hanging on the back of the bedroom door. Today, it's coarse black fabric sewn with cheap glass stones. Yesterday, I dazzled the courtiers in midnight satin and blood-red rubies, fitted to show every curve. I looked amazing. I *was* amazing. And papa was so proud. But that was then; in daylight the romance and magic drains away.

Well, not entirely. If he'd given me the choice I would have kept the dress and lost the face. This intsy-winsy mouth would look better on a trout than a girl and these wide, trusting eyes make me look like a lost puppy. Shame magic sticks to flesh better than it does to cloth or glass. So I'm left with a peasant's costume and a princess's looks - at least while the sun's up. I imagine I'll get used to it.

May as well tidy up. Anything to stop him going into one of his strops when he gets home. I know him: after the party, the comedown. Despite the success of this latest scheme he'll be off again soon enough, pacing and muttering over injustices only he remembers, raging about vengeance for ancient slights.

If only I could stop thinking about Siggy. That wasn't a side-effect either of us foresaw. It's so dumb. *He's* so dumb. But the silly boy's also very... cute. And he's a prince, of course. A real live, blue-blood, no-brain, pert-buttocked prince. When papa gets back I'm going to ask when I can see him again. After all, he loves me now: naturally he'll want to see me again. It can't end here. And if I do go back to the palace to see Siggy again, then that would make the revenge all the sweeter. That's what I'll say, soon as papa gets back.

While I wait, I light the fire. I sweep the floor while the water's heating, then I put the plates in to soak, wash some socks and shirts and finally have a go at scraping papa's work-table clean, though it'll take more than warm water to shift all this fat and dried blood.

When the sun starts to sink behind the trees and there's still no sign of papa, I begin to fret. Remembering the odd feeling I had this morning – it's a wise sorcerer's daughter who listens to her intuition – I put on a cloak and shoes and go out.

I know where he'll be. I'm in such a hurry to get round the lake that it's a while before I notice how empty the water is. Not a swan in sight, even though it's still light. Something is wrong.

On the far side I come across footprints. Footprints made by delicate, girlie feet, the sort born to wear embroidered slippers and be carried across thresholds by adoring princes. Dozens of pairs, all running away from the lake. Which can mean only one thing. The birds have flown. Or rather, not being birds anymore, run off.

My heart begins to patter. I call papa's name, but get no answer. I won't panic. A sorcerer's daughter never panics.

Then I find him.

He's lying face-down in the reeds. I almost stumble over his body.

A noise, an ugly thoughtless squeal, breaks from my throat. Birds burst up from the willows at the sound. Then I'm crying, the tears rolling off my face like the first fat drops of a summer storm.

After a while I get control again and make myself look more closely. His right wing is broken and he's been shot through the heart with a crossbow bolt.

A crossbow bolt.

Siggy?

I never thought my silly, pretty prince had it in him. That's love for you. Not love for *me* though. I know that now. I might have turned his head when I danced for him in the glow of papa's magic, but the one he really wanted was *her*, the leader of the cursed princesses. Her white innocence, her effortless grace; her pathetic need. He killed my papa to free the stinking princess from papa's enchantment. And it worked too. Her and all the other girlies, back in human form all the time, no longer doomed – hah, doomed! – to be swans in the daylight.

I start crying again. This time the tears are all for me. I don't fight them.

When I came out of the lake this morning I had a father – not a good or loving father, but the only one I've known –

and the love of a prince. Or so I thought. Turns out I don't have either! I rage at the trees, the sparrows, the reeds. I curse the world.

The world ignores me.

Finally I run out of anger and tears. I sniff, then drag papa's body down to the shore. On his left side, he's got an arm, not a wing, and I wonder what this means. After all, if murdering him lifted the curse on the princess and her cronies, what will it do to me? They were normal girls once, back before papa found them. I don't think I was ever a normal girl, not given the way papa changed the subject whenever I mentioned mothers or birthdays. Now he's dead so the spell's broken and they're human all the time. What about me? Do I have to spend the rest of my life as this leggy, flightless girl-thing?

But when the last flashes of the sun disappear behind the mountains I feel the familiar tingle, soft as downy feathers and urgent as the need to pee. I hurry to get papa into the water. As soon as he's free of the shore the lake pulls him out of my hands. He slips silently down into the dark, chill depths.

My skin is crawling now. I undo my cloak, pull my dress over my head and wade out further. Tiny buds of black are bursting out all over my body, unfurling into sleek feathers, a thousand pin-pricks becoming dark flowers. I raise my chin and my neck grows longer, filling my head with the sound of cracking bones. My knees twitch, then break cleanly and start to heal themselves, reversed.

It hurts. Every time, I forgot how goddamn much it hurts, until it happens again.

But it's a good pain. It's the pain that makes me what I am.

At the final moment I sweep my arms back, and now they're no longer arms, but wings. I plunge chest-first into the water.

When I come up, I'm a swan, black as a moonless night.

For a while I simply glide around, listening to the night-calls and the gurgles and the splashes; the life of the lake. It isn't that I *can't* think when I'm a swan. I just can't be bothered to.

I see light on the water, a sudden burst of gold, shockingly pretty. For a moment the sight foxes me.

Then I realise it's a reflection and look up, just as a red flower explodes above the trees, its mirrored twin glittering in the surface of the lake. Fireworks. Fireworks to celebrate a royal wedding.

Well, they didn't waste much time. Fall in love one day, marry the next. Hell's curse on them both.

Then, suddenly, I know why they're – why *she's* - in such a hurry.

Another thing people don't know about magic is that there are some forces it can't stop. Like death. Or time. Oh, it can make people think nothing's changing, stick a nice comfortable illusion in front of reality. Magic can even put some things on hold for a while. But in the end, there's always a price to pay. I don't know how old I am but since I've started counting the years I've been through my fingers and toes twice, and I'm back to fingers again. The white swans have been living on the far side of the lake for as long as I can remember, and papa once told me that *she* was their leader because she's the oldest of them all.

Now father's dead and the spell's broken. Given I'm a swan again it would seem I've enough magic of my own to keep me going but as for her... any day now, time's going to start catching up with her. I bet she can feel it in her bones. She knows she doesn't have long. That's why she's so desperate to wed my Siggy at once.

It might be a week, a month, maybe even as much as a year, but one morning soon my poor, brave fool of a prince will wake up next to a woman older than his grandmother. Let's see true love survive that.

I can wait. It'll happen, sure as night follows day. And when it does I'll be here. After all, we swans mate for life.

At times like this, I almost wish I had a mouth to smile with.

THE FIRST WITCH OF DAMANSARA

Zen Cho

Vivian's late grandmother was a witch — which is just a way of saying she was a woman of unusual insight. Vivian, in contrast, had a mind like a hi-tech blender. She was sharp and purposeful, but she did not understand magic.

This used to be a problem. Magic ran in the family. Even her mother's second cousin, who was adopted, did small spells on the side. She sold these from a stall in Kota Bharu. Her main wares were various types of fruit fried in batter, but if you bought five pisang or cempedak goreng, she threw in a jampi for free.

These embarrassing relatives became less of a problem after Vivian left Malaysia. In the modern Western country where she lived, the public toilets were clean, the newspapers were allowed to be as rude to the government as they liked, and nobody believed in magic except people in whom nobody believed. Even with a cooking appliance mind, Vivian understood that magic requires belief to thrive.

She called home rarely, and visited even less often. She was twenty-eight, engaged to a rational man, and employed as an accountant.

Vivian's Nai Nai would have said that she was attempting to deploy enchantments of her own — the fiancé, the ordinary hobbies and the sensible office job were so many sigils to ward off chaos. It was not an ineffective magic. It worked — for a while.

There was just one moment, after she heard the news, when Vivian experienced a surge of unfilial exasperation.

'They could have call me on Skype,' she said. 'Call my hand phone some more! What a waste of money.'

'What's wrong?' said the fiancé. He plays the prince in this story: beautiful, supportive, and cast in an appropriately self-effacing role — just off-screen, on a white horse.

'My grandmother's passed away,' said Vivian. 'I'm supposed to go back.'

Vivian was not a woman to hold a grudge. When she turned up at KLIA in harem trousers and a tank top it was not through malice aforethought, but because she had simply forgotten.

Her parents embraced her with sportsmanlike enthusiasm, but when this was done her mother pulled back and plucked at her tank top.

'Girl, what's this? You know Nai Nai won't like it.'

Nai Nai had lived by a code of rigorous propriety. She had disapproved of wearing black or navy blue at Chinese New Year, of white at weddings, and of spaghetti straps at all times. When they went out for dinner, even at the local restaurant where they sat outdoors and were accosted by stray cats requesting snacks, her grandchildren were required to change out of their ratty pasar malam T-shirts and faded shorts. She drew a delicate but significant distinction between flip-flops and sandals, singlets and strapless tops, soft cotton shorts and denim.

'Can see your bra,' whispered Ma. 'It's not so nice.'

'That kind of pants,' her dad said dubiously. 'Don't know what Nai Nai will think of it.'

'Nai Nai won't see them what,' said Vivian, but this offended her parents. They sat in mutinous silence throughout the drive home.

Their terrace house was swarming with pregnant cats and black dogs.

'Only six dogs,' said Vivian's mother when Vivian pointed this out. 'Because got five cats. Your sister thought it's a good idea to have more dogs than cats.'

'But why do we have so many cats?' said Vivian. 'I thought you don't like to have animals in the house.'

'Nai Nai collected the cats,' said Vivian's sister. 'She started before she passed away. Pregnant cats only.'

'Wei Yi,' said Vivian. 'How are you?'

'I'm OK. Vivian,' said Wei Yi. Her eyes glittered.

She'd stopped calling Vivian jie jie some time after Vivian left home. Vivian minded this less than the way she said 'Vivian' as though it were a bad word.

But after all, Vivian reminded herself, Wei Yi was 17. She was practically legally required to be an arsehole.

'Why did Nai Nai want the pregnant cats?' Vivian tried to make her voice pleasant.

'Hai, don't need to talk so much,' said their mother hastily. 'Lin — Vivian so tired. Vivian, you go and change first, then we go for dinner. Papa will start complaining soon if not.'

It was during an outing to a prayer goods store, while Vivian's mother was busy buying joss sticks, that her mother's friend turned to Vivian and said,

'So a lot of things to do in your house now ah?'

Vivian was shy to say she knew nothing about the preparations afoot. As the eldest child it would only have been right for her to have been her mother's first support in sorting out the funeral arrangements.

'No, we are having a very simple funeral,' said Vivian. 'Nai Nai didn't believe in religion so much.'

This was not a lie. The brutal fact was that Nai Nai had been an atheist with animist leanings, in common with most witches. Vivian's mother preferred not to let this be known, less out of a concern that her mother would be outed as a witch, than because of the stale leftover fear that she would be considered a Communist.

'But what about the dog cat all that?' said Auntie Wendy. 'Did it work? Did your sister manage to keep her in the coffin?'

Vivian's mind whirred to a stop. Then it started up again, buzzing louder than ever.

Ma was righteously indignant when Vivian reproached her.

'You live so long overseas, why you need to know?' said Ma. 'Don't worry. Yi Yi is handling it. Probably Nai Nai was not serious anyway.'

'Not serious about what?'

'Hai, these old people have their ideas,' said Ma. 'Nai Nai

live in KL so long, she still want to go home. Not that I don't want to please her. If it was anything else ... but even if she doesn't have pride for herself, I am her daughter. I have pride for her!'

'Nai Nai wanted to be buried in China?' said Vivian, puzzled.

'China what China! Your Nai Nai is from Penang lah,' said Ma. 'Your Yeh Yeh is also buried in Bukit Tambun there. But even if he's my father, the way he treat my mother, I don't think they should be buried together.'

Vivian began to understand. 'But Ma, if she said she wanted to be with him—'

'It's not what she wants! It's just her idea of propriety,' said Ma. 'She thinks woman must always stay by the husband no matter what. I don't believe that! Nai Nai will be buried here and when her children pass on we will be buried with her. It's more comfortable for her, right? To have her loved ones around her?'

'But if Nai Nai didn't think so?'

Ma's painted eyebrows drew together.

'Nai Nai is a very stubborn woman,' she said.

Wei Yi was being especially teenaged that week. She went around with lightning frizzing her hair and storm clouds rumbling about her ears. Her clothes stood away from her body, stiff with electricity. The cats hissed and the dogs whined when she passed.

When she saw the paper offerings their mother had bought for Nai Nai, she threw a massive tantrum.

'What's this?' she said, picking up a paper polo shirt. 'Where got Nai Nai wear this kind of thing?'

Ma looked embarrassed.

'The shop only had that,' she said. 'Don't be angry, girl. I bought some bag and shoe also. But you know Nai Nai was never the dressy kind.'

'That's because she like to keep all her nice clothes,' said Wei Yi. She cast a look of burning contempt at the paper handbag, printed in heedless disregard of intellectual property rights with the Gucci logo. 'Looks like the pasar malam bag. And this slippers is like old man slippers. Nai Nai could put two of her feet in one slipper!'

'Like that she's less likely to hop away,' Ma said thoughtlessly.

'Is that what you call respecting your mother?' shouted Wei Yi. 'Hah, you wait until it's your turn! I'll know how to treat you then.'

'Wei Yi, how can you talk to Ma like that?' said Vivian.

'You shut up your face!' Wei Yi snapped. She flounced out of the room.

'She never even see the house yet,' sighed Ma. She had bought an elaborate palace fashioned out of gilt-edged pink paper, with embellished roofs and shuttered windows, and two dolls dressed in Tang dynasty attire prancing on a balcony. 'Got two servants some more.'

'She shouldn't talk to you like that,' said Vivian.

She hadn't noticed any change in Ma's appearance before, but now the soft wrinkly skin under her chin and the pale brown spots on her arms reminded Vivian that she was getting old. Old people should be cared for.

She touched her mother on the arm. 'I'll go scold her. Never mind, Ma. Girls this age are always one kind.'

Ma smiled at Vivian.

'You were OK,' she said. She tucked a lock of Vivian's hair behind her ear.

Old people should be grateful for affection. The sudden disturbing thought occurred to Vivian that no one had liked Nai Nai very much because she'd never submitted to being looked after.

Wei Yi was trying to free the dogs. She stood by the gate, holding it open and gesturing with one hand at the great outdoors.

'Go! Blackie, Guinness, Ah Hei, Si Hitam, Jackie, Bobby! Go, go!'

The dogs didn't seem that interested in the great outdoors. Ah Hei took a couple of tentative steps towards the gate, looked back at Wei Yi, changed her mind and sat down again.

'Jackie and Bobby?' said Vivian.

Wei Yi shot her a glare. 'I ran out of ideas.' The *so what?* was unspoken, but it didn't need to be said.

'Why these stupid dogs don't want to go,' Wei Yi muttered. 'When you open the gate to drive in or out, they go running everywhere. When you want them to chau, they don't want.'

'They can tell you won't let them back in again,' said Vivian.

She remembered when Wei Yi had been cute — as a little girl, with those pure single-lidded eyes and the doll-like lacquered bowl of hair. When had she turned into this creature? Hair at sevens and eights, the uneven fringe falling into malevolent eyes. Inappropriately tight Bermuda shorts worn below an unflatteringly loose plaid shirt.

At seven Wei Yi had been a being perfect in herself. At seventeen there was nothing that wasn't wrong about the way she moved in the world.

Vivian had been planning to tell her sister off, but the memory of that lovely child softened her voice. 'Why you don't want the dogs anymore?'

'I want Nai Nai to win.' Wei Yi slammed the gate shut.

'What, by having nice clothes when she's passed away?' said Vivian. 'Winning or losing, doesn't matter for Nai Nai anymore. What does it matter if she wears a polo shirt in the afterlife?'

Wei Yi's face crumpled. She clutched her fists in agony. The words broke from her in a roar.

'You're so stupid! You don't know anything!' She kicked the gate to relieve her feelings. 'Nai Nai's brain works more than yours and she's dead! Do you even belong to this family?'

This was why Vivian had left. Magic lent itself to temperament.

'Maybe not,' said Vivian.

When Vivian was angry she did it with the same single-minded energy she did everything else. This was why she decided to go wedding dress shopping in the week of her grandmother's funeral.

There were numerous practical justifications, actually.

She went through them in her head as she drove past bridal studios where faceless mannequins struck poses in clouds of tulle.

'Cheaper to get it here than overseas. Not like I'm helping much at home what. Not like I was so close to Nai Nai.'

She ended up staring mournfully at herself in the mirror, weighted down by satin and rhinestones. Did she want a veil? Did she like lace? Ball gown or mermaid shape?

She'd imagined her wedding dress as being white and long. She hadn't expected there to be so many permutations on a theme. She felt pinned in place by the choices available to her.

The shop assistant could tell her heart wasn't in it.

'Some ladies like other colour better,' said the shop assistant. 'You want to try? We have blue, pink, peach, yellow — very nice colour, very feminine.'

'I thought usually white?'

'Some ladies don't like white because — you know—' the shop assistant lowered her voice, but she was too superstitious to say it outright. 'It's related to a not so nice subject.'

The words clanged in Vivian's ears. Briefly light-headed, she clutched at the back of a chair for balance. Her hands were freezing. In the mirror the white dress looked like a shroud. Her face hovering above it was the face of a mourner, or a ghost.

'Now that I've tried it, I'm not sure I like Western gown so much,' said Vivian, speaking with difficulty.

'We have cheongsam or qun kua,' said the shop assistant. 'Very nice, very traditional. Miss is so slim, will suit the cheongsam.'

The jolt of red brocade was a relief. Vivian took a dress with gold trimmings, the highest of high collars and an even higher slit along the sides. It was as red as a blare of trumpets, as red as the pop of fireworks.

This fresh chilli red had never suited her. In it she looked paler than ever, washed out by the vibrant shade. But the colour was a protective charm. It laid monsters to rest. It shut out hungry ghosts. It frightened shadows back into the corners where they belonged.

Vivian crept home with her spoils. That night she slept and did not dream of anything.

The next morning she regretted the purchase. Her fiancé would think it was ridiculous. She couldn't wear a cheong-sam down the aisle of an Anglican church. She would take it back to the boutique and return it. After all, the white satin mermaid dress had suited her. The sweetheart neckline was so much more flattering than a mandarin collar.

She shoved the cheongsam in a bag and tried to sneak out, but Wei Yi was sitting on the floor of the laundry room, in the way of her exit. She was surrounded by webs of filigreed red paper.

'What's this?' said Vivian.

'It's called paper cutting,' said Wei Yi, not looking up. 'You never see before meh?'

On the floor the paper cuttings unfurled. Some were disasters: a mutilated fish floated past like tumbleweed; a pair of flirtatious girls had been torn apart by an overly enthusiastic slash. But some of the pieces were astounding.

'Kwan Yin,' said Vivian.

The folds in the goddess's robes had been rendered with extraordinary delicacy. Her eyes were gentle, her face double-chinned. Her halo was a red moon circled by ornate clouds.

'It's for Nai Nai,' said Wei Yi. 'Maybe Kwan Yin will have mercy on her even though she's so blasphemous.'

'Shouldn't talk like that about the dead,' said Vivian.

Wei Yi rolled her eyes, but the effort of her craft seemed to absorb all her evil energies. Her response was mild: 'It's not disrespectful if it's true.'

Her devotion touched Vivian. Surely not many seventeen-year-olds would spend so much time on so laborious a task. The sleet of impermanent art piled around her must have taken hours to produce.

'Did Nai Nai teach you how to do that?' Vivian said, trying to get back on friendlier ground.

Wei Yi's face spasmed.

'Nai Nai was a rubber tapper with seven children,' she said. 'She can't even read! You think what, she was so free she can do all these hobbies, is it? I learnt it from YouTube lah!'

She crumpled the paper she was working on and flung it down on the floor to join the flickering red mass.

'Oh, whatever!' said Vivian in the fullness of her heart.

She bought the whitest, fluffiest, shiniest, most beaded dress she could find in the boutique. It was strapless and low-backed to boot. Nai Nai would have hated it.

That night Vivian dreamt of her grandmother.

Nai Nai had climbed out of her coffin where she had been lying in the living room. She was wearing a kebaya, with a white baju and a batik sarong wrapped around her hips. No modern creation this — the blouse was fastened not with buttons but with kerongsang, ornate gold brooches studded with pearls and rhinestones.

Nai Nai was struggling with the kerongsang. In her dream Vivian reached out to help her.

'I can do!' said Nai Nai crossly. 'Don't so sibuk.' She batted at the kerongsang with the slim brown hands that had been so deft in life.

'What's the matter? You want to take it off for what?' said Vivian in Hokkien.

'It's too nice to wear outside,' Nai Nai complained. 'When I was alive I used safety pins and it was enough. All this hassle just because I am like this. I didn't save Yeh Yeh's pension so you can spend on a carcass!'

'Why do you want to go outside?' Vivian took the bony arm. 'Nai Nai, come, let's go back to sleep. It's so late already. Everybody is sleeping.'

Nai Nai was a tiny old lady with a dandelion fluff of white hair standing out from her head. She looked nothing like the spotty, tubby, furiously awkward Wei Yi, but her expression suddenly showed Vivian what her sister would look like when she was old. The contemptuous exasperation was exactly the same.

'If it's not late, how can I go outside?' she said. 'I have a long way to go. Hai!' She flung up her hands. 'After they bury me, ask the priest to give you back the kerongsang.'

She started hopping towards the door, her arms held rod-straight out in front of her. The sight was comic and horrible.

This was the secret the family had been hiding from Vivian. Nai Nai had become a kuang shi.

'Nai Nai,' choked Vivian. 'Please rest. You're so old already, shouldn't run around so much.'

'Don't answer back!' shouted Nai Nai from the foyer. 'Come and open the door for Nai Nai! Yeh Yeh will be angry. He cannot stand when people are late.'

Vivian envisioned Nai Nai hopping out of the house — past the neighbourhood park with its rustling bushes and creaking swings, past the neighbours' Myvis and Peroduas, through the toll while the attendant slumbered. She saw Nai Nai hopping along the curves of the Titiwangsa mountains, her halo of hair white against the bleeding red of the hills where the forests had peeled away to show the limestone. She saw Nai Nai passing oil palm plantations, their leaves dark glossy green under the brassy glare of sunshine — sleepy water buffalo flicking their tails in wide hot fields — empty new terrace houses standing in white rows on bare hillsides. Up the long North-South Expressway to her final home.

'Nai Nai,' said Vivian. *Don't leave us,* she wanted to say.

'Complain, complain!' Nai Nai was slapping at the door-knob with her useless stiff hands.

'You can't go all that way,' said Vivian. She had an inspiration. 'Your sarong will come undone.'

Whoever had laid Nai Nai out had dressed her like a true nyonya. The sarong was wound around her hips and tucked in at the waist, with no fastenings to hold it up.

'At my age, who cares,' said Nai Nai, but this had clearly given her pause.

'Come back to sleep,' coaxed Vivian. 'I'll tell Mummy. Bukit Tambun, right? I'll sort it out for you.'

Nai Nai gave her a sharp look. 'Can talk so sweetly but what does she do? Grandmother is being buried and she goes to buy a wedding dress!'

Vivian winced.

'The dress is not nice also,' said Nai Nai. 'What happened to the first dress? That was nice. Red is a happy colour.'

'I know Nai Nai feels it's pantang, but—'

'Pantang what pantang,' snapped Nai Nai. Like all witches, she hated to be accused of superstition. 'White is a boring colour! Ah, when I got married everybody wanted to celebrate. We had two hundred guests and they all had chicken to eat. I looked so beautiful in my photo. And Yeh Yeh... '

Nai Nai sank into reminiscence.

'What about Yeh Yeh?' prompted Vivian.

'Yeh Yeh looked the same as always. Like a useless play-boy,' said Nai Nai. 'He could only look nice and court girls.'

'Then you want to be buried with him for what?'

'That's different,' said Nai Nai. 'Whether I'm a good wife doesn't have anything to do with what he was like.'

As if galvanized by Vivian's resistance, she turned and made to hit the door again.

'If you listen to me, I'll take the dress back to the shop,' said Vivian, driven by desperation.

Nai Nai paused. 'You'll buy the pretty cheongsam?'

'If you want also I'll wear the kua,' said Vivian recklessly.

She tried not to imagine what her fiancé would say when he saw the loose red jacket and long skirt, embroidered in gold and silver with bug-eyed dragons and insectoid phoe-nixes. And the three-quarter bell sleeves, all the better to show the wealth of the family in the gold bracelets stacked on the bride's wrists! How that would impress her future in-laws.

To her relief, Nai Nai said, 'No lah! So old-fashioned. Cheongsam is nicer.'

She started hopping back towards the living room.

Vivian trailed behind, feeling somehow as though she had been outmanoeuvred.

'Nai Nai, do you really want to be buried in Penang?'

Nai Nai peered up with suspicion in her reddened eyes as Vivian helped her back into the coffin.

'You want to change your mind, is it?'

'No, no, I'll get the cheongsam. It'll be in my room by tomorrow, I promise.'

Nai Nai smiled.

'You know why I wanted you all to call me Nai Nai?' she said before Vivian closed the coffin. 'Even though Hokkien people call their grandmother Ah Ma?'

Vivian paused with her hand on the lid.

'In the movies, Nai Nai is always bad!'

Vivian woke up with her grandmother's growly cackle in her ears.

Wei Yi was in the middle of a meltdown when Vivian came downstairs for breakfast. Ma bristled with relief:

'Ah, your sister is here. She'll talk to you.'

Wei Yi was sitting enthroned in incandescence, clutching a bread knife. A charred hunk of what used to be kaya toast sat on her plate. The *Star* newspaper next to it was crisping at the edges.

Vivian began to sweat. She thought about turning on the ceiling fan, but that might stoke the flames.

She pulled out a chair and picked up the jar of kaya as if nothing was happening. 'What's up?'

Wei Yi turned hot coal eyes on Vivian.

'She doesn't want to kill the dogs wor,' said Ma. 'Angry already.'

'So? Who ask you to kill the dogs in the first place?' said Vivian.

'Stupid,' said Wei Yi. Her face was very pale, but her lips had the dull orange glow of heated metal. Fire breathed in her hair. A layer of ash lay on the crown of her head.

'Because of Nai Nai,' Ma explained. 'Wei Yi heard the blood of a black dog is good for Nai Nai's ... condition.'

'It's not right,' said Wei Yi. 'It's better for Nai Nai if she goes peacefully. But *you* won't understand one!'

Vivian spread a layer of kaya on her piece of bread before she answered. Her hands were shaking, but her voice was steady when she spoke.

'I think Ma is right. There's no need to kill any dogs. Nai Nai is not serious about being a kuang shi. She's just using it as an emotional blackmail.' She paused for reflection. 'And I think she's enjoying it also lah. You know Nai Nai was always very active. She likes to be up and about.'

Wei Yi dropped her butter knife.

'Eh, how you know?' said Ma.

'She talked to me in my dream last night because she didn't like the wedding dress I bought,' said Vivian.

Ma's eyes widened. 'You went to buy your wedding dress when Nai Nai just pass away?'

'You saw Nai Nai?' cried Wei Yi. 'What did she say?'

'She likes cheongsam better, and she wants to be buried in Penang,' said Vivian. 'So I'm going to buy cheongsam.

Ma, should think about sending her back to Penang. When she got nothing to complain about she will settle down.'

'Why she didn't talk to me?' said Wei Yi. Beads of molten metal ran down her face, leaving silver trails. 'I do so many jampi and she never talk to me! It's not fair!'

Ma was torn between an urge to scold Vivian and the necessity of comforting Wei Yi. 'Girl, don't cry — Vivian, so disrespectful, I'm surprise Nai Nai never scold you—'

'Yi Yi,' said Vivian. 'She didn't talk to you because in Nai Nai's eyes you are perfect already.' As she said this, she realized it was true.

Wei Yi — awkward, furious and objectionable in every way — was Nai Nai's ideal grandchild. There was no need to monitor or reprimand such a perfect heir. The surprise was that Nai Nai even thought it necessary to rise from the grave to order Vivian around, rather than just leaving the job to the next witch.

Of course, Nai Nai probably hadn't had the chance to train Wei Yi in the standards expected of a wedding in Nai Nai's family. The finer points of bridal fashion would certainly escape Wei Yi.

'Nai Nai only came back to scold people,' said Vivian. 'She doesn't need to scold you for anything.'

The unnatural metallic sheen of Wei Yi's face went away. Her hair and eyes dimmed. Her mouth trembled.

Vivian expected a roar. Instead Wei Yi shoved her kaya toast away and laid her head on the table.

'I miss Nai Nai,' she sobbed.

Ma got up and touched Vivian on the shoulder.

'I have to go buy thing,' she whispered. 'You cheer up your sister.'

Wei Yi's skin was still hot when Vivian put her arm around her, but as Vivian held her Wei Yi's temperature declined, until she felt merely feverish. Her tears went from scalding to lukewarm.

'Nai Nai, Nai Nai,' she wailed in that screechy show-off way Vivian had always hated. When they were growing up Vivian had not believed in Wei Yi's tears. They seemed no more than a show, put on to impress the grown-ups.

Vivian now realized that the grief was as real as the volume deliberate. Wei Yi did not cry like that simply because she was sad, but because she wanted someone to listen to her.

In the old days it had been a parent or a teacher's attention that she had sought. These howls were aimed directly at the all-too-responsive ears of their late grandmother.

'Wei Yi,' said Vivian. 'I've thought of what you can do for Nai Nai.'

For once Wei Yi did not put Vivian's ideas to scorn. She seemed to have gone up in her sister's estimation for having seen Nai Nai's importunate spectre.

Vivian had a feeling Nai Nai's witchery had gone into Wei Yi's paper cutting skills. YouTube couldn't explain the unreal speed with which she did it.

Vivian tried picking up Wei Yi's scissors and dropped them, yelping.

'What the—!' It had felt like an electric shock.

Wei Yi grabbed the scissors. 'These are no good. I give you other ones to use.'

Vivian got the task of cutting out the sarong — a large rectangular piece of paper to which Wei Yi would add the batik motifs later. When she was done Wei Yi took a look and pursed her lips. The last time Vivian had felt this small was when she failed her first driving test two minutes after getting into the car.

'OK ah?'

'Not bad,' said Wei Yi unconvincingly. 'Eh, you go help Ma do her whatever thing lah. I'll work on this first.'

A couple of hours later she barged into Vivian's room. 'Why you're here? Why you take so long? Come and see!'

Vivian got up sheepishly. 'I thought you need some time to finish mah.'

'Nonsense. Nai Nai going to be buried tomorrow, where got time to dilly-dally?' Wei Yi grasped her hand.

The paper outfit was laid in crisp folds on the dining table. Wei Yi's scissors had rendered the delicate lace of the kebaya blouse with marvellous skill. Peacocks with uplifted wings and princely crowns draped their tails along the hems, strutted up the lapels, and curled coyly around the ends of the sleeves. The paper was chiffon-thin. A breath set it fluttering.

The skirt was made from a thicker, heavier cream paper. Wei Yi had cut blowsy peonies into the front and a contrasting grid pattern on the reverse. Vivian touched it in wonder, feeling the nubby texture of the paper under her fingertips.

'Do you think Nai Nai will like it?' said Wei Yi.

Vivian had to be honest. 'The top is a bit see-through, no?'

'She'll have a singlet to wear underneath,' said Wei Yi. 'I left that for you to do. Very simple one. Just cut along the line only.'

This was kindness, Wei Yi style.

'It's beautiful, Yi Yi,' said Vivian. She felt awkward — they were not a family given to compliments — but once she'd started it was easy to go on. 'It's so nice. Nai Nai will love it.'

'Ah, don't need to say so much lah,' Wei Yi scoffed. '"OK" enough already. I still haven't done shoe yet.'

They burnt the beautiful cream kebaya as an offering to Nai Nai. It didn't go alone. Wei Yi had created four other outfits, working through the night. Samfu for everyday wear; an old-fashioned loose, long-sleeved cheongsam ('Nicer for older lady. Nai Nai is not a Shanghai cabaret singer'); a sarong for sleeping in; and a Punjabi suit of all things.

'Nai Nai used to like wearing it,' said Wei Yi when Vivian expressed surprise. 'Comfortable mah. Nai Nai likes this simple kind of thing to wear for every day.'

'Four is not a good number,' said Vivian. 'Maybe should make extra sarong?'

'You forgot the kebaya. That's five,' Wei Yi retorted. 'Anyway she die already. What is there to be pantang about?'

They threw in the more usual hell gold and paper mansion into the bonfire as well. The doll servants didn't burn well, but melted dramatically and stuck afterwards.

Since they were doing the bonfire outside the house, on the public road, this concerned Vivian. She chipped doubtfully away at the mess of plastic.

'Don't worry,' said Ma. 'The servants have gone to Nai Nai already.'

'I'm not worried about that,' said Vivian. 'I'm worried about MPPJ.' She couldn't imagine the local authorities would be particularly pleased about the extra work they'd made for them.

'They're used to it lah,' said Ma, dismissing the civil service with a wave of the hand.

They even burnt the fake Gucci bag and the polo shirt in the end.

'Nai Nai will find some use for it,' said Wei Yi. 'Maybe turn out she like that kind of style also.'

She could afford to be magnanimous. Making the kebaya had relieved something in Wei Yi's heart. As she'd stood watch over the flames to make sure the demons didn't get their offerings to Nai Nai, there had been a new serenity in her face.

As they moved back to the house, Vivian put her arm around her sister, wincing at the snap and hiss when her skin touched Wei Yi's. It felt like a static shock, only intensified by several orders of magnitude.

'OK?'

Wei Yi was fizzling with magic, but her eyes were calm and dark and altogether human.

'OK,' replied the Witch of Damansara.

In Vivian's dream a moth came fluttering into the room. It alighted at the end of her bed and turned into Nai Nai.

Nai Nai was wearing a green-and-white striped cotton sarong, tucked and knotted under her arms as if she were going to bed soon. Her hair smelled of Johnson & Johnson baby shampoo. Her face was white with bedak sejuk — powder moistened and spread over the face as a cooling paste.

'Tell your mother the house is very beautiful,' said Nai Nai. 'The servants have already run away and got married, but it's not so bad. In hell it's not so dusty. Nothing to clean also.'

'Nai Nai—'

'Ah Yi is very clever now, har?' said Nai Nai. 'The demons

looked at my nice things but when they saw her they immediately run away.'

Vivian experienced a pang. She didn't say anything, but perhaps the dead understood these things. Or perhaps it was just that Nai Nai, with 65 years of mothering behind her, did not need to be told. She reached out and patted Vivian's hand.

'You are always so guai,' said Nai Nai. 'I'm not so worried about you.'

This was a new idea to Vivian. She was unused to thinking of herself —magicless, intransigent — as the good kid in the family.

'But I went overseas,' she said stupidly.

'You're always so clever to work hard. You don't make your mother and father worried,' said Nai Nai. 'Ah Yi ah ….' Nai Nai shook her head. 'So stubborn! So naughty! If I don't take care sekali she burn down the house. That girl doesn't use her head. But she become a bit guai already. When she's older she won't be so free, won't have time to cause so much problems.'

Vivian did not point out that age did not seem to have stopped Nai Nai. This would have been disrespectful. Instead she said,

'Nai Nai, were you really a vampire? Or were you just pretending to turn into a kuang shi?'

'Hai, you think so fun to pretend to be a kuang shi?' said Nai Nai indignantly. 'When you are old, you will find out how suffering it is. You think I have time to watch all the Hong Kong movies and learn how to be a vampire?'

So that was how she did it. The pale vampire-like skin had probably been bedak sejuk as well. How Nai Nai had obtained bedak sejuk in the afterlife was a question better left unasked. Vivian had questions of more immediate interest anyway.

'If you stayed because you're worried about Wei Yi, can I return the cheongsam to the shop?'

Nai Nai bridled. 'Oh, like that ah? Not proud of your culture, is it? If you want to wear the white dress, like a ghost, so ugly—'

'Ma wore a white dress on her wedding day. Everyone does it.'

'Nai Nai give you my bedak sejuk and red lipstick lah. Then you can pretend to be kuang shi also!'

'I'll get another cheongsam,' said Vivian. 'Not that I don't want to wear cheongsam. I just don't like this one so much. It's too expensive.'

'How much?'

Vivian told her.

'Wah, so much ah,' said Nai Nai. 'Like that you should just get it tailored. Don't need to buy from shop. Tailored is cheaper and nicer some more. The seamstress's phone number is in Nai Nai's old phonebook. Madam Teoh.'

'I'll look,' Vivian promised.

Nai Nai got up, stretching. 'Must go now. Scared the demons will don't know do what if I leave the house so long. You must look after your sister, OK?'

Vivian, doubtful about how any attempt to look after Wei Yi was likely to be received, said, 'Ah.'

'Nai Nai already gave Ah Yi her legacy, but I'll give you yours now,' said Nai Nai. 'You're a good girl, Ah Lin. Nai Nai didn't have chance to talk to you so much when you were small. But I'm proud of you. Make sure the seam-stress doesn't overcharge. If you tell Madam Teoh you're my granddaughter she'll give you discount.'

'Thank you, Nai Nai,' said Vivian, but she spoke to an empty room. The curtains flapped in Nai Nai's wake.

On the floor lay a pile of clothes. Moonlight-sheer chif-fon, brown batik, maroon silk and floral print cotton, and on top of this, glowing turquoise even in the pale light of the moon, the most gilded, spangled, intricately embroi-dered Punjabi suit Vivian had ever seen.

A CHANGE OF HEART

A Babylon Steel story
Gaie Sebold

I leant on the ship's rail and stared at grey rain hitting grey water, feeling somewhat sorry for myself. I was running. It was something I did a lot back then. Not, this time, from anyone who wanted to kill me; just the end of an affair. We'd both served as bodyguards to a local merchant, and had a lot of fun – rather more than fun, at least on my part. But he'd cooled off. Instead of hanging about with the risk of seeing that face I still loved around the next corner, I decided to get moving.

It wasn't helping yet.

In this part of the planes they have a legend concerning Meriasen of Kyr, a healer who came from another land to heal a sick queen. She arrived safely but there was a terrible war, and she could never go home. She was so heartsick she had her heart cut out of her breast and placed in a crystal cage on top of a mountain, where she could no longer feel its pain. Right now that sounded like a pretty attractive proposition.

In the absence of somewhere else to put my heart, I'd decided to hang up my sword for a while, metaphorically, at least, and go back to whoring. I was heading for Coriath, where I'd heard that a friend, Deralis, was doing well as a courtesan. I hoped she might see her way to showing me around, help me get set up, maybe introduce me to a decent client or two. I could do with the break, and the healing qualities of some nice, healthy, uncomplicated (emotionally uncomplicated, that is) sex.

Coriath looked chilly and grim, but then a dockside in the rain is seldom the most appealing place from which to view a town. There were a few miserable-looking freelance whores huddled in warehouse doorways; fewer than I was used to seeing, even in this sort of weather. I approached one and she gave me the once-over any half-sharp doxy gives a potential client, but this had a little extra edge to it.

'Looking for an amourette, love?' Interesting word. Of all the many I'd encountered it was one of the prettier ones, even if it did sound like some sort of biscuit.

I asked for directions to Deralis' place. 'Her? She's expensive, sure you wouldn't rather have a nice cosy tumble wi' me?' The banter was standard, but her face was strained and she kept glancing past my arm.

'I'm in the business, honey.'

She glanced up at me, startled. 'You are?' She assessed me again, not as a client this time. I saw her noting the weaponry – the visible weaponry, at least - and something passed over her face, a lightening, the promise of sun behind a cloud. 'Maybe you'll bring us luck, eh? Hey, I like those hair clips. You wanta sell 'em?'

I touched the pair of nicely carved curving steel clips I wear. 'Sorry, love. These are my lucky clips. Can't bring anyone else luck if I get rid of my own.' The clips were made for me by a friend. They're more than just pretty. They come apart, to reveal a pair of very small but effective blades. The sort of thing you can keep discreetly to hand on the bedside table for emergencies without putting the wind up your clients.

She told me the way and I felt her gaze on my back as I walked up the wide, wet street away from the docks.

The house was cosy-looking, built of warm pinkish stone, with a dark green trim. I knocked, and stood as far as possible under the eaves, waiting. Nothing happened.

'She's not there.'

I turned around. A young woman in a long leather coat stood behind me, biting her lip, rain running off her wide-brimmed hat. 'You a client?'

'No. A friend.'

She was looking me over in a wary, assessing way. I was beginning to get a bad feeling, after the way the dockside doxy – excuse me, amourette – had responded. Something was going on here. 'I met Deralis a year or so back,' I said. 'Over in Thrallick. We kept in touch, and I was hoping to see her, get some pointers on setting up here. Whoring's legal, here, isn't it? That's what her letters said.'

'Yes, it's legal.'

I held out my hand. 'Babylon Steel.'

She took it. Her grip was strong; a spatter of small, shiny scars marked the skin of her hand. 'Liva Tare.' She sighed. 'You'd best come in before we drown.'

She unlocked the door, and led me in. It was nicely appointed, if a bit heavy on the gilt and furbelows for my taste. But that was Deralis all over. If you could paint it gold, add lace to it, or stick sequins on it, she liked it.

'I'm sorry,' Liva said, 'that you've come all this way for nothing.' She took off her hat and coat and hung them on a stand near the fire. She had a strong, attractive face, big brown eyes and a firm chin, but those eyes were sunken in shadowed hollows and her lips had been bitten raw. 'She wouldn't mind if I offered you a drink, at least.'

'Nice place. She's doing well.'

'She… yes.' Liva took glasses from a cabinet and a bottle from another, but her movements were distracted, and she kept pausing as though she'd forgotten what she was doing. Eventually I had a drink in front of me and my boots were steaming. I eased my boots off – the one with the handy little knife sheathed inside always took longer to dry – and put them closer to the fire.

All very comfortable, it should have been, but it wasn't. Something was definitely up. 'So, any idea when Deralis is likely to come back?' I said.

Liva shook her head, then sat down abruptly and put her face in her hands. 'It's been ten days,' she said. 'Ten days, and another woman dead, and I… *gods.*'

I waited, then when I was sure she could answer I said, 'How about you start at the beginning?'

They'd met a few months ago. 'It wasn't… I wasn't one of her clients,' Liva said. 'I'm an alchemist.' That explained the burn scars on her hands. 'She came to me because she thought I could help her with a potion. I sorted it out for her, and we got talking… she kept coming back, for the silliest things…' she smiled, sadly, and shook her head. 'I was so stupid, it took me forever to realise that wasn't why she was coming to the shop. In the end she just had to ask me straight out. We've been seeing each other ever since. I wanted her to stop...' she looked up at me, flushing dark. 'It wasn't because I mind, you know, what she does. Only, two amourettes were killed, and then another, and I asked her to just stop, for a while, you know? I could support us both. At least until they caught whoever was doing it. And she said she would but she had three clients booked who she didn't want to turn away, so... I waited. She said she'd come to the shop, and I waited. I waited. Then I came here. And that was ten days ago, and they've found another body and I keep waiting for the next one to...to be her.'

'You said until they caught whoever's doing it. You think it was all the same person?'

'Gods, I hope so,' she said. 'Whoever it is takes...' she swallowed. 'Takes their hearts.'

'What?'

'Whoever kills them cuts their hearts out.'

Liva insisted on getting me another drink, and then she cooked a meal, waving away my objections. 'Deralis would want me to,' she said. 'And it... I like cooking. It helps.' We all have our ways of coping.

After a good dinner which I devoured and she barely touched, she asked me if I'd stay.

'What, me?' I said. 'Here? Why? I mean, I'd be happy to, but...'

'You could keep an eye on the place. I've got my own rooms over my shop, I can't be here all the time. Make sure that if... when she comes back, it isn't all closed up and empty. And...' she looked up at me, something in her eyes that was a lot closer to desperation than hope. 'You knew her, and maybe you can think of something. I've asked everyone I can think of, but no-one knows anything.'

'What about local law?'

'Oh, they're useless. We've got a city guard but it's just a retirement sinecure for former palace guards. If no-one rich gets hurt they can barely be bothered to turn out.'

'So…' *who's going to catch him?* I thought, but managed, just, not to say.

'*Please,*' she said, her hands twisting together in her lap. 'I don't know where to go for help. I'd ask a mage but the only ones we've got are necromancers, and one of those is just starting out – anyway, I don't see what they could do.'

'The first place I'd look would be her clients,' I said. 'Do you know any of them?'

'No. Well, I've met a few since… but she usually booked them for the evenings and when I knew they were going to be here I didn't come over.'

'Did she keep a client list?' I said.

'I don't know,' Liva said. 'If she did, it's probably in her bedroom.'

I followed her up the stairs. A graceful back and neat muscular calves above practical boots. Deralis had good taste.

She also had a book tucked into a chest at the bottom of the bed. Clients' nicknames, preferences and visiting dates were carefully detailed. Thankfully, she was picky and charged high, so there weren't a huge number.

Like a lot of us in the business, Deralis didn't write down their real names: that can cause all kinds of trouble if the wrong person gets hold of them. I started to read out the nicknames. 'Red Head – Cane – Baldy – know who any of these are?

'I recognise Red Head. He dyes his hair. He just came yesterday, looking for her.'

'Have you been here much?' I said. 'Since she disappeared?'

'Every evening, just in case … that was when her clients usually came. I was waiting to ask them if they'd heard any-thing, but even when they'd talk to me they couldn't help.'

'All right. You tell me if anyone else has come looking since she disappeared, and I'll see if I can match 'em up with the list. Limp… well, I assume that means he walks with one, but…'

'Oh, yes. There was a man with a limp here two days back. What about from before she disappeared?'

'Not yet. Just these for now.'

'Why only these?'

'Because they thought she was still here. Anyone who didn't...'

'...might know she wasn't.' Liva nodded. There was a slightly feverish gleam in her eye. 'See, I *said* you could help!'

We went through the rest of the list, and ended up with three who hadn't turned up, or weren't recognisable. 'Big Nose Hairy Ears,' I read. 'He... OK that's a new one. Mr Fancy Pants. Maybe he's a good dresser... oh, no, I see. That's not a lot of help. This one's been crossed out. It looks like Rev...Revive? *Too much,* that's all I can read of the rest.' Well, everyone has lines they prefer not to cross.

'Let me see.' Liva jumped to her feet and reached for the book.

I hesitated.

I mean, not minding that your lover beds other people is one thing, but reading the details of the services they provide can be a little disconcerting.

'What?' Liva said. 'Oh for the gods' sake, I know what she does, I'm not going to...' she glanced at the page, and said, 'besides, I don't even know what that *means.'* She understood the next bit though, because she flushed, coughed, and said, 'Oh. *Really?'*

'Some people like it.' People liked much stranger things than she'd just read, and that was just the humans, but I didn't think this was the time or place to go into it. 'Right. Well, we can't exactly go around asking people what they're into, but...'

'You could,' Liva said. 'Couldn't you?'

'What?'

'You could. Set up here, and tell people you offer the same services, as these three want...' she looked so pleased with her idea I almost went along with it, but I wasn't *that* depressed over my affair ending.

'There's a problem with that,' I said.

'What?'

'Look, Liva, I like you, and I'm fond of Deralis, but I don't really want to end up with my heart cut out. I'm still using it.' However bruised it currently felt.

'Oh. Oh, I suppose... I'm sorry, I should have thought. It's just...' she closed the book, and dropped it on the bed.

I picked it up again. 'Did she talk about any clients who were giving her trouble?'

'One, but she wouldn't tell me who. Just that he was getting insistent.'

I looked at that last page again. Revive, crossed out. Some other things, more heavily crossed out – presumably his particular bedroom preferences. And that phrase, *too much.* 'Revive,' I said. 'Does that one mean anything?'

'Revive? No, not a thing.'

'Liva… do you know if anyone offered her something more permanent?'

'I don't…'

'An exclusive contract, say?'

'Someone did, yes. But she said no.'

'Any idea who?'

'She wouldn't say, only that he was persistent but she thought he'd got it. You think… But she'd never have done it without telling me! Even if she didn't want to see me any more, she'd have *told* me. Besides, we…' she shook her head and looked away. 'She'd never do that. Not to me. And what about her things?' She gestured at the pretty room overcrowded with flamboyant ornaments and gilded lamps. 'Why would she leave all her things?'

'It's not that. If she was taking a contract, she'd probably let her current clients know, that's just good manners, and good business. It's just… sometimes, people don't like being turned down. You *sure* you don't have any idea who it was?'

'I never asked…' she looked miserable. 'I didn't want to know about the clients. I should have asked.'

'You couldn't know,' I said. 'All right, I'll see what I can find out tomorrow. Talk to some of the other amourettes. Try and track down those last three clients.'

'Thank you.' She gripped my hand, hard; hers felt work-worn and too thin. 'I'd better go, I've got orders to fill at the shop. But please stay here. I'm sure she'd want you to.'

So I did.

I couldn't settle for a long time. I sharpened my blades, wandered around, found the small back area where a vase lay shattered on the ground. Black, plain, presumably thrown over the wall by a neighbour, not Deralis' style at all. Looking at the shards gave me the creeps. There had been a bonfire too – the rain pattered on fragments of burned cloth, black and white, puddled wax. Water darkened with ash ran between the stones. Cheery.

Deralis' bed turned out to be the most comfortable thing I'd failed to sleep in for a long time.

I lay listening to the endless rain hitting the window and running in the gutters. It's a lonely sound when there's too much empty bed. Liva's face, marked with shadows, drifted through my mind. I wondered what she looked like when she was happy; when she was with Deralis, that big, delicious woman who could play the virgin with any clients who fancied the idea, but who also had a loud, rich laugh and a fund of jokes that even I found astonishingly dirty. I thought of those other women, women whose faces I didn't even know. Did families, friends, lovers, lie awake tonight, trying to remember those faces, trying not to think of what had been done to them?

And why had it been done? Why that way? Why the hearts?

I finally fell asleep, and dreamed of cold rain falling into the space where a heart should be.

'Deralis? No, no, I don't know anyone of that name.' The City Councillor had guilt written all over him, but not a murderer's guilt. He fitted the physical description in Deralis' book so well that I'd just had to ask a few of the freelance whores for 'big nose, hairy ears...' They really were *incredibly* hairy, as though he had a small grey animal living in each one.

I leaned over his desk and whispered, '*juko fruit.*'

He paled, glanced around, although there was no-one else there, and said, 'What do you want? Money? I won't succumb to blackmail.'

'You succumbed to other things quite enthusiastically, I understand' I said. 'Look, I just want to know when you saw her last. Was there was anything odd? Did she seemed worried, distracted?'

'I can't remember when it was.'

'Try.' I stood up. I'm taller than a lot of people and broad in the shoulder, I can loom quite effectively. Especially if I put hand to hilt and glower. 'Try hard.'

He leaned back in his chair, blinking. 'All right, all right! I'm thinking!'

I leaned back a little, but kept my hand on the sword hilt, where he could see it.

'Dofrei! It was just before Dofrei, the Festival of the Dead. It was odd, because she had decorations in the parlour but she was taking them down, before the Festival.'

'Did she say why?'

'She said they weren't hers.'

Perhaps Liva had put them up. 'So when is the Festival of the Dead?'

'Fourteen days ago.'

'And you haven't been back, to visit?'

'No!' He leaned forward. 'Look, promotion cycle's coming up, I have to be *discreet.*'

'I thought whoring was legal here?'

'It is. But if anyone knew about...' he glanced down. 'The thing. With the fruit. Or the... People wouldn't understand.'

'Sounds like a good reason to want someone out of the way,' I said.

'No! I just...I have to be careful, I was planning to go back. Do you really think something's happened to her?'

'You are *aware* that five amourettes have been found with their hearts cut out?'

'But they're street girls,' he said. 'Not like Deralis.'

I had a blade to his throat before either of us could think about it. I managed, just, to keep from cutting him. 'They're women,' I said. 'People. They matter. It would do you good not to forget that, *Councillor.*'

He swallowed, his throat bobbing against the blade.

'Now,' I said. 'You're a man of influence. I want to see the bodies. Get me that, and I'll take you at your word that you don't know anything more about it.' I took the blade away.

'You have no authority here,' he said.

I smiled at him, and said, 'juko fruit.'

'I'll make arrangements.'

Liva had told me where to find her shop. The look of min-
gled hope and dread on her face when I walked in was hard
to take.

'Have you…'

'I went to see the bodies – well, the one that's left. Two
have been claimed by family and two are burned already.
I was only just in time, they're burning the last one
tomorrow.'

'Yes, it's the custom here. Those poor women. And the
last was Jathis… she has a little boy…'

'You saw the bodies?'

'After Deralis disappeared, I had to check… I saw the last
two.'

I debated whether to tell her I'd seen… well, not worse,
but as bad, on the battlefield. Except this was different. This
wasn't the result of someone trying to kill someone else any
way they could – there was no other wound anywhere, and
the hearts had been extracted neatly, not simply hacked at.
There was no sign the victims had fought against a blade; no
cuts to the hands. Unconscious? Drugged? And there hadn't
been much blood where each body was found. Which either
meant something magic was going on, or they were killed
somewhere else, then dumped. 'Whoever did this, I think
they just wanted the heart. Nothing else.'

'What are they *doing* with them?' She looked at me, hor-
rified. 'They couldn't be, I don't know, *eating*… oh, gods.'

'I don't know. Some places when they hunt a big preda-
tor, they believe that whoever gets to eat its heart will get its
power. But why these women?'

'They were all amourettes.'

'Yes…' I tried to think. Would someone think that
taking a whore's heart would give them some sort of sexual
power? The story about Meriasen of Kyr drifted through my
mind. Hearts, and power. It felt as though it should mean
something but what, I had no idea.

'Oh, by the way,' I said, 'did you and Deralis argue, over
anything? Other than you wanting her to take a break, I
mean.'

'We didn't… don't, argue.'

'Even silly things? Festival decorations for example?'

'*Festival* decorations? Why would we argue over something like that?'

My turn to shrug. It probably meant nothing. Maybe Deralis had put them up and then decided they didn't go with the décor.

'I need to talk to these necromancers you mentioned,' I said. 'They might know about hearts, mightn't they? If they're used in a ritual or something.'

'What is it?' Liva said.

'*Revive,*' I said. 'Sound like a necromancer's nickname to you?'

'You think…'

'I don't know. Where's the nearest?'

'The young one, Tarek.'

I don't know what I expected from a necromancer, but it wasn't the flushed, round-faced young man with a small green furry beast attached to his robe who opened the door. 'Yes?'

'I'm looking for Tarek.'

'That's me.'

'You got a minute? I need to ask some questions.'

'You're interested in the Art?' Tarek smiled. 'Come in.' He unhooked the small beast from his robe. 'You've *been* fed,' he told it. It made squeaky protests as he carried it through into a room that was furnished mainly with books. A string of shabby paper skeletons was draped across the mantel, and a few mouse-nibbled candles in the shape of skulls lay here and there. The room smelled of dusty paper and something faintly acrid.

'So many people just make *assumptions,*' he said. 'All skeletal armies and forcing spirits to do one's evil bidding. I'm interested in the practical applications.'

'In some circumstances a skeletal army might be quite a practical application.'

'But it would give such a bad impression. I'm trying to get people to understand necromancy differently.'

'So what are those?' I pointed at one of the paper skeletons. 'That's the sort of thing that's going to give people the wrong impression, surely?'

'Oh, they're just Festival decorations. I forgot to take them down. It's… Well, I believe in paying respect to the traditions, you know, even if one is trying to modernise, we need to acknowledge what's gone before. Here.' He picked up a book with the hand not holding the small creature, and thrust it at me. 'It's a good basic text, for beginners. Oh, and maybe Nuthrin, and Bofredik, and… Where's that copy of the Modern Necronomicon…'

'I don't actually want to study necromancy,' I said, backing away slightly. 'I just want to know if it involves body parts. Hearts, particularly.'

'Well, it can do, of course. That's what I'm trying to *tell* people. It's a healing art, applied correctly.'

'How would taking someone's heart be healing?'

'It wouldn't, unless you had another one to put in its place. That's what the revivification process is for. The body's like a cart,' Tarek said.

'A cart.'

'If a wheel comes off, you fit another one. Well, if someone's heart stopped working, and you could find one that did, replace it, revive the body'.'

'You've done this?'

'It worked on the dog,' Tarek said. Then his round face went mournful. 'Well, briefly.'

'So what about humans?'

'Oh, that's much more complicated.'

'No,' I said. 'No, it isn't.' I'd had a long morning and a bad night and my temper was getting the better of me. '*Have you tried it on humans.* Specifically, amourettes. Amourettes who are now dead due to someone thinking they had a better use for their hearts.' I had him backed against a pile of books by this time.

'No! What? What amourettes? Don't hurt Smoffy!' He held the small beast as far away from me as he could. It meeped. Books were beginning to cascade from the pile behind him.

'I'm not going to hurt… Whatever that is. However I would like an answer. Now.'

'No!' He glanced down at the blade and swallowed. 'I mean, yes, you can have an answer, but it's no, I've never tried it on a human.'

'And you don't know anything about the amourettes.'

'No. I don't. I've never… my studies keep me very busy!' he said.

'Do you know a woman called Deralis?' I was fairly sure that 'I've never' was indicative, but…

'Who?'

'A courtesan. A friend.'

'No. Was she one of the ones who got killed? That's… Look, I don't know. I haven't been out of here for days. I've been... I can show you more easily. An experiment. My landlady's been bringing my meals. Could you move the sword, please?'

I sheathed. 'All right.' Tarek had gone very pale. 'Show me this experiment.'

It was in the next room, and proved to involve a frog. Which looked quite cheerful considering it only had a head, connected by wires to a bottle with some stuff inside I didn't want to look at too closely. It blinked at me. This was where the acrid smell had come from.

'I've kept it alive for twelve days!' he said. 'This is cutting-edge stuff, you know. But it's why I haven't been out. I have to renew the wards every hour.'

'I'm sorry I disturbed you,' I said.

'I'm sorry too,' Tarek said. 'I… The amourettes talk to me sometimes. They seem nice. I hope your friend's alright.'

'Where does the other necromancer keep himself?'

'Sulvan? Fringal Street, the other side of town. He's *very* old fashioned, though. I mean, you want a skeletal army, he's probably your man. I tried to talk to him about moving with the times, I even lent him some books, but he just didn't seem to want to *know*.'

On my way over, I talked to some of the freelance amourettes. The usual run of clients, the usual occasional one who gave them the creeps. But Deralis' clients were mostly upper-end, the kind who preferred, and could afford, a discreet arrangement and a comfortable house instead of a doorway or a single grubby room where the sheets hadn't been changed.

'One of her clients did come around, though,' one said,

a little whip of a thing, who barely came to my shoulder, standing outside a neat friendly-looking inn. 'Sulvan, the necromancer.'

'When was this?'

'Yesterday,' she said. 'He said did I know where Deralis had got to. I was a bit short with him. I mean, it's not very flattering, is it.'

'He didn't…'

'No, he just said he'd made a mistake and walked off.'

'All right, thank you.'

Well, that was Sulvan off my list. If he'd been asking after Deralis, several days after she disappeared, he obviously didn't know where she was.

'If you hear or think of anything? I'm staying at her place,' I said. I felt thoroughly fed up, and more and more certain I'd arrived too late to be any use to poor Deralis. 'Meanwhile… Is this inn any good? All right, for the next hour I'm going to be in there with a big drink.'

I got wine, and sat at a table and brooded. I'd run out of ideas. All that was left was Mr Fancy Pants, and the idea of going through the whole town checking out male underwear had a lot less appeal than usual.

'Excuse me,' said a voice. 'I understand you're a friend of Deralis. Could I speak with you?'

I looked up.

He was a quietly dressed, clean-shaven young man, a little pale, not bad-looking. I gestured him to sit down. 'I'm trying to find her,' I said, 'or at least, what might have happened to her. Can you help?'

'I wish I could.' He sighed. 'I've been so worried about her.'

'You know her?' I said.

'Oh, yes.'

'Do you have any ideas, then?'

He shook his head. 'It's a mystery. I don't understand it.' He leaned forward. 'You know her well?'

'I knew her back in Thrallick,' I said.

'You remember Thrallick? That's splendid. Could I buy you a drink?' he said.

Something about that struck me a little odd. What was

splendid about remembering Thrallick? 'That's kind,' I said. 'But I have one. Thank you.'

'Oh, yes, I see you do,' he said.

That was the last thing I remembered.

I woke up somewhere chilly, with the sound of water dripping, and a candle-flame flickering at the edge of my vision.

It stayed there, because I couldn't move.

I was lying on my back, arms at my sides, on something flat and hard. Above me was a rock ceiling. It didn't have the reek of a prison cell. It smelled quite clean; just odd. There was a tickling, acrid scent, faintly familiar and... Meat.

And breathing. Deep, regular breathing.

I was not feeling very good about this.

Approaching footsteps.

A pale face appeared in my vision. The man from the tavern. 'Is it you?' he said. 'It is, isn't it? When you mentioned Thrallick... see, I knew you couldn't resist giving yourself away, eventually. It's meant. We'll soon have you back where you belong.'

Feeling, along with a really serious case of pins and needles, was coming back into my hands and feet. I realised I was tied up; hands and feet both bound to some sort of fastening at the side of whatever it was I was lying on. My chest was cold.

My shirt was open to the waist.

He hadn't been looking at my breasts. It wasn't those he was interested in.

I remembered the body, the gaping bloody cavity where a heart should have been.

Well, now I knew who I was in a room with, and getting the arse out of there was becoming pretty bloody urgent. Obviously I'd been drugged. How the hells had he got me out of the tavern without anyone noticing? The pins and needles suggested the drug was beginning to leave me; but the ropes were tight and tough. I wriggled my hands, turned my wrists. Not completely tight, not loose enough to get out of without help.

I could see my weapons lying a few feet away, just chucked in a pile.

Well, most of 'em. He hadn't taken my boots off.

With both hands and feet tied, reaching my boot-knife was going to be tricky. I couldn't reach my hair ornaments either.

I turned my head to one side, and started rubbing it against the slab. If I could work one or both of the ornaments out of my hair I could, maybe, use my face and body to shuffle it down as far as my hand, and cut the rope.

I kept glancing at my captor. He was bending over another slab – no, not a slab, a bed; satin sheets and plump pillows. And ropes. Whoever was on that one might be getting more comfort, but they were still tied up.

I heard him tutting. 'You're getting bruised. If only you'd been *sensible*. All this nonsense, darling. You're just running away. What's the point of running?'

He moved, and I saw.

It was Deralis. She was alive; it was her breathing I could hear. She was surrounded by symbols, stands of burning herbs, unpleasant-looking dried things.

She was naked to the waist. There was a great ragged scar down the centre of her chest, rising and falling as she breathed.

He moved over to the pile of my things he'd put on a chair, and picked up Deralis' client book. He flicked through it, shaking his head. 'Why did you let them do these things? Once you had me…' the book fell open at the last page, the one with the three final clients. He looked down at it, and his mouth twisted horribly. His hands clenched, tearing the book's pages. 'Too much? *Too much?* My love, my wealth, my eternal devotion. Too much?' He made a visible effort to calm himself, and smiled, shaking his head. '*Silly* darling,' he said. 'Nothing I could give you could be too much. Well, you won't need this anymore.' He threw the book on the fire.

Then he turned, and came over to where I was lying. I hadn't quite managed to work the ornament down towards my hand yet. 'I know you're in there,' he said.

'You're Sulvan,' I said. 'The necromancer.'

'Well who else would I be, my dear?'

'Who do you think's in here?'

'You, Deralis.' He looked towards the still, slow-breathing form on the other bed. 'Or at least, your heart, my silly darling. Trying to hide it from me, pretending it had changed, and you didn't love me any more. I knew. I knew you'd just hidden it.'

Things suddenly became horribly clear.

'She didn't want your contract,' I said. He turned away. He wasn't listening to me. He hadn't listened to Deralis either.

Some people can't hear 'no'. Slides right off 'em.

'I thought you must have put it in one of the street girls,' he said. He moved away, out of range of my vision, and something clinked. 'Some of them were kind to me, the way you always were, and so I thought… But then when she woke up, after, she just cried and was silly, so I knew I hadn't found it.'

The first hair ornament slid out, I could feel it hard and cold under my cheek. I shuffled, trying to push it towards my hand.

It slid into the hollow between my neck and shoulder and disappeared. I couldn't feel the damn thing anymore.

One left. Careful, Babylon. Ear. Cheek. Chin, scraping against metal and stone. Not good for the complexion, this.

Under the shoulder. Careful.

'It's that girl Liva's fault,' Sulvan said. Good, keep chattering, you bloody madman, hide the sound of metal moving over stone. 'She turned you against me. Maybe it wasn't you. Maybe *she* hid your heart away, is that it? I'll have to deal with her. She can't be allowed to come between us again.'

In all my career I don't think I've never put so much effort into a bit of a wriggle. Under my upper arm. Lower arm.

The hair ornament slid into my palm. I managed to free the blade, bent my hand as far as it would turn, sawing at the rope, couldn't see what I was doing, hoped I wasn't going to accidentally open a vein.

Sulvan turned around. He had a vial in one hand. The other was holding a big, serrated blade.

'I don't know why you'd do this to yourself,' he said, coming towards me.

I slashed out. The blade was only a couple of inches long, but it caught him across the fingers. The vial dropped to the floor. Pungent fumes wafted up. I held my breath, not quite fast enough. My vision began to waver.

But he was closer to the fumes, and smaller than me. He staggered. I grabbed the boot-knife, slashed at the rest of the ropes. He came again. 'You're only hurting yourself,' he said.

I got him in the side, not deep enough, my aim was all messed up. He looked shocked, then resentful. 'I'm doing this because I love you!'

'That's not love,' I said.

There was a crash. I wasn't sure if it was real, or the drug, but then Liva and Tarek burst into the room. Liva leaped on Sulvan's back and Tarek took a wild swing with his staff, and, amazingly, caught Sulvan a cracker across the knees, felling him like a tree. I'm not sure which of them was more taken by surprise.

'Don't kill him,' I said, through the big soft waves that were rolling over my vision. 'Tie him up. Don't kill him.'

'How the hells did you and Tarek find me?' I said. Liva and I were sitting either side of Deralis' bed.

'I knew you were going to call on the necromancers,' Liva said. 'When you didn't come back, I went to Tarek first, and then we spoke to the girl at the inn. She'd seen you coming out with Sulvan and she thought you were drunk.'

Deralis fingered the scar on her chest. Liva gently moved her hand away.

Deralis looked pretty good, considering, but she was still a way from her tough, raucous self. 'He kept bringing me things,' she said. 'Even after I told him I didn't want the contract. I came home one day and found him putting up Festival of the Dead decorations in the parlour. He must have got hold of a key, had a copy made – I asked for it back. He gave it to me, but I never thought he might have more than one. I burned the decorations. I tried to give him back the things he'd given me but he wouldn't take them so I burned those too. As though that would make him go away.'

'I still don't understand,' Liva said. 'Why did he do it?'

'He kept a book of his own,' I said. 'I read it. Some of it. It was a mess. You know the legend of Meriasen of Kyr?'

'She kept her heart in a cage, didn't she?' Liva said.

'Yes. And there's other legends like that – people keeping their hearts somewhere else so they can't be hurt, or killed. Sulvan believed them. Or believed some version of them. When Deralis told him she didn't want to take his contract offer, didn't even want him coming around anymore, he convinced himself that she'd hidden her heart from him, that she'd put it somewhere else. Because really, in her real heart, she had to love him. Because he wanted her, she had to want him back. She was only pretending she didn't, hiding her heart.'

'But that…' Liva shook her head, gripping Deralis' hand more tightly. 'That makes no sense.'

'It made sense to him.'

'He killed them all, looking for my heart. Thinking I'd wake up, and tell him I loved him, tell him it had all been a mistake.' Deralis started to cry. Again. 'Those poor women. If I'd known, I could have pretended … told him I loved him, waited for a chance to get away. Every time I woke up I just begged him to let me go, I didn't know what was happening. It's my fault he kept killing. If I'd just *known*.'

'*No.*' Liva and I spoke together. We looked at each other, and she gestured for me to go on.

'It's his fault,' I said. 'His. No-one else's. His fault he couldn't take no for an answer, and his fault he'd rather murder than admit the person he wanted might turn him down. Just his.'

'At least you got to Jacinth before they burned the body,' Deralis said. 'Is she…'

'So far as I know she's fine. She doesn't remember any of it – which is probably just as well,' Liva said. 'And Babylon managed to talk to that councillor and get the records of her identity removed, so no-one's going to wonder why she's walking about. Amazing how effective just mentioning fruit can be.'

'You and Tarek did brilliantly,' I said. They had, bribing the guards at the public morgue to get Jacinth's body before they burned it. Getting it to Sulvan's, and especially the next bit, which was messy. But now Jacinth was back home with her little boy, and Sulvan's workshop had, unfortunately, burned to the ground. Along with whatever was in it. Apart from a few books that might have found their way into Tarek's collection.

'He's a bit useful, that young Tarek,' I said. 'He might never have done it before, but he did all right.'

Deralis gave a shadow of her usual smile. 'He's not so bad, is he?'

'Quite cute, actually,' I said. 'In a fresh-faced virgin sort of way. And he's been working ever so hard. Perhaps he could do with a little recreation. What do you think?'

Liva rolled her eyes. 'Is she always like this?' She asked Deralis.

'I don't know why she thought she needed *me* to find clients for her,' Deralis said.

'Actually I think I might offer him a freebie,' I said, 'what with him coming heroically to the rescue and all.'

Deralis ran her fingers over the scar again. 'Mine doesn't feel any different. I wonder if Jacinth's does.'

'No reason why it should,' I said. 'There was nothing wrong with his *heart.*'

CONTRIBUTORS

ARTIST

Sarah Anne Langton draws things, writes and scribbles a lot about comics. Qualified Astronaut. Part time archaeologist. Full time geek.

Sarah has worked as an Illustrator for Hodder & Stoughton, Forbidden Planet, EA Games, The Cartoon Network, Sony, Marvel Comics and a wide variety of music events. Written and illustrated for Jurassic London, Fox Spirit, NewCon Press, Anachron Press and 'The Fizzy Pop Vampire' series. Hodderscape dodo creator and Kitschies judge. Daylights as Web Mistress for the worlds largest sci-fi and fantasy website. Her work has featured on io9, Clutter Magazine, Laughing Squid and Creative Review.

Fine her online at http://www.secretarcticbase.com

AUTHORS

A. R. Aston is a speculative fiction writer from former industrial town of Swadlincote, located deep in the Heart of England (in the left ventricle if you must know...). An avid student of history and english literature, he has always had a passion for the written word. When not writing, he can be found reading voraciously, creating a functional time machine, and composing spurious facts about himself... For more of his work, visit his author page on amazon:

http://www.amazon.co.uk/A.-R.-Aston/e/B00AKG2IEK

Or alternatively visit his blog, The Tentacled Tribunal, at: http://lordlucan1.wordpress.com

Stephanie Burgis lives in Wales with her husband, fellow writer Patrick Samphire, their two children, and their crazy-sweet border collie mix. She has published over thirty short stories in various SF and fantasy magazines and anthologies as well as a trilogy of Regency fantasy novels for younger readers, The Unladylike Adventures of Kat Stephenson. You can find links to her other short stories and excerpts from her novels on her website: http://www.stephanieburgis.com

Zen Cho is a Malaysian writer of SFF and romance living in London. She was a finalist for the Campbell Award for Best New Writer in 2013. Her short story collection *Spirits Abroad* was published by Buku Fixi in June 2014.

Her website can be found at http://zencho.org

Jaine Fenn is the author of the Hidden Empire series of far future SF novels published by Gollancz, which began with *Principles of Angels*. She also writes short stories in other genres, and is a sucker for a retold folk tale. Her website can be found at http://www.jainefenn.com

Tom Johnstone's fiction has appeared in various publications, including the *Ninth* and *Tenth Black Books of Horror* (Mortbury Press), *Brighton – The Graphic Novel* (Queenspark Books) and *Supernatural Tales*, #27. He also co-edited the austerity-themed anthology *Horror Uncut: Tales of Social Insecurity and Economic Unease* with the late Joel Lane, published in September 2014 by Gray Friar Press.

Juliet E McKenna's love of other worlds, other peoples, fantasy, myth and history was nurtured by childhood viewing of programmes such as Doctor Who, Star Trek and UFO. After studying Classics at Oxford University, she worked in personnel management before a career change to combine motherhood and book-selling. Her debut novel, *The Thief's Gamble,* was published in 1999, the first of *The Tales of Einarinn*. That series was followed by *The Aldabreshin Compass* sequence, beginning with *Southern Fire* and *The Chronicles of the Lescari Revolution*, starting with *Irons in the Fire*. She writes diverse shorter fiction and always enjoying the challenge of something new, she wrote a serial story for Aethernet magazine in 2013. She is currently exploring the possibilities and opportunities of independent ebook publishing alongside traditional methods.

Check out her website at http://www.julietemckenna.com

Christine Morgan works the overnight shift in a psychiatric facility, which plays havoc with her sleep schedule but allows her a lot of writing time. A lifelong reader, she also reviews, beta-reads, occasionally edits and dabbles in self-publishing. Her other interests include gaming, history, superheroes, crafts, cheesy disaster movies and training to be a crazy cat lady. She can be found online at http://www.christine-morgan.org

Gaie Sebold's debut novel introduced brothel-owning ex-avatar of sex and war, *Babylon Steel* (Solaris, 2012); the sequel, *Dangerous Gifts*, came out in 2013. *Shanghai Sparrow,* a steampunk fantasy, came out in 2014. She has published numerous short stories, had a variety of jobs (some more unusual than others) and is a member of T Party Writers. She now writes, runs writing workshops, grows vegetables, and procrastinates to professional levels. She has also been known to commit performance poetry and to run around in woods hitting people with latex weapons, though seldom both at the same time.

Extracts from Shanghai Sparrow and the Babylon Steel novels can be found on her website: http://gaiesebold.com.

Follow the latest scandal and tidbits from the world of Babylon Steel at http://scalentine.gaiesebold.com.

Sam Stone is the award-winning author of *The Vampire Gene Series.* Her latest works include the first part of her new apocalypse trilogy, *Jinx Town,* a short horror novel that first appeared in audio, *The Darkness Within,* and her latest Steampunk novella*, What's Dead PussyKat.*

A prolific and eclectic genre writer, Sam's short fiction has appeared in many collections and anthologies as well as her own collection *Zombies in New York and Other Bloody Jottings*. She is currently working on the second Jinx book.

Sam lives in Lincolnshire with her partner David and their cat, Jinx.

Visit her at: http://www.sam-stone.com

Adrian Tchaikovsky is the author of the acclaimed Shadows of the Apt fantasy series, from the first volume, *Empire In Black and Gold* in 2008 to the final book, *Seal of the Worm*, in 2014, with a new series and a standalone science fiction novel scheduled for 2015. He has been nominated for the David Gemmell Legend Award and a British Fantasy Award and his first full length science fiction novel, *Portia's Children* comes out in 2015. In civilian life he is a lawyer, gamer and amateur entomologist.

Find him online at: http://shadowsoftheapt.com

Jonathan Ward is a science-fiction, horror and fantasy writer hailing from the sprawling urban metropolis of Bedford. He has wanted to be an author since the age of eight, though it's questionable whether his writing talents have improved since then. When not writing he can be found reading a good book, out exploring new places, or in the pub being sarcastic to his closest friends.

Jonathan's Author Central page containing links to all of his published work: http://www.amazon.co.uk/Jonathan-Ward/e/B002BLQ8HA/ref=ntt_dp_epwbk_0

Jonathan's Facebook writing page: http://www.facebook.com/pages/The-Written-Ward/339336243357

Chloë Yates is a writer of odd stories. Having peppered her way across the Fox Spirit landscape with stories in all three of Kate Laity's Noir series (*Drag Noir* will be out soon), work appearing (and to be appearing) in all but one of the Fox Pockets, and becoming a *Girl at the End of the World* (Vol. 1), she is currently working on her first novel and a collection of short stories for the upcoming *Feral Tales* trilogy. She lives in the middle of Switzerland with her bearded paramour, Mr Y, and their disapproving dog, Miss Maudie.

Find her online at: http://chloeyates.com

EDITORS

Jenny Barber is an editor and writer with a particular fondness for short fiction. Along with Jan Edwards she has co-edited *The Alchemy Press Book of Ancient Wonders, The Alchemy Press Book of Urban Mythic #1* and *Urban Mythic #2*. As a writer she has had fiction published with various small presses including Fox Spirit Books and Elektrik Milk Bath Press and has written non-fiction for the *Girl's Guide to Surviving the Apocalypse* blog.

When not doing any of that, she's a minion of all trades for the family business and can usually be found wrangling spreadsheets and walking around rented houses talking to herself.

Brave souls can find her at: http://www.jennybarber.co.uk

Jan Edwards is a writer with a passion for folklore and mythology; has thirty-six fantasy shorts published in almost every form (with first collection coming very soon); was short-listed for a BFS Award for Best Short Story; lives in North Staffs with other half Peter Coleborn plus the cats and chickens, but was born and raised in West Sussex; is a Reiki Master and Meditational Healer; taroist par excellence; edits for the award winning Alchemy Press (with the inimitable Jenny Barber - The Alchemy Book of Ancient Wonders (2012) and Alchemy Press Book of Urban Mythic vol 1 (2013) and vol 2 (2014); has one mainstream novel out under a pen name and a fantasy novel as Jan Edwards arriving shortly.

For more details go to http://janedwardsblog.wordpress.com/

If you enjoyed Wicked Women here as some other titles by Jan Edwards and Jenny Barber:

The Alchemy Press Book of Ancient Wonders;

Discover standing stones, burial mounds, ruined castles or sunken cities: the ancient sites that litter our landscapes; the ancient wonders that possess a mysterious appeal that cannot be denied.

The Alchemy Press Book of Urban Mythic

There is magic out there on the street and the Mythic are alive and well and creating chaos in a city near you. Fourteen fabulous authors bring you tales of wonder and horror, with ancient curses and modern charms, strange things in the Underground, murder and redemption, corporate cults and stalwart guardians, lost travellers and wandering gods, fortune tellers and urban wizards, dragons, fae and unspeakable beasts.

The Alchemy Press Book of Urban Mythic 2.

In the footsteps of volume one, here are a further twelve tales of myth and magic, of legendary creatures, set in the modern age, with stories from: Sarah Ash, James Brogden, Carl Barker, Andrew Coulthard, KT Davies, Pauline E Dungate, Chico Kidd, Tanith Lee, Christine Morgan, Lou Morgan, Marion Pitman and Adrian Tchaikovsky.

For details go to http://alchemypress.wordpress.com/

Foxspirit.co.uk

'After nourishment, shelter and companionship, stories are the thing we need most in the world.' Phillip Pullman

Skulk: *noun* – a pack or group of foxes

Fox Spirit believes that day to day life lacks a few things, primarily the fantastic, the magical, the mischievous and even a touch of the horrific. We aim to rectify that by bringing you stories and gorgeous cover art and illustrations from foxy folk who believe as we do that we could all use a little more wonder in our lives.

Here at the Fox Den we believe in storytelling first and foremost, so we mash genres, bend tropes and set fire to rule books merrily as we seek out tall tales that excite and delight us and send them out into the world to find new readers.

With a mixture of established and new writers producing novels, short stories, flash fiction and poetry via ebook and print we recommend letting a little Fox Spirit into your life.

 @foxspiritbooks

 https://www.facebook.com/foxspiritbooks

 adele@foxspirit.co.uk